PRIMA FACIE

PRIMA FACIE

A NOVEL

SUZIE MILLER

HENRY HOLT AND COMPANY
NEW YORK

Henry Holt and Company
Publishers since 1866
120 Broadway
New York, New York 10271
www.henryholt.com

Henry Holt® and Ⓗ® are registered trademarks of Macmillan Publishing Group, LLC.

Distributed in Canada by Raincoast Book Distribution Limited

Library of Congress Cataloging-in-Publication Data

Names: Miller, Suzie, author. | Miller, Suzie. Prima facie.
Title: Prima facie : a novel / Suzie Miller.
Other titles: Prima facie (Novel)
Description: First U.S. edition. | New York : Henry Holt and Company, 2024.
Identifiers: LCCN 2023024658 (print) | LCCN 2023024659 (ebook) |
    ISBN 9781250292209 (hardcover) | ISBN 9781250292216 (ebook)
Subjects: LCGFT: Novels. | Legal fiction (Literature).
Classification: LCC PR9619.4.M5685 P75 2024 (print) |
    LCC PR9619.4.M5685 (ebook)
LC record available at https://lccn.loc.gov/2023024658
LC ebook record available at https://lccn.loc.gov/2023024659

Our books may be purchased in bulk for promotional, educational, or
business use. Please contact your local bookseller or the Macmillan Corporate
and Premium Sales Department at (800) 221-7945, extension 5442, or by
e-mail at MacmillanSpecialMarkets@macmillan.com.

First U.S. Edition 2024

Designed by Meryl Sussman Levavi

Printed in the United States of America

1 3 5 7 9 10 8 6 4 2

For all the women who comprise the 'one in three'

Boldness be my friend.
SHAKESPEARE (from *Cymbaline*)

Courage is the most important of all
the virtues. Because without courage,
you cannot practice any other virtue
consistently.
MAYA ANGELOU

Fortune favors the bold,
VIRGIL

PRIMA FACIE

BEFORE

CHAPTER 1

Thoroughbreds. Every single one. Primed for the race, every muscle pumped; groomed in expensive, understated, designer gray or navy suits, classic white shirts, black robes. All these top legal women have a sort of swagger, an ironic way of owning the space, a satchel flung from one shoulder to the opposite hip. Nude or red lipstick, not too much mascara. Cool earrings, and designer boots, or cheeky heels bought on a trip overseas. I study them all. Have done so for years. Copy them. I'm a good mimic, before eventually I become better at 'being a barrister' than the ones born to it. The top women do law differently than the men, subtly different, and it takes a while for me to compute the various ways they own the space. All the little details are secret code for 'we're here but we're doing it our way, not like the crusty old male barristers of the past.' And these accumulate the more confident you become, the more you own your space in court. Barrister bags in pink or blue are placed around the court, like loyal dogs beside their owners: blue for baby barristers of fewer than twenty years, the pink ones are a badge of honour, given to a junior barrister by a KC who has singled them out for praise. I was granted a pink one, and I treasure it, but I use mine more ironically than anything else. White, thick, soft ropes of a certain length and texture act as handles, blazoned with hand-stitched initials in the only font permitted, and lined with court-approved ticking. A barrister bag was once a thing of pride, supposed to be used for carrying briefs and materials for court—they might have been useful centuries ago—but now really there for the show. Symbols of the elite, handed down from father to son to son. Sometimes a daughter received her father's bag, but those barristers—the women who grew up with law in the family—they don't have the same uncomfortable relationship with these things that I do. They also don't love the law like I do either. They don't see it as a tool for power in the way I always have; don't hold on to it tight. Sure, they know it is 'powerful,' but most slipped into the law as if settling into an old family leather armchair, and think of it more as a family business, not a desperate arena to fight for justice.

It's easy to pick these women. They mostly don't do criminal law, nothing grubby. Nothing *risky*. If they do opt for a criminal practice, it's usually a tame version, and often chosen more out of curiosity than life experience, chosen more for the excitement than the desire to fight for clients on the lowest rungs of social standing.

For those of us beyond the barrister bag accoutrements, the satchel is a much better statement: confident, unfazed, a symbol of having made it well past the need for a security blanket, our own little badge of honor.

Yet there are some things we all have in common: the horsehair wigs that cover our well-cut, warmly colored styles that give all women barristers the same unfortunate case of 'six p.m. wig-hair' at the end of a long day. Something the male forebears didn't account for when they enshrined it as legal costume. For the men, the only way they can differentiate from each other is the color of their tie. Every now and then some unusual glasses frames or an interesting watch.

In a glance, I can tell who's who in the court foyer. What cases they have run, won, lost; what cases are listed today. If it's a certain group of barristers, then it's all white-collar crime in corporate finance cases, their instructing solicitors trail behind them with trolleys of white binders.

And then there's those of us who ride the lifts to the criminal courts. We circle, heads held high. All of us trained and ready for the sprint. Not jumpy but wired, like a horse, excited, restless. Waiting for the starting gun. I walk into court with my client, take in a rabble of police leaning into the prosecution barrister. Arnold Lathan is prosecuting. Good. I'm glad it's him, dare I say this is now perhaps a winnable case. I nod to Arnold briefly and he nods back. My blood rises but I have to hold back, keep it together, don't get too excited. Arnold's always prepared, but he's just not as quick once things unfold. I don't recognize any of the police. That's also good. They have no idea what to expect. My client is lagging. Tony. He's a tall guy, big, this isn't the first time I've acted for him, but it is the first time on a matter like this. Tony's charge of stealing and assault is based entirely on the evi-

dence of one man, someone whom he once played football with. A
compromised witness who maintains a major grudge against him. He
dislikes Tony, looks down on him; approached him in the bar and has
made a statement that leaves out the abuse and assault Tony endured
at this man's hands. The police clearly believed the story against Tony,
and so here we are. The witness's word against Tony's. Tony is dressed
as I told him, but he still doesn't cut it. A suit from Primark, a cheap
no-brand shirt, and a tie he must have got free with the shirt on sale
somewhere. Still, at least he tried. He's hidden all his tatts of snakes
and knives under that layer of polyester. Good. It's always a shock to
me when these tough guys walk into the foyer of a court. And Tony is
no different. They run the streets out there, confident, cocky, reading
all the signs, but in here, the signals are different, and each of them
say 'you have no power.' I told him to 'bring your toothbrush' and
he told me this morning that he actually did. He pulled it out of his
pocket, a blue Tesco brand with some fluff from the pocket of his new
jacket layering the bristles.

　　No, Tony, it's just a saying.
　　But you told me—
　　It's just lawyer talk.
His eyes are glued to my lips, trying to work out what I'm saying. I
explain it.
　　It means 'the cops have a good case.'
　　But you said—
　　Tony, they won't actually let you take your toothbrush into
　　prison with you!
　　They won't?
He's scanning me for any sort of hope.
　　Don't panic just yet.
Tony is scared. Like, little-boy scared. Of course he is. For him this
is not an everyday thing, not a familiar place. He's been up all night,
drinking and vomiting, he's had to iron that shirt, and ask his girlfriend or his mum to put the tie on for him. He probably caught the
train in and ate Maccy-D's around the corner, not knowing where
he'd spend the next night. This is big, he could go away for a few
years if he goes down.
The truth is, keeping them afraid is useful. They listen more, tend

toward being a bit in awe of you, and it acts as a buffer in case they go down. It means once they know jail is possible, you're all they have. If we walk out of here today, I am his favorite person; if he goes inside, it won't be a shock. I can see so much of my brother in Tony. Out of place, in a terrible situation that looks like it can only get worse. I head over to him.

Hey, Tony.

As he hurries to stand up, I see he is sweating.

You okay?

Yeah. Yeah.

Anyone coming to be with you?

His tongue moistens his lips. He's just twenty-five.

Mum's on her way.

Good.

I am the only thing familiar in this room. There is laughter from a group of barristers, another calling loudly for his client. Confidence and power surround Tony, but he has none of it. His eyes are soft and for the first time since I met him, he has neither gum nor cigarette in his mouth. I see the child in him. Not the asshole in the police brief, the thug who drank too much, lost his cool, and is in over his head.

Do you think there's any hope your witness will arrive?

He has an ex-girlfriend who witnessed it all, saw that it was not Tony who threw the first punch.

Dunno. Maybe. Shall I call her again?

Yeah, you do that. Tell her we're in the list for ten a.m.

I know there's no hope. She's been AWOL for the last month. Truth is she doesn't want anything to do with this case. She's scared to give evidence. No one likes to be cross-examined. At least calling her will give Tony something to do as he waits for his mum. Gives me a chance to review the main points, a trip to the loo, straighten my wig and makeup.

When Tony takes his seat in court, he pulls the chair up to the bar table beside me. I have to reprimand him. A look, 'no, you can't sit here.' I turn to him and explain he is to sit in the dock, I direct him over to the court officer. He complies meekly, he's shaking. The man described in the police brief as a dangerous, violent, drunken thug in a bar is this scared twenty-five-year-old shaking like a boy. The narratives do not reconcile. This is the truth of the law. Then, Tony's mum enters, takes a seat halfway down in the gallery. She is alone too. Texting. I gesture to her to 'turn off your phone.' She doesn't understand. I give up. I turn and look at the court clock. Court is starting to hush, judge is late but not much. It's just after ten. I hear the chatter in the gallery behind me, but now that I'm on the job I push it into background noise. Flick through my papers, pour some water from the jug on the bench into a tumbler, arrange my notes.

The energy in the room every case I run: this is the moment before— when the charged space around me has a current of excitement and dread. This is where my skill set gets to flex its muscle. I draw all my energy into the same place, make the bar table my own. Blinkers on; only focused on what is ahead. Face confident, giving nothing away. So much of this is theater. All the details of the case are in my head, no room for anything else. I am holding it together, holding back, keeping my blood at just the right temperature. Just below boil. Waiting. Waiting. Then bang.

The court officer calls out:

   All rise.

We all leap to our feet. Nodding our respect as the judge arrives. He takes his seat, and we take ours. The prosecutor and I, pumped, both in our own lane, both utterly aware of each breath the other takes, but never acknowledging each other unless, 'I refer to my friend, the prosecutor, Your Honor.' No eye contact.

We are out of the stalls and it's on. It's a long race so I hold back, know when to have restraint. Nothing worse than jumping in too early out of a desire to win a point that ultimately undermines your case. The prosecution opens, stands, and looks at the jury. The best chance for Tony is if the prosecution case can't be made, where the evidence can be undermined by the defense and there's the chance to make an argument for no case to answer. That means the case fails, Tony 'walks.' I have the whole course mapped in my mind, yet ready to tear it up at the first surprise. The prosecutor stands and lists the charges. At the bar table my eyes graze the bench, performing practiced nonchalance at the prosecution's accusations. My face gives nothing away, sit still, straight back, focus on what's before me, poised, watching, waiting, nerves taut. Every word uttered I am processing, interrogating, filing away, all the while feigning boredom. Breathe. Eyes gentle but listen to every word, interpret every physical signal, looking for an opening. The theater is not just to impress the clients, not just to show who is in charge, it's part of the game. I sit slightly back, head cocked to one side, leaning on the back of my chair, but all my muscles are tightly wound, waiting to spring.

Then I spy an opening: the prosecution witness is drifting away from just answering questions and is elaborating in ways that he isn't asked to. I can see Arthur, the prosecutor, is tempted to ask something he knows is ambiguous. His hesitation is key. It's starting to open up, wait, wait . . . let some more open up. This is the measure of my skill set, the waiting, the calm before.

And there it is, instinct pushes me forward, I leap to my feet. Measured, but clear.

Your Honor.

I hold everything in one place, and eyes, eyes are all looking at me. I can't see anyone, but I feel the shift. Standing tall, waiting, and the judge focuses in on me. I hear my own voice.

I'm so sorry to rise, sir, but I believe my friend at the bar table, counsel for the prosecution, is leading the evidence from his witness. The prosecution case rests solely on the evidence of this man, this witness here. A witness, the defense will argue, is severely compromised.

Strong and sure, explaining my objection, making my application to disallow a line of questioning. The prosecutor tries to maintain his momentum, I feel the urge to say more but rein it in. Less is more, I've made my point, keep them guessing. The judge momentarily pauses, like he has just felt the energy of the game, his eyes resting on me again; he knows me, he has seen me in action before. Is that respect? He hasn't been on this side of the bench for a long time, but he loves the fight, he loves a muscular argument, and this one is shaping up. He leans forward. Application granted.

Yes! In my mind I am cheering, but anyone watching me won't see it. My instructing solicitor sits in a chair near mine at the bar table. He is a man almost as young as Tony, from a nice private school, with the neatest haircut in the room. I don't need him at all, but he thinks I do, so he pores over his notes just to be ready. I see Tony look at me from the dock as I turn back to take my seat. He doesn't quite know that I have won a significant point, but he feels it, a subtle shift. The witness in the box is someone Tony once knew well, but after this there is no friendship left. This man has moved a long way from when he and Tony played football together. He wears sharp cologne and works in property now, some sort of estate agent. He is the 'bastard' that the Tonys of this world always lose to. To Tony this man is everything wrong with his life, a lifetime of built-up hostilities leading to this moment where the witness sits in court trying to get Tony sent to jail. For me, though, the witness is just the witness, a pawn in the bigger game. I sit down while the prosecutor continues to examine his witness, he has botched something, and he is patching it up as best he can. There are other barristers in court, sitting in the gallery as they await their own court matters, alert to the arguments, curious to see how another one of their own uses their skills. The judge speaks.

It's your witness, Ms. Ensler.

And this is the moment. The witness is mine, oh yeah, the witness is mine now. The witness breathes in, wary, sizing me up. He is computing everything about me, taking in what I am wearing, how I look at him, whether I am the sort of woman he can charm, or ridicule. My neurons are firing, words being formed; I'm carefully selecting phrases as tight as a drum. The courtroom is silent, charged, waiting for me. I drink up this moment. I stand and take a moment, move my robes and do up the button on my suit jacket. The courtroom is still. I can hear my own voice in my head. 'Keep it cool, Tessa, keep it cool.' I can see in my periphery the witness still taking the measure of me. I look small to him, young. But he can't quite figure me out. I let everyone wait just a second more than they expect, then I launch. Cross-examination is the best part. It's all instinct. Yes, you need the information, the map of the journey forward, but once you're on your feet you need to be nimble. Need to be flexible. Turn on a beat. I focus in on the witness. Inside I'm poised, ready for the play ahead. But the witness has no idea who I am, perhaps he was warned by someone of my various techniques, but by now he has forgotten it all. I ask the witness a question, he turns to the judge and answers the question quickly.

I ask the same question in a different way, watch his face, a flicker.
He repeats his answer, a dismissive wave at me, before quickly eyeing
the judge. I repeat his answer. I don't look but I feel the prosecutor
stir slightly at the bar table next to me.

I repeat the answer again, quizzically. The witness looks right at me,
thinks I am getting mixed up. I flick through some papers, let him
think I've lost my way.

He jumps in, tries to explain his answer, his voice patronizing. He
lets it be known with the pacing of his words that he thinks 'this one
is a bit slow in understanding.'

I hear myself breathing, then a barely audible snicker from the prosecution.

Good. Very good.

Again, I flick through pages in my file, check Tony in the dock, he
moves uncomfortably.

Good.

I ask a similar question and watch the witness relax. His shoulders
roll back, eyes dart around, a smirk. 'This one doesn't seem to know
what she's doing.' Check the judge. Expressionless. But this judge
has seen me before, he's seen the likes of me. He's quietly observing
the performance. Question one.

Question two.

Look worried about the answers. This emboldens the witness. He
looks around the gallery, looking for an audience. Flashes me a look
and condescends, then . . . is that a hint of flirtation? I nod at his
answers, flicking through pages, fumbling. I watch him, yes yes, here
he goes.

I let the witness talk, overtalk. I let the witness 'clarify.' Good.

         Thanks for that, sir, I wasn't sure . . .

And he goes further. He's in his element. His eyes dismiss me; 'This
one must be straight out of uni or something; she's not that good,'
he thinks. He's putty in my hands now. He relaxes, thinks he has
the upper hand. And so now he is not careful, not afraid, no longer
vigilant.

He says something inconsistent.

I nod, and look confused, let him explain it to me, but inside I am on alert. This is the break in his serve, this is where I take my lead. He's explaining and I'm nodding as he digs himself in more deeply.

Okay, I see. That's a bit clearer now . . .

Oh, he volunteers more information. It's all too easy, he has talked himself into a total mess. I dare to turn and momentarily clock the prosecutor. I see him put a finger to his forehead. Yes, he knows. And I know, but the guy about to bury himself talks on and on. In my mind's eye I am circling him, nodding approval. I ask for further clarification.

Oh, I see, but why did that happen?

The witness is so obliging! He is 'helping the woman out.' I quickly check the judge; my face is a mask—but the judge knows. Turn back to the witness, there is blood in the water and I just let the witness swim on. He has gone beyond the point of return, no one can help him now.

When he's done, he sits back, flash of confidence across his face. I let him feel his control, feel in charge of the moment. I let him indulge in feeling safe and secure.

Then, I breathe in and out, remind myself to tiptoe through the next bit, really pace the impact.

The witness crosses his arms. I have stopped flicking through pages, I am standing very still yet I am circling him. The judge and the other lawyers know what's coming. They silently cringe for him, but they love it, they lean forward. The people in the public gallery are a little bored, they see incompetence in me, someone lost, they have no idea what is happening. And the witness, there in the witness box, the man I am talking to, he still has no clue. No. Fucking. Clue.

I'm sorry, but just to clarify. I do have one more question. I hope you don't mind; it will help me get the full picture . . . The smallest of eye rolls from the witness. Perfect. This is exactly where I need him to be. But if the witness were watching the prosecutor, the guy sitting next to me at the bar table, he'd sense something is amiss. The prosecutor turns his face down toward the bar table. I stop moving, stop paper shuffling, stop fawning confusion. I look right at the witness.

I ask my question.

A strange movement across his face, he looks to the prosecutor for reassurance; the prosecutor can't say anything, but his eyes, they are begging him to be careful, begging the witness not to fall into the trap laid out before him. I see all this and then I fire four questions like bullets at the witness.

Bang, bang.

Bang. Bang.

His face registers the shock. Utter annihilation; he looks at me.

For the first time this witness sees me. Sees who I really am.

I watch the slow dawning, followed by a fury. Fury at me, at being taken for a ride. I stand up tall, let him see my power. He thought he had this but here I am. I like that he had dismissed me, I like that he had rolled his eyes, decided I was lousy at my job. I like it all for this moment. This moment where I have won the game and he is forced to look at me, and to realize that he had completely underestimated whom he was dealing with.

He doesn't like it.

I watch the witness sweat as he thinks of an answer. The people in the gallery are not bored anymore. They have just seen a cross-examination in action, one as brilliant as they see on the television. I can feel the shift in them, they might be behind me, but they are now looking at me with respect, curiosity. 'She's good.' But I'm not done yet.

My first movement is to look over at my client, he stares at me awestruck, he had long given up, he beams at me, but I continue as if I haven't seen him. I am not done yet.

      Answer the question, please, Mr. Bateman.

I say this in the most professional voice I have. The witness does not speak. I relish this last moment and take my time. The prosecutor has his head down almost touching the bar table, his case destroyed. He knows it, I know it, and the judge knows it, but the performance still must reach its finale. I press on in the sweetest voice I can muster.

      Your Honor, the witness is not answering my question.

The judge reminds Mr. Bateman that he must answer the question. I turn to Mr. Bateman and wait. He is cornered and I wait. He mumbles something. I lean in.

      I'm sorry, I didn't hear that.

The judge speaks wearily.

You must speak into the microphone for the recording, Mr.
    Bateman.
I gesture to the witness to bring the microphone closer to his face, smiling benevolently. By now Mr. Bateman is very wary of me. He answers.
    Yes, I was.
    So, your answer is a yes then, sir?
The judge has had enough, the man is destroyed and tells me I have
my answer. I do! And I like it. The prosecutor shakes his head when
he is asked whether he will reexamine. He doesn't even stand. There's
nothing he can do to save his case. The judge lets the witness go and
as he leaves the witness box, he tries to make eye contact with the
prosecutor. What just happened? He is confused, fumbling, he is
enraged. With me. His face is shaken as he walks past me, he has no
idea what went down. It's not emotional for me, it's just the game of
law. I stand up again and request that the case against my client be
dismissed. Tony doesn't know what is happening, but he senses it's
good. I address the judge, neutral.
    I submit that there is no case to answer, Your Honor.
The judge is swift, he dismisses the case. He turns and explains to Tony
that the case cannot be proved and that he, Tony, is free to go. Tony
shakes his head, beams, but doesn't walk from the dock until I beckon
him. As I pack up my paperwork I turn and nod to his mother. She
also stands to leave. The barristers' rule is you can't flaunt a win. Every
winner might lose the next day. We don't even call it losing, it's too
hard for us to wrap our mouths around that word, instead we call it
'coming second.' Today the prosecutor came second. I nod a thank-
you and acknowledge the prosecutor, try not to make eye contact.
Put my papers in my satchel and cross it over my chest, undo my suit
jacket and make my way toward the door of the courtroom. Everyone
who saw me win is watching me. I saunter. Mentally cue applause;
it feels good. When I get to the door, I turn, nod to the judge. Tony
and his mother are on either side of me, I motion for them both to
nod too, and they do. This big thug of a man and his mum are in my
thrall. I am the one who leads the way through this strange system,
puts them on a path to home. When we are outside the courtroom I
dare to strip away the artifice, not all of it though, they still need me
to be in charge.

Tony, you can brush your teeth at home now.

Tony looks at me, questioning me.

You're free to go home, Tony. They didn't have a case. It's all
over.

I realize Tony and his mother, despite hearing the judge dismiss the
case, still do not quite know the outcome. Tony's mother bursts into
tears, she grabs my hand and puts it to her heart. There's suddenly
a warmth, a strange closeness to this mother and her son. It's too
familiar. I start to falter. This mother, her boy, such love between
them. Her relief is so palpable. I wonder how many sleepless nights
she has had worrying about what would happen today, I also wonder
how she can bear it. There will be another time for Tony in court,
of that I have no doubt, but for today she can take her boy home.
Tony's mum is not letting go of my hand, I put my other hand over
hers and gently take it off her chest, gradually releasing her grip.

I must run, another case to prepare.

Keep it professional. Turn to Tony.

As for you. I don't want to see you in here, ever again.

I say this to a grown man, to someone towering over me. I say this
to Tony, still in his badly ironed shirt, sweat marks now under each
arm. He nods almost violently. He won't be here again, he is sure.
I'm not. But in this moment, he grabs my hand and shakes it. This
giant thug of a man is filled with respect for me. In this moment, I
have power.

CHAPTER 2

Outside court I turn on my iPhone and call Alice's number to debrief.
Alice and I are so different, but our chambers rooms are next door,
and it creates an intimacy of sorts. We bear witness to each other's
lives, notetakers of the ins and outs of each other's court diaries,
cases, and occasionally each other's love affairs. The adrenaline kick
of winning a matter makes it impossible to settle until you have
had the chance to speak to someone, a listener who understands the
game. It's been trickier lately because Alice has not been doing well.
I hesitate, then dial. It would be weird if I didn't, I know she would
be expecting it. Her number rings but the voice that picks up is not
Alice's. It takes a moment, and then I realize it's Julian.
He tells me:

Alice is in the loo, she left her phone at the photocopier.
How'd it go?

I smile to myself.

I won.

I wonder to myself whether I sound arrogant. I don't mean to. I'm
still computing that I'm debriefing with Jules. He is slightly out of
reach for me usually, a bit of a hero at the bar, a guy who is very at
home there. A cab slows down nearby. I jump in, duck down, and
rip off my robe and wig, laughing on the phone as Julian's voice manages a hint of humor, then he says:

What's new?

I ask the cabbie to head to St Pancras station. Jules asks me for details.

Did your guy give evidence?

Didn't have to. I called for no-case. The primary witness fell over
in a hot mess. He's laughing but impressed, I'm packing my wig in
my Tupperware box, folding my robes into my barrister bag. It feels
good to be able to tell someone who is also on a winning streak.

Julian is a better barrister than Alice, more dynamic. He responds to details around my killer cross-examination. I tell Jules the witness obviously thought he was dealing with some brainless twat. Julian says:

Big mistake. Serves him right, he underestimated one of
the best.

Without warning I feel a warm jolt. I hop out of the cab, and the driver calls me back.

Love, you don't get to ride for free!

I forgot to pay, forgot it wasn't an Uber. I'm embarrassed, find a twenty in my pocket.

So sorry, here, keep the change.

As an afterthought I add:

My uncle drives a cab where I'm from.

The cabbie smiles at me, gives me a wave. I return to Jules on the phone. Feel a little exposed, perhaps he heard the comment about my uncle, but I'm soon distracted by the conversation. I've never spoken to Julian on the phone before, and I don't think we have ever had a conversation that didn't include someone else at chambers. Truth is, Julian is someone I would never hang out with normally. And I most certainly wouldn't call him and tell him about a case I had won. I was on a high, out of court, rushing to the train to jump on and head to Mum's place.

Can you tell Alice the brief for the matter she's taking on
for me tomorrow is on my desk.

Sure.

Julian tells me his day was all corporate clients, boring as batshit, wishes he could get to court on a juicy criminal matter like me. I have to tap my phone ticket app to board the train, the noise drowns out the last thing Julian says, but when I end the call I linger slightly on the concept of Julian.

Julian is born to this world, takes it all in his stride. Father is a King's Counsel, the most senior barrister of all; godfather *also* a KC.

Throw my barrister bag with my robes inside on the luggage holder above and settle into a window seat, satchel at my feet. Settle in for the ride to Mum's. I dare to think I'm starting to make a mark. I mean, if Julian, one of the most well educated, confident men at the bar, compliments someone on their work, then you have to take it as a good sign. I smile inwardly as the train pulls out of the station. I take the elastic out of my hair, wriggle out of my suit jacket, lean my head against the window.

It's a long ride to Mum's, the train makes its way out of London before winding its way through familiar countryside; I feel the gloss of my legal life melt into the seat on the carriage. A tea trolley arrives, I sip milky white tea and wonder why Mum has called me for tea. She rarely calls me, it's always me leaving messages for her. She can't pick up her phone at work, the cleaning company she works for either has a nanny cam watching employees all day or they have some extra sense about who has been on their phones. It makes Mum crazy worried she'll lose her job. She says if I really want to talk to her, I should call back again after it goes to voicemail, two calls and she will pick up. I do this all the time and it drives her crazy. It's supposed to be for emergencies only, but I never know for sure whether she is at work or the supermarket, or just at home and missed the first call. I put in my AirPods and listen to some music and watch the world outside the window race by.

When the train arrives at Luton, it's like I am back to the same person who started out, there's no pretending here. Everything is too familiar, everyone too familiar. I leave the station, consider buying a sausage roll, then think better of it. Walk down the high street, there's a small dog on a lead staring at me, I stare back and smile before winding my way through the back streets to the place I grew up in.

I can see Mum's housing estate and drop quickly into the corner shop; a familiar waft of vanilla-scented cleaning products rises up at me. The man behind the counter is Sharn. He's much older now, been here for years. I grab a bottle of Fanta, Mum's favorite drink, and head to the register.

Evening, Sharn, how are you?

Well, hello there, long time no see, hey? Is that really little Tessa Ensler?

I laugh along.

Well, it's nice to see you. I tell all the young ones who come in, you know a girl from up the road here took herself to Cambridge, and now she's a lawyer in London. I know he's being kind but it feels awkward. He remembers more than just this. He remembers me as a small girl, coming in with scraped knees, or with my brother, Johnny, clutching a pound coin if I was lucky. He remembers my father. We talk about the new Tesco Metro on the corner and how Sharn's business is suffering. I nod sympathetically but I know that even my mum, who loves Sharn, shops there now. It's just cheaper. I feel guilty so I buy some expensive chocolates and Sharn must climb a ladder to reach them, which makes me wonder whether they might be past their expiry date. He's still talking about Cambridge.

I tell them all about you going off and studying law there. About how they could do it too if they wanted to. I nod, but I feel uncomfortable. I earn so much more than Sharn these days. Sharn with his 24/7 business, living out the back with his kids, his wife, and his mother. All of them working the shop, his kids starting early, and although they went to the same state school I did, we steadily avoided each other, knowing that a sort of intimacy through the shop could somehow betray us. I think about how sad that was. What secrets did I really know? That they struggled? So did my mum both before Dad left and then much more so afterward. It was all too hard to navigate, easier to just disconnect. I pay for the Fanta and the chocolates, ask Sharn about his mother, who I then instantly remember has already passed away. I tell him I thought she was lovely, because she was, although I don't remember a single conversation I ever had with her. Sharn's mother never spoke any English, but she sometimes would look at you like she understood the intricacies and privacies of your sadness. I shiver at what she must have known about my parents.

CHAPTER 3

THEN

Johnny carries in the last Tesco bag of books and puts them by my desk. He has looked uncomfortable all day at Cambridge, but now here in my room he fills the space. He's strong, so he's made good time unpacking. Too good time. There's a silence that none of us can fill. I sit on my bed, feeling melancholic, I know that Johnny can tell. He speaks almost too cheerily.

Well, that's the last of it!

I look up at his face. I can't say anything. He knows though.

Gonna miss you, kiddo.

I feel my eyes hot and bite my lip so I won't cry. I don't want to be pathetic. I gather my thoughts and toss my hair back.

Yeah, sure you will, you'll never have to share the remote!

I want to keep up the bravado, but the thought of Johnny and Mum leaving is suddenly too hard. Mum is putting a few last things into my tiny fridge, her back to us. I look at Johnny and I can't help myself.

Think I'll make any friends here?

I try to sound cool, but it comes out as a plea. Johnny quips back quickly.

Not a chance.

He knows how to make me laugh. He comes over and pats my hair, then awkwardly moves in to hug me. It's exactly what I crave but this is not what our family does, so it's a brush of my back. It's enough though. Johnny tries to keep things light, he points over at his old BMX, he's letting me have it to get around campus.

Don't let anyone steal my bike, okay?

I want to laugh because we both know that bike is worth nothing,

but I keep my mouth firmly closed, nod at him. If I move anything
more, I will cry. He avoids my face, probably to save me the humiliation. Mum is still busying herself washing a glass in my tiny sink.
Johnny speaks at the wall.

> Show 'em what you're made of, Tess.

Silence, then I dare to ask exactly what I am thinking.

> Johnny? Maybe I shouldn't . . .

Johnny looks alarmed. He doesn't like this vulnerability. It's spoken,
which is not how we do it.

> Hey! You've got a fucking good brain, Tess. We can't both
> be stuck painting houses.

I roll my eyes at him. There's an act of generosity in him acknowledging his own lack of options.

> You'd be so rubbish at it if you had to, anyway!

I laugh. Mum comes over to me and hands me some sandwiches.

> For when you're hungry later.

She looks like she might cry. I tell her:

> I'm eighteen, Mum, I'll be okay.

Our family can't say 'I love you' but it's there, and in this moment I
feel it so strongly it hurts. It feels sharper and more intense because
we don't say it. Johnny's face is trying to shape his chin and mouth
into something manly, and Mum lets a few tears escape. I cling to her
for a moment. Johnny has moved away. He looks around my room.
Bags of books everywhere, clothes hung in the closet by Mum. Me
on the single bed being left behind. He has to change the mood.

> And just so you know, there's no hanging around over
> Christmas with new posh friends. You gotta come home
> or I'll sell all your stuff on eBay!

Then they are gone.

CHAPTER 4

I don't knock when I reach Mum's place, just use my key. I can tell as soon as I walk in that she has vacuumed because of the lingering odor, a sort of aftertaste our home Hoover has always had. I always wonder how, after cleaning offices all day, she can bear to vacuum at home. I call out.

    Hiya.

Head into the kitchen, the telly is blaring about how someone collected too much social security. I hate the stuff Mum listens to, the poor bastard with too much payout is being humiliated and berated on the screen. Mum is washing vegetables at the sink. I turn off the telly and she spins around to see me. Why does Mum still register fear at the first surprise?

    Hi, Mum.

I plonk down the Fanta and the chocolates. She smiles at me. Tired, worn.

    Finished court early so I thought I would come and help
        you prepare.

She's staring at the Fanta, squinting.

    It's not sugar-free, love.

'Fail,' I think to myself.

    Johnny around?

She ignores this and gestures to the vegetables.

    I got those potatoes you like.

She hands me a knife, and I start chopping right there in my suit. She asks:

    How was your day, love?

I consider whether to tell her, decide why not?

    I won a case.

She doesn't miss a beat.

Ah, so you got more criminals out on our streets again
        then, did ya?
I tell myself there's nothing to add, I just chop. Silence between us
as the knife slices through potatoes and carrots, hitting the chopping
board with dull, quick sounds. Mum pats the meat with a tea towel,
puts it in the baking dish. The oven is already heating. I change
topics.
        Johnny not home then?
She washes her hands under the tap and dries them on a dishcloth.
        I've got something for you.
Mum leaves the kitchen, I'm stunned. What could she possibly have
for me? She comes back with a plastic shopping bag, stands in front
of me, I take it as a message to wash my own hands. Then Mum
hands the bag to me tentatively. I take it, confused. She never buys
me things for no reason. I briefly think it's a late birthday present but
that's not possible because my birthday was ages ago.
        What is it?
Mum steps back, takes her lighter from the window ledge, and lights
up a fag. She leans toward the open window. She's nervous.
        Saw it on special.
I pull out a shirt. It's a bright pink and one hundred percent polyester. I'm still taking it in when she speaks up again.
        Said to myself, looks like what a lawyer would wear?
Her voice trails off slightly, anxious. This is not what a lawyer would
wear, and most certainly not what I would wear. I am afraid of
betraying this truth so all my effort goes into the delight I feign.
        Oh wow, Mum, thank you so much.
She's tentative, but I sense something else, a relief, a quiet joy.
        Do you like it?
I hold it up.
        Mum! I love it!
Her face, the happiness it gives her, it makes me start to tear up. I
suddenly love this disgusting shirt. I take off my own shirt and pull
on the pink one. Then I tuck it into my suit trousers. This is a step
beyond what my mother would have hoped for and I play it perfectly. Parade around. As I walk past her, I grab her in a hug, she can't

help it, always stiffens when she is touched, but her face glows, for just a moment, before it clouds over. I am close enough to her that she can whisper to me.

Your brother got into a fight last night, up at the pub.
I stop in my tracks. Everything has changed. I am seething.

What? Again?
This is no response, but the intimacy between us is broken. She has unburdened herself and passed the worry, the fear onto me. Yet for me it presents as fury. Mum stubs out her cigarette, takes off her cardigan. Her uniform has her name inscribed on her left breast pocket, 'June.' She washes her hands again and starts to chop.

Mum, he's going to end up in jail.
She busies herself. I never know why she tells me these things only to hope I won't react. It only provokes me further.

What the hell is wrong with him? He should be working,
        paying his way.
I pick up my knife and start to chop carrots with force. It's unnerving for Mum but I can't help it.

He's such a loser.
I don't know whether it's instinct or a small sound that alerts me, but I turn to see Johnny standing in the doorway in old tracksuit bottoms and a T-shirt. Over his brow is a dried bloody mess; he looks tired. I flinch, no one wants to deal with Johnny when he is like this. He bellows at me.

Says who?
I just stand there. He moves toward me and breathes his words down at me. I stand defiantly. He continues.

Says the fancy fucking lawyer in her fancy fucking pink
        shirt.
I want to laugh, the fancy pink shirt for God's sake. I can't make that joke in front of Mum but I hear myself lash out:

At least I have a job.
This enrages him, he stomps into the kitchen. Mum and I both flinch. Mum yells.

Stop it! Stop it, both of you!
She looks terrified, and both Johnny and I know where that look

comes from. It makes me angrier at Johnny. His alcohol breath is stale and dirty, but I do not show any fear. I realize that he is hungover from the night before. I spit it at him:

What's wrong with you?

I realize the only reason Mum told me about the fight is because I would see his face, and she figured introducing it carefully might manage my reaction. I'm never scared of Johnny, even now when perhaps I should be. I yell right into his face.

What, are you going to hit me or something? Is that how you communicate now?

Mum screams out.

Stop this, both of you.

Johnny is shocked at what I said. He stares at me uncomprehendingly.

I'd never hit a woman.

My retort comes so hard, fast, and cruel that I'm shocked at myself.

You're doing everything else he did though, aren't ya?

Johnny tells me to fuck off. Mum chastises me, quiet but stern.

Tessa, that's enough.

We all know I have gone too far. Johnny looks at me, and beneath the fury I see confusion, hurt. What happened to us? He used to be my best friend. I'd follow him everywhere, all my childhood. It was me who sat with him every Saturday as he searched the spectators on the live TV football footage, looking out for a specific Everton supporter. We both knew whom he was looking for. I didn't have the heart to tell him that even if I saw our dad, I wouldn't recognize him anymore. I feel a wave of longing, but my eyes meet his, close, firing off each other, and I will not back down. Johnny flails a little, then in a different voice he challenges me.

When did you turn into such a bitch?

It stings. I can tell Johnny doesn't know what to do next with his feelings, he lurches past at the bench, with a bang swiping everything off. A plate smashes, Mum screams and starts to cry. There is nothing else for me to do but gather my stuff.

I'm . . . just going to go.

I look back as I leave the kitchen, Johnny is leaning with his eyes closed against the wall. Mum is trying to pick up pieces of potato, carrot, and broccoli.

Mum? I'm sorry.

She shakes her head. I want to make things all right, but I can't. The last thing I see is my mum on the kitchen floor, on her hands and knees. At the front door I take two fifty-quid notes out of my bag and slip them into Mum's handbag. I let myself out, pulling the door closed behind me.

CHAPTER 5

THEN

The university is gobsmackingly beautiful, more than I could ever have dreamed. So many incredible old buildings, and areas of carefully mowed grass. I keep saying to myself, over and over in my mind, 'Cambridge,' 'I'm at Cambridge.' It feels like a forbidden sweet in my mouth, a delightful secret. I am now a resident in a college that has housed centuries of students, it's overwhelming to even think about this. I must organize my subject timetable and attend a compulsory law induction lecture.

While I'm not keen on entering the massive dining hall for supper, eventually hunger takes over and I slide in. I watch the other students vigilantly. They carry their meals to long tables, greet each other, chat, and laugh. I sit alone, eat some fish with potato, then creep back to my room. A single bed, a desk, wardrobe, small fridge, sink, and a window. I stare through the window, which looks out onto a pretty area of the university. I want to enjoy it, to take it all in, but as I gaze out at my new world, I'm struck only by my own face reflected. Everything feels suddenly eerie and lonely. I long for something that I can't quite put my finger on. This is everything I have worked for: this place, Cambridge. And yet, this strange longing persists.

The next morning, I eat cereal in my room and dress for the induction lecture. Despite leaving ample time to arrive, I still manage to be late.

When I finally reach the correct lecture hall, I take my name tag from the table and affix it to my jumper. Wearing my new jeans, trainers, and the jumper Mum bought me specially, I venture into the lecture hall.

There are only a few seats available other than those in the very front row. I quickly assess whether to take a single seat in the middle of a row or a seat at the front. I decide the fear of being called upon is so great that I will find my way through all the other seated students to the middle of a row. I squeeze my way, apologizing and sliding simultaneously, until I reach the one spare seat. Sandwiched between a boy and a girl, I feel a strange shift. 'This is me in the induction lecture at law school at Cambridge,' I dare to tell myself.

I'm dumbfounded by how everyone seems to know someone else, some even clustered in groups. 'Where do all these people come from?' I think as I look about me. Two hundred faces and each of us must have had top marks at A levels. Other than teachers at school, I'd never been in a room before with people who finished A levels.

I can't help but ask myself, 'How am I here?' No one ever believed I would end up here. All summer, adults had been telling me that I was 'lucky to have such a huge opportunity'; always 'lucky,' no recognition of how hard I'd worked to get the grades to get in. There was a seam of something else running through their acknowledgment, a sense that I could only go so far, or that I would probably screw it up so I should 'not put on any airs and graces, Tessa.' They felt I was somehow upsetting the natural order of things, and hated that I had no response when these flashes of resentment appeared. But even I had various backup plans, because I knew that even if I was accepted, the only way I could take up the offer was to secure a scholarship. When that news arrived, I was able to really own it.

I was going to Cambridge.

Today the faces about me seem confident, with an air of expectation. It occurs to me that their parents and grandparents had probably been here too. 'That's okay, I'm here now, I just have to do what they do, and I'll belong here.' For now I am pretending, but I'll get the hang of it. Hawklike, I zoom in on a group of suited staff hovering at the entrance. Involuntarily I start, a wave of primal fear descends. Maybe I fluked it, and one of those suited people is going to barge in with a list and call out my name. 'Tessa Ensler? I'm *so* sorry, there's been a terrible mistake.'

I imagine all eyes upon me as I struggle to get up and push my way out of the middle of this middle row. Humiliated, a failure already.

Even as I regain my focus and push such thoughts out of my mind, my nails dig into my palms. A hush takes over the room before the dean enters. She moves toward the podium and I feel a thrill of excitement. 'This is happening.' Her voice is loud and crisp.

You are the crème de la crème.

She actually says that, and it is the first time anyone has said anything like that about me. I want to laugh in embarrassment, but as I watch the others, everyone is nodding, seriously contemplating this idea. She moves on to remind us that we are at the top law school because we have top marks, inferring that we are also top people. I store all of this in my mind, thinking how I will mimic her back home at the pub with some mates. 'Crème de la crème.' Then it occurs to me it might not be funny to my mates back in Luton, they are not here being called the top people. All this happens in an instant before I am back with the dean. She speaks earnestly.

You will be the ones to change the country.

She says this and pauses. Just as lawyers on TV do. They say something big, then make you wait. I lap it up. This is what I am here to learn, to make this many people hang on your every word. I take out my notebook but then realize nobody else is taking notes.

She starts to speak again.

But.

I don't like this. But? What is the but?

Look to the person on your left.

I feel terribly shy. I dare to turn. It's the boy, and 'fuck, he is bloody gorgeous.' I can tell he's from a posh school. He must already know he will 'change the country.' Probably already has! I try to look unimpressed, shake my hair a bit and pick my chin up. Eyes at him, as he turns back around from the person he was looking at. He takes a quick glance at my outfit, yet somehow makes a full appraisal. The jumper gives me away, it's obvious that I am not where he is from. I feel a familiar wave of something. Not humiliation, but close, and it feeds a self-hatred. I haven't figured out the code yet, I have given myself away. I wither.

The dean continues.

Then look to the person on your right.

I'm glad to turn from the boy. The girl on my right has a haircut

that screams 'private school.' She is wearing clothes that are supposed to look worn, but I know they are brand-new. She has layers
of clothing, layers of necklaces, her makeup is earthy, bloody hell
her makeup is contoured. She welcomes the boy on the other side
of her, then turns and looks right at me. I hold back. I am not going
to give anything of myself, I will not let her look at me like the boy
did. But she's different. She looks at me warmly, smiles a big goofy
smile, and then pulls a face. I try to stifle a snort, but it comes out
anyway. 'For God's sake, Tessa, just be normal, won't you?' Still,
'Mia,' as her name tag denotes, seems happy to see me. Then the
dean again.

Look back at me and hear this.

Mia's arm brushes mine as she turns back. I'm still cringing at the
snort.

One of the three of you will not make it. Yes. One of the three
of you will fail. Make no mistake. You are all in competition
with each other.

The dean pauses again. For effect. Then:

You are not friends; you're fighting each other. And the
game starts . . . NOW.

I can't look at Mia, or the boy. I feel myself redden. The other two,
they think it's going to be me! I'm the one who won't make it. Because
you can tell I don't belong here. I feel angry at both.

Mia types into her phone, the latest model, I notice, super expensive.
I assume we won't talk again after today. She'll end up being a top
lawyer and she won't remember my name. It's fine. I don't care. But
I feel the familiar fury rise in my throat. I feel the fight in me start.
No more of this 'you could screw this up.' I have all A stars and I am
going to show the world.

The dean starts again.

Out of those of you who even make it to bar school, only
one in ten of you will get pupillage. Only five of those
might get silk, and only one has a chance of being a judge
each decade.

I turn to the boy. See the sticker carefully attached to his chest.
'Benedict.' Of course he is called Benedict. He glances at me, but
nothing. He has already dismissed me. 'Fuck you,' I think to myself.

He becomes the person I most want to beat. The dean again. She's talking 'the law.'

Never assume anyone is telling you the truth—even yourself.
There is no real truth, only legal truth. Don't trust your gut instincts, only your legal instincts. You will get it wrong if you think you know what will happen.

This time I start to write it all down. The dean gathers her papers, makes a dramatic exit, leaving us with one last pearl.

You are the best of the best, prepare yourselves for the fight of your life, because law school is just the beginning.

Years later I reflect on the notes on this writing pad just before I toss it out.

Benedict, the guy on my left, graduated and ended up working as a powerful banking lawyer, just as I expected. He was always headed right there.

The girl on my right—Mia. She dropped out after first year to go to acting school, but before she left, we became best friends. For life.

As I read the notes I scrawled way back on that first day at Cambridge, I realize that the dean was right. Instincts can be wrong. I had assumed that Mia would never talk to me again after that day. That we were worlds apart and she would never give me another thought. How wrong I was.

And then, on the next page of the notes, I spy something else: 'Never assume you are telling yourself the truth. Don't trust what you "think" you know. This is not life, this is law.' I rip the page from the notebook and pin it above my desk. That might have been the truest thing I ever learned at Cambridge.

CHAPTER 6

Up at the bar on the corner, I order our drinks as I wait for Cheryl. She texted me the name of a fancy mocktail that she likes. Cheryl arrives just as I put our drinks down. She's the same as always, laughing eyes, colored hair, tight clothes, bounding up to me. She might be Johnny's girlfriend, but she was mine first. We met in primary school and she has stuck by me ever since, even when I never came home in the last year of uni, even after I moved to London. She's like a sister to me. We're like sisters to each other. Even more so since she started dating Johnny—though maybe this is what changed with me and Johnny, now I think about him as a man, think about how he's treating her. Cheryl herself will never leave town, she's not even keen for a weekend at mine in London. She tells me about her work up at the call center, about some antics the staff all get up to. She says she doesn't hate it as much as she used to, she's quite good at selling stuff, she tells me. She's drinking her mocktail in large gulps. I tease her about her drink; she used to drink the real thing. Cheryl laughs. Then there is a silence we both know is Johnny. I know she knows what went down, and she knows I know she knows. She puts her drink down.

Tess, it's his first fight in years.

I realize she is standing up for Johnny. I feel ever so slightly betrayed.

That we know of!

I'm being smart, not thoughtful, and Cheryl speaks quietly as she looks into her glass.

Some asshole called me a fat pig at the pub.

Fuck.

I feel furious on behalf of Cheryl, mad at my mother for not offering this context, although perhaps she didn't know. Cheryl jumps in.

Anyway, Johnny's going to step up now.

She seems cheerful, but I'm still engulfed in anger and regret. Cheryl pulls a piece of paper out of her bag and lays it before me. An ultrasound image of a baby.

No way! You're joking?

You're going to be an aunty.

I pick it up. There's a baby right there. We squeal, hug.

That explains your virgin cocktail.

We were going to tell you over dinner.

I feel the weight of understanding. Mum had asked me to dinner because she knew; she was setting a scene where Johnny and Cheryl were going to break the big news. Cheryl looks over my shoulder and frowns. I turn and there's a man with a beer, he leers toward me, drunk and clumsy. Cheryl speaks up.

Way out of your league, buddy!

The man sneers at me and I turn back to Cheryl. We both roll our eyes.

Johnny said he's going to put a ring on it.

Cheryl volunteers this as if it has just occurred to her that it's something she might be interested in. We both know she has been waiting for years.

That's awesome.

Cheryl can't contain herself.

SISTERS!

We laugh ourselves silly, talk about how at eight we tried to convince everyone that we were sisters, it was just that I had been adopted to another family. After a belly laugh, I lean back. I am so grateful to Cheryl.

Thanks for meeting me here.

Cheryl shrugs, gestures to her virgin cocktail.

I'll meet anyone anywhere for a free drink, even if there is
no alcohol in it.

After relating every ache and pain, every urine test and internal examination, Cheryl must go home. She wants to drive me to the station, but I want some air. I start the walk to the last train to London. The streets are dark and cooler now. Empty, with all the shops closed and few cars. I walk briskly, so I am sure I won't miss the train. Then behind me on the street, I see the guy from the pub. He's on the other side of the road but catching up; I start to walk faster.

Heart pumping. Breathing fast, in, out. I try to look nonchalant, bold, confident, but he is gaining and I panic. He calls out to me:

Hey.

I ignore him, silently berating myself for not taking Cheryl's offer of a lift. I am walking fast now, almost running, but I won't break into a run because then he'll know I am afraid. Because I am afraid. A quick glance behind and he is now on the same side of the road as me, the station is still a ways away. Do I press on or cross over and sprint back to the pub? He waves at me. The guy breaks into a sprint. He's tall, heavyset. I also break into a run; I consider taking a turn, but the streets are small and dark. He is just behind me, and I stop abruptly, panting, mind racing. I tell him:

My boyfriend is waiting at the station for me.

He holds something up, but it's dark and I can't see what he has. Is it a knife? He is panting but I make out what he says.

You left your phone behind.

I see he has my phone in his hand, held aloft. My heart is still thumping but my brain catches up. He is returning my phone. My hand is shaking as I accept the return. He is not pursuing me to hurt me, to rape me, to stab me. He is pursuing me because I left my phone at the pub. I speak to him in a professional voice, but I can hear my own desperate relief.

Thanks.

I stand but don't want to continue the conversation. I brace myself for any further advances, but this time he is done. He turns to go.

No problem.

He walks away.

I continue to the station. When I tap in to catch the train, I briefly stand and catch my breath. My hand still charged and shaky. My breathing is nearly normal as the train pulls out.

CHAPTER 7

I grab a sausage roll on the walk into chambers the next morning. It's nine when I get there, and Alice is in a total flap. She grabs me as soon as I enter, pulls me to one side.

Where have you been?

I'm confused.

I went to my mum's last night.

I've been texting you.

I realize my phone volume is right down.

Have you got the PNC for the drug case you flicked me?

It dawns on me. The case I gave her runs today. She needs the Police National Computer printout of the defendant's previous convictions. I remember I spoke to Julian on Alice's phone. Seems he hasn't passed on the message!

I told Julian to tell you, it's on my desk.

We walk in tandem to my room, it's so messy Alice does a double take. I shrug; mess means a barrister is busy; she knows this. I find the file with the PNC and hand it over.

He's been inside twice before.

Alice sighs. She leaves quietly, flicking through pages. I grab another file and put it in my satchel. Julian hovers nearby. This is unusual, he is rarely around this part of chambers. Julian is chatting to Adam in the hallway and turns as if to have only just noticed me. Julian smiles at me.

Hey?

I smile back, he is so cocky. He doesn't take his eyes off me. Julian continues,

Word is Kingston, King's Counsel, no less, was on Tinder, get this, IN COURT. Swiping away!

The image makes me smile. A KC on Tinder is too human, too of this world.

Left, or right?

Julian laughs. It feels good to have him laugh at my quip.

He's been reported. His client took offense.

I'm shaking my head. Thinking, 'As you would be if you were paying him to run your case!' In a private case those clients are shelling out thousands of pounds a day. Julian looks at me again.

Coming out for drinks this week?

I shrug. He puts his head to one side flirtatiously. I feel a strange tingle.

Maybe.

I see Adam looking at me too, catch his eye. We go way back, were at law school together, we talk files and cases, shared ideas. His parents are educated, both teachers, but he understands about layers of privilege that the others don't. I've been nominated for the Chambers' Bar Awards for Criminal Barrister of the Year this year, but Adam already won it last year. I must admit Adam is the best barrister our age that I know; he can quote whole sections of the Criminal Code Act by memory. He's a freak! He's someone who cross-examines clients so brilliantly too, just leads them to where he wants them to go. Now that I have so many sexual assault cases, I rely on his style to cross-examine alleged sexual assault victims. It helps because as a barrister you look better to the jury; so many of the male barristers still come across as rabid, accusatory, angry—but Adam has a better way. Just suggest the mistakes in their testimony, pick up on inconsistencies, and put those to the witness complainant—they're usually so uncorroborated anyway that it's easy to pick up on inconsistencies. Test their story. He never goes in for the kill, he just lulls them with sympathy, then analyzes their answers. If there's any doubt, then it's just about uncovering it. It's helpful to talk to Adam, makes me a better lawyer. The idea is to stand outside it, don't take 'sides,' just test the law, test the testimony against the law. Test it. Test it. If the story has holes, then point them out. Because it's not just your case, it's the law that's at stake. And the law is there to protect everyone. Protect those who accuse, protect those who are accused, protect those police who don't cut corners, so the ones who do are exposed. We can't just prejudge someone. And if a few guilty people get off, then it's because the police or the prosecutors at the Crown Prosecution Service didn't do their job well enough. Due process is everything.

He asks:

>	What have you got on this morning?

I respond to Adam as if Julian is not even there.

>	Three sentence matters. Up at inner court. You?

>	I'm still in the giant case up at the Old Bailey.

There is a warmth there between Adam and me, real respect, friendship. Julian jumps in.

>	And you were on the news last night, old Adam, weren't
>		you?

>	In the background.

I jump in.

>	Double point for TV too, I'm not even in print yet! You're
>		well in the lead, Adam.

Adam is modest but he's also studying what is happening. Julian and
me. I feel slightly embarrassed. Julian jumps in.

>	Hang on, hang on, I've got that South Kensington knife
>		case coming up. All media are onto it.

Adam laughs.

>	You'll be shoving senior counsel to the curb every day,
>		pushing your face into the cameras!

I laugh, he's right. Julian is laughing as well.

>	Well, gotta win the bet. You'll both see, you'll be paying for
>		my drinks all year.

Adam smiles, we both groan. I tease Julian.

>	Read the 'rules, Jules'; even if you win, it's drinks for only
>		three months!

Julian is watching me. I suddenly feel awkward and take my satchel.

>	Good luck today then.

I walk back to Alice's room; she is about to leave too—groaning
about having to catch the train to Snaresbrook Crown Court, but
happy to have the case. We move toward the lifts together. I glance
back at the men; they are gone. Alice reminds me that after court we
were all going to help our new pupil with some basics. It's been six
years since I was a pupil and I like helping the good ones. Phoebe is
better than most, she's smart and has exactly what you need to run
defense. She can think quickly on her feet, pivot when the case starts
to falter, holds her ground in court, and knows the law.

She is also hungry for criminal cases; she likes being nimble, likes running the unpredictable race that defense barristers experience. There's nothing else like it and she has that same hunger, that same need to be the best. This is something all criminal defense barristers need. You can't take someone's life in your hands unless you are prepared to go for broke, to fight for them as hard as you can.

Once I was trying to explain this to Mum and her mate Kathy, that it's my role as a defense barrister, but she wasn't buying it. I explained that my job is to take the client, hear their story, and tell the court the best version of that very story. Mum was all:

But what if he did it?

I reminded her:

They are not all 'he's,' and it's not my job to know whether they did it or not.

She didn't understand, not because she can't but because it defies her own logic. I told them my job is to tell the best version of my client's story, and the prosecutor tells the best version of the police story, and the jury decides which story is more likely. That's it. Simple. I just tell a story, a storyteller. The jury decides, not me.

Kathy was enthralled, but Mum wasn't so sure.

And what if your story is wrong?

Really, Mum, I just play within the rules and do the best I can. If we all play by the rules, then justice will be done. And if some guilty people get off, that's because the prosecutor didn't do their job well enough. My job is to make sure that innocent people don't go to jail. That's what matters. Everyone deserves due process.

I might be laying it on thick, but I know Mum's weakness. She wants to think everyone has a fair go. Although it was never my brother Johnny's experience. When Johnny was first arrested as a juvenile, he took the rap for someone else despite Mum begging him not to. I understood why he did it. But now I know that by taking the rap that time, he then became 'known to police' with a criminal record. That meant not only were his job prospects sunk, but his chances of being arrested again increased. And true to this, he was actively pursued after that; they would always come talk to him whenever there was a robbery or a break-and-enter in the area. Johnny didn't stand a chance after that first conviction, and now even in his early thirties it still follows him. The law is supposed to test a case, but sometimes the police set up their reporting of the facts so that the case looks better. The defense job is to be able to uncover that.

When the afternoon comes around, I have managed to get two sentence matters heard, both guilty pleas for assault occasioning actual bodily harm, and another sentence matter on a sexual assault guilty plea put over for a social work report. The two resolved sentences had remarkably successful outcomes. I smashed it in court—I had so much narrative context on the lives of the guys I was repping and I argued so strongly that I wound up diverting both of them from full-time custody. It felt good. Sometimes it's as much about listening to a client's background and life story, finding ways for rehab or engagement, as much as it is about knowing the law. Just go that extra mile and set something up for them that the judge can't easily turn down.

We're all in Alice's room, hers being larger and neater. I'm giving Phoebe a refresher on police cross-examination, because Julian told her I am the best at cross-examining police. It sort of embarrasses me, this unadulterated praise, but the truth is that secretly I love it. Julian's here too, with Alice. They are good mates, were in some tennis club together in high school for years, well before the bar. I know Julian did well in court this morning because he has a swagger about him. It's the way he holds himself. Alice didn't do great, she ended up adjourning because she could see the writing was on the wall. She's now nursing a headache and a somber mood. Adam wanders in after court. I ask him how the Bailey was that day. He shrugs.

Inconclusive.

I feel the need to be better at explaining things to Phoebe now Adam is here.

I tell Adam:

Jump in if I miss anything?

Adam leans against the wall. He's astute; I bring in my best game plan.

Phoebe, the thing is that the police officers all show each other their statements.

Julian pipes in.

They're not as smart as us, no matter how much they try to
stitch things up.
He makes a fail sign, thumbs-down. Continues.
They hand us reasonable doubt on a silver platter.
I jump in.
If you try to play God in the system you're damned, but
the police forget. They think they ARE the system.
Julian is nodding, Alice is distracted. I look directly at Phoebe.
The trick when you cross-examine them is to get under
their skin.
Yes, but how?
Come with me tomorrow. I have a really difficult police officer
who is in exactly this situation. I can tell things don't line up
with his junior. They've fixed it. It will be over in no time.
Phoebe is delighted. I explain a quick outline summary of the case
for her. Julian tells Phoebe he has a footballer case coming up she
might be interested in. I flop onto a chair across from Alice, watch-
ing while Julian performs as he talks about his matter. He makes a
big deal of the fact that he is doing it pro bono, for free, as a com-
munity gesture of goodwill. I roll my eyes at Adam, who smiles.
Julian notices.
What?
I laugh.
You can't possibly call that pro bono!
Everyone laughs, even Phoebe. Julian isn't offended at all. He goes
along with it.
Why not? I do it for free.
He beams at me, challenging me. I roll my eyes.
Oh my God. What, for a posh football club! That, my
learned friend, is not pro bono! What Adam does for the
Refugee Legal Centre, now that's pro bono. The cases I
take for the kids from the estates . . .
Julian rolls his eyes. Turns to Phoebe and says:
Trust me, Phoebe, stick with me. I get free tickets, the
corporate box no less, and caviar, while this lot are eating
at Pret!
Adam lets out a laugh. Julian pretends to be fake betrayed by Adam.

What, you too? Come on!
Adam can't help himself.
    Mate. You donated a 'get off a drunk-driving charge' to a
        football fundraiser last year!
I hadn't heard this; Alice and I are gobsmacked. Julian jumps in.
    Got some laughs too.
Alice rolls her eyes; I jump in.
    Bet you loved the attention.
Julian turns to me.
    Maybe.
Phoebe questions:
    Did they use it?
Julian is quick.
    The very next week.
I can't help myself.
    That's borderline encouraging bad footballer behavior.
Julian ponders this.
    But it was worth it because I was briefly considered by the
        players to be cool!
I like this self-deprecating side of Julian. It's a sweet gesture from such a privately educated, entitled guy. He knows we are all laughing at him, and he not only lets us but takes the piss out of himself. Adam warns him.
    You're actually lucky no one reported you to the bar
        standards board. I can just see the headline.
Julian does a great face of terror, then can't help responding with great delight.
    At least I'd increase my media!
We all laugh. I like us all like this, the banter, the collegiality. Alice notices Phoebe shift slightly.
    Hey, we're here to help Phoebe, not to encourage Julian's
        ridiculous ideas.
Julian casts his eyes to Phoebe; he knows how to make anyone feel like the center of the room.
    Of course we are. Phoebe, the floor is yours, what's your
        case?
Phoebe glances from face to face. Nervous?

I have a sex case in a fortnight. My first, I need to know
    how to cross the complainant.
There's a weirdly charged pause in the room. I'm not sure why. But
Phoebe continues.
    Can I play the complainant, and someone crosses me, and
        I get the feel?
Alice speaks. Gently.
    I won't do that to you!
Phoebe turns to the men.
    Julian? Adam?
Julian is considering it when Adam jumps in.
    Tessa, you do it.
Eyes look right at me. I consider it, but no. I have another offer.
    Better idea. Come watch my sex case next week. It's a
        consent defense.
The mood has shifted. No real reason why, we are probably thinking
the same thing. How awkward it would be to cross-examine Phoebe
on this. I try to break the mood.
    For God's sake don't let Julian show you how! He got into
        big trouble with Spanx in his last case.
Julian exaggeratedly covers his eyes and groans. Success, mood bro-
ken. Phoebe asks:
    What?
I fold my arms and put Julian on the spot.
    Jules?
Julian is shaking his head. Alice jumps in.
    To be fair, it wasn't Jules's argument, it came from the silk
        leading him.
I turn to Phoebe but speak loudly enough that it's easy for everyone
to know I am speaking to them all.
    Jules was assisting a KC who told the jury that the woman
        rolling down her Spanx while she slept was her partially
        taking off her underwear, and therefore consenting.
Julian, face in his hands.
    And the KC—or *Julian*—didn't realize until the jury came
        back—a jury of eight young women mind you!—what
        the issue was.

I'm never going to live this down, am I?
Well other than the Spanx argument it was a hard case to
        lose!
Jules considers this.
        True. I acknowledge a mistake when it has been made.
I turn to Phoebe,
        Remember at law school, they always said 'never assume
                you know something, never assume what you think you
                know is true'?
Phoebe laughs.
        Yeah.
I turn my palms up.
        Exactly!
Julian shrugs.
Alice spots a cleaner outside her door and speaks up.
        If you're taking out the rubbish, can you take this too?
I flinch a little. I see the cleaner, expressionless; she moves over
to Alice, takes the bin Alice gestures toward. Julian is engaged in
explaining to Phoebe.
        The thing is the story must make consistent LEGAL truth.
                Never forget that.
Alice doesn't make eye contact with the cleaner, instead turns back to
her desk. I hear Julian in the background.
        When the debate centers on consent, you don't have to
                prove that she consented, just that HE DID NOT
                KNOW there WAS NO CONSENT. That it was
                reasonable for him to think it was okay.
Phoebe knows this, but she hangs on everything Julian says. As the
cleaner exits the room with Alice's bin, I meet her eye. Smile, mouth
'thanks.' I think about how the police think they are God until they
are caught out, about how I will catch out the officer tomorrow with
Phoebe watching me.
My eyes trail after the cleaner as she makes her way down the hallway
in her pale blue uniform, carrying a bin containing the remnants of
Alice's breakfast. I hear the tail end of Julian justifying the KC's cross
examination.
        I mean, we made a big mistake, should have made more

of an effort to understand the regime of women's support underwear, I guess. Or been more alert to who was
on the jury.
I reflect upon seeing Jules cross-examine in the past; I consider that
he has learned his style from most of the male KCs he has assisted
in court. Jules has this slightly annoyed manner about him when he
cross examines, which I'm not sure he even realizes he uses. The tone
might only be picked up by the likes of me, that tone that men in
power use when they doubt you. It's hard to explain unless you can
hear the slight putdown in it. I interrupt.

So, the KC—and our Julian here—didn't know that
women can't bear to sleep in tight, ugly Spanx, and that
of course you roll them down because otherwise they're
so damn tight that you can't sleep. He tells the jury, most
youngish women, mind you, that she rolled down her
Spanx because she was consenting to him putting his
hand inside her.
Phoebe giggles.
Oh God. You've obviously never worn Spanx!
Julian rolls his eyes.
Clearly, Phoebe. Clearly!
Adam explains to Phoebe:
His client went down. He's serving time.
Julian looks guilty. Phoebe notices.
Was he innocent?
We all groan.
Phoebe!
Julian doesn't miss a beat.
No way. But still, he shouldn't have lost!
Julian gives us all a cheeky grin, then throws his arms up in the air.
Enough. So, let's lock in drinks at the posh place on the
river, the one with the music.
I'm keen, so is Alice. She tells Phoebe:
It's the new place, Inflation.
Julian nods.
If you're all super lucky I'll invite some footballers too!
Alice laughs, turns to Phoebe.

He always says that, but they never come, do they, Julian?
Julian plays the loser. Makes me laugh. I look over at Adam questioningly.

>Not me, sorry, I'm with the baby so Saskia can get some
>>time out this week.

He shrugs.
The cleaner returns with Alice's bin, empty now. Alice and the others
move out toward the noise in the hallway. Someone out there has
called Julian to see something. I stand, see the name tag pinned on
the cleaner's uniform: 'Penny.' I take the bin from her before she puts
it down. She nods. I wonder whom she is supporting at home, where
she lives. I read her tag out loud.

>Penny!

>Sorry? Oh, I'm not Penny, this is someone else's tag,
>>couldn't find mine.

She pauses, I nod. She speaks up again.

>I'm Magda.

>Thanks, Magda.

She shrugs. Smiles. Leaves.

CHAPTER 8

THEN

I head off to work just off campus in the town center. Riding there on Johnny's old bike, I weave through the green of Cambridge University. I love the feel of the cool wind smacking my face. Marks & Spencer lets me bid for all my shifts in advance; I can do more shifts during term time, fewer over exam periods. I ride up through groups of students, some outside drinking coffee, some kissing, others on their phones on the grass. I still don't know many people, but I know my way around parts of the college and the university now. Keeping up with my classes; my marks are better than I would have hoped for. Everyone complains about the food, and to fit in I sometimes complain too, but the truth is I can't believe my scholarship includes board and meals. Every meal is like a restaurant to me. The men's business shirts and ties department is a completely new world for me. It occurred to me during training that I have never known anyone who would wear any of it. With no dad around, and Johnny—who I have never seen in a business shirt in my life, a tie out of the question (the only time he was ever out of jeans was at my granddad's funeral)—it's just an alien area of clothing. I lock up my bike outside and see there's two guys from one of my classes. I feel embarrassed, shy. I don't want them to see me in my black outfit with my work badge pinned on. None of the other students seem to have part-time jobs, although two of the other scholarship students do tutor in French and German. I've never learned another language. As I turn to head inside, Mia, the girl from induction, rocks up to the boys, lights up a cigarette, and starts chatting. Mia might be the most natural person I have ever seen. She just appears in places, dressed like she is, and every time I learn something new about her. She's also super friendly, and we really have a laugh when I see her. She's funny, and she thinks I'm funny, which kind of makes me be funny! I didn't realize she smoked until I saw her light up just now, and while her hair was red last week, it's now a different color. A brownie gold. I sat behind some other girls in lecture who pointed her out and talked about her family. I strained my ears out of curiosity and heard various mentions of their notoriety. Wealth, well known, involved in philanthropy. I leaned back. 'That's enough,' I thought. I don't want to know any more, or I might not feel so comfortable around her. As I walk past the guys, Mia jumps out to greet me.

  Just the person I need to talk to.
I smile.
  Sorry, I've got work, I'm almost late.
  I know, I'm going to hang about until you have a break.
  Okay?
  I don't know when my break is.
She shrugs. Like time is something she has in abundance. I imagine without having to work as a student there must be lots of time to hang about.
  Okay.
  You still in men's business attire?
The two guys look up. Check me out.
  Yeah. I think I'm measuring the necks of all the men in
   suits.
She laughs her wild laugh without a single measure of self-consciousness.
  Well, that's one way to strangle the patriarchy!
We both laugh. I am so fond of her; she has been a steadfast presence since I began uni. She sidles up to me at meal times, sits next to me in classes, despite being in huge demand. She introduces me to others as her mate and tells me 'you're so hot, you know that, right?' which makes me blush because people don't say 'hot' where I come from. Especially other girls. I tell Cheryl on the phone one day that girls say that to girls here. Cheryl asks me whether Mia is a lesbian.
  No, I don't think so, I think she would say something if she
   was. She always has a boy around too.
Cheryl sighs.

> Wouldn't you like to be that sort of girl, one that just
> knows they can get whatever they want. I hate her on
> principle.

I coerce Cheryl into meeting her one day when she comes up on the
train with my mum to visit, and the three of us get drunk together
in Mia's room. Later Cheryl agrees with me.

> I know she's posh but she's not posh posh. She's fucking
> awesome.

Cheryl even spent a morning giving her a facial. When I'm on the
floor at work, the other servers always ask me to help some color-
blind guy choose a tie to match his suit and shirt choice. I have
made a name for myself now as the 'color whisperer' but it's all
intuitive. I have so much confidence in this now that I believe my
own hype and do it in lightning speed. Just hope I'm not sending
them all out dressed wrong. My break comes early today, which is
not great because then you're on your feet until the shop closes. But
at least Mia won't have to wait for hours to chat. I grab my backpack; I've pinched some pastries from the college breakfast table and
stashed them in a plastic box in my bag. She's meeting me where
she was earlier; I approach and see a different set of guys surround-
ing her. Mia bolts toward me and we make our way to a green spot
where there's a park bench. As we walk over, she points out a cute
guy. I know she is expecting me to use my new skill set to pick his
neck size at a distance. I'm pretty good at it, but even if I wasn't she'd
never know. I just have to sound confident.

> Sixteen-inch.

We laugh. She pinches some of my stolen croissant. I'm still baffled
as to why she waited to see me. She's more pensive as we walk. I wait
it out. Eventually.

> Tess, tell me.

We sit. I wait for her to explain.

> Why'd you choose law?

I'm confused, try to think of an answer, and then, remembering it is
Mia, just tell her the truth.

> I think it began as an idea when my brother was arrested at
> seventeen. He hadn't done anything so I assumed he would
> get off, but he was convicted. Had a rubbish lawyer.

Mia takes this in.

> You've got a passion for it?
>
> Mmm.

Mia lights up a cigarette.

> I'm dropping out.

I'm stunned.

> What? Why?

I wait to hear that she is pregnant or something. Why would she give up when she has this opportunity?

> Acting school.
>
> What?

I'm genuinely confused.

> I got into RADA, the Royal Academy of Dramatic Art. It's
>> in London.

I'm catching up. She looks so excited that I smile encouragingly. But really, I am selfishly upset that I am losing the one person I really like here at uni. That I'll have to start again.

> I don't want you to leave!

She throws her arm around me. Squeezes me in and I nearly choke on a bit of croissant.

> You're the best thing about this whole experience.

I'm shocked. But completely enthralled.

> The funniest, smartest, most authentic person I have ever
>> met.

She looks teary. I panic.

> I'm not going anywhere. You can visit anytime.

She smiles.

> Friends for life, okay?
>
> For sure.
>
> The thing is Tess, my parents are not going to like it.
>
> Why?
>
> They like the idea of me becoming a lawyer.
>
> Oh.

I'm surprised that her parents have any say in what she decides to do. I can't imagine Mum advising me on what I study. I shrug.

> Thing is, it's your life!

Mia beams. It's like she's never heard this before.

I guess I'm the one in three that didn't make it as a lawyer.

That gets you off the hook, you can relax now!!

She's joking, but after work as I cycle back to change and meet Mia at a bar somewhere, I take this as a sign that I will make it in law. I reflect back to induction and the dean telling us that we can't trust our instincts, just our legal instincts. She was right. Once more I thank my lucky stars; because if I'd trusted my instincts, I would have never made friends with Mia.

CHAPTER 9

Phoebe is standing outside in the courtroom foyer in the morning, waiting for me. She has shown such eagerness to watch me in court that she has shown up to see me cross-examine the police. She looks different; tells me she has bought a new suit and wanted to try it out. It's a nice look, though it has slight embellishments that tend to highlight her junior pupil status without her realizing it. The trick is to dress as plainly, yet as upmarket, as possible. Nevertheless her suit looks expensive. There's something about Phoebe that I like, I can't put my finger on it; perhaps like Mia she is more than a product of the privilege she came from? Perhaps she really loves the law like I do, I'm not sure. Phoebe is confusing.

People like myself do defense cases because they believe in protecting people from the police. They believe defense work is social justice work, a way of fighting for rights, and they want to fight for the underprivileged. I saw what went on around me, how people from the estate were targeted by police, like my brother.

Adam and I are both of this ilk, and while Adam's family have never had issues with the law, Adam has a philosophical stance, a deep commitment to what is right. I like to think that mine has evolved into something philosophical too. Fight for the underdog and all that. But sometimes I'm just acting for underdogs because I was one. Then there are those like Julian who love the fight of it, the game of law, and who see working in criminal law as an exciting way to fight. Alice is more in Julian's camp, but she is losing her confidence. And confidence in court is everything. Especially in criminal law. Phoebe talks as if she is a social justice warrior, but her family are the most privileged bankers I have heard of. It confuses me. Where did she find this fire to defend? She is passionate about defense, brutal about prosecution matters—and it seems to come from a fire deep in her belly.

When my cross-examination of the police officer begins, Phoebe is taking notes behind me. The police officer is hostile, he is staring me down. Old-school. This means he is going to be a pushover. It's the ones who are perfectly polite, unemotional, and not defensive that I have to worry about, but this guy, this police officer with his red face and flared nostrils, is an easy target.

I decide to take my time to nail him so that Phoebe can witness it. I stand, smile kindly as he scowls back at me. No bother. The truth is that cross-examining police is sort of . . . fun. I would never say that to anyone who isn't a barrister, but we all know it can be. It sounds bad to say it, but there is something very rewarding about methodically undermining their evidence by pointing out what looks manufactured, then presenting them with their own lies. Once you find a way under their skin, they get defensive, and they make mistakes. That is the gold right there, the mistakes they make on the stand. Because once they are caught out lying, everything else they have said before is suddenly much less reliable, if at all. My role is to test the case, just test it, and test it over and over. Find the inconsistencies. And when the police leave themselves wide open, it is all instinct and practice that lets you bring it home, land that plane.

I have extracted all I needed from the junior officer who came before him, so when the sergeant walks up to the stand, I fear it might all be over too quickly, that Phoebe won't see me at my best. The big police officer clears his throat. I wait until he is ready. Then jump right in.

> I suggest, Constable, that you are a man who is quick to
> anger.
> No. And it's not constable, it's sergeant.
> I suggest that you are an officer who is likely to make
> mistakes, Constable.
> No, and it's sergeant.
> But you did make some inconsistent statements in court
> today, haven't you, Constable.

I take a moment. Holding my hand up to stop his answer.

I'm so sorry. SERGEANT.

I look at him, making my point clear. A constable making mistakes is one thing, a sergeant making mistakes is a 'problem.' He doesn't flinch.

>I made a simple mistake, that's all.

>But you did read your partner's statement before your
>>own, didn't you . . . SERGEANT?

He hesitates. Does he admit this or not? I stand unwavering.

>I don't know.

Ah, too easy. I tilt my head to one side.

>Oh, but I think you do know, sir. Take your time.

I do not move a muscle except to straighten my neck, eyes right at him. He is figuring out what I might know; he concludes that something has been said, that someone has messed up, and that it is up to him to fix it. It's a mind game right now. Confidence and daring. He ventures an answer.

>Yes.

>Yes, you did read your partner's statement before you wrote
>your own.

>Glanced at it.

I let that sit.

>So, when you *glanced* at it, was this done in full knowledge
>>of your partner?

He's confused. His face red.

>Yes.

>So, he gave you his statement to read, or did you ask for it?

>I can't remember.

Cock my head to one side again.

>I might have asked for it.

I look confused, then:

>Well, that's strange, because your partner said here in court
>today that under no circumstances would he share his statement
>with you to read, and that you would never ask for it. So then,
>one of you is lying here in court today, aren't you, Constable?

He shoots me a look of pure hatred.

>It's SERGEANT.

I nod. Take a moment, then smile at him.

Oh, I am sorry, sir. I didn't mean to make you ANGRY.
I glance back at Phoebe; she is grinning, trying hard not to.

Later, when we meet Adam at the Pret up the road for lunch, she
delights in recounting it. Phoebe has a visceral distrust of the police,
like me. It's quite a strange connection.
There is a line of solicitors in the Pret. Phoebe wants to know how I
can tell. I point out the women in silk shirts, and the men in really
nice Italian ties. Adam comments.
     They're a different breed. All corporate contracts and
          building agreements.
I laugh and make an exaggerated yawn. Later, as we walk back to
chambers with our lunch, I tell Adam and Phoebe the story of one
of the pupils we had a few years back: Sophie.
     She was taking a statement from an accused, I was listening
          in, and she asked the client, no word of a lie: 'But tell
          me, did you do it?'
Adam bites into his sandwich, shaking his head. Through cheese and
ham he mumbles:
     What did you do?
     I dragged her away, like, 'Excuse me, can you come with
          me a moment, Sophie?' And then I say to her, 'What the
          fuck do you think you're doing?' She's all, 'What? What?'
          and I tell her, 'If he now says he did it, you can't act for
          him, you will have to send him to someone else.'
Adam shakes his head.
     You know what she said? She said, 'So, I don't want to act
          for someone who did it, do I?'
We're laughing.
     So I tell her, 'Sophie, it's not your job to know, you just
          take instructions and do the best job with what you have.' I
          mean, did she even go to law school?!
Phoebe asks:
     What happened to Sophie?
I can't remember.
     I think she left, just never came back!
When we arrive at chambers, it's a long Thursday afternoon preparing

cases for Monday. Julian appears at my room for the second time this week.

Hey, we're all heading over to the river place now. Coming?
I nod. Yes, it's exactly what I need: unwind, drinks, and a bit of a dance.

At eight I check my lipstick in the loo, rescue my wig-hair, then head over to Alice's room. Together we walk over to the bar, chatting about work, and when we arrive it is pumping. There are loads of people we know, mostly young barristers from our chambers, everyone except Adam; he never goes out anymore, now that he has a baby. Seems to be able to work from home and still get incredible results. I put on some mascara that gets stuck in my eye. I hate this, the sting, the need to wash it out and then clean up and begin again. I stand there waiting for the sting to go. Red eye. Wonder about how lawyers are all so comfortable with each other, I guess because other people don't understand the system of defense. How innocent people are arrested because they are poor, powerless, and struggling. How there are two laws—one for those living hard and one for those who have money. I've seen in court how easy it seems to be for rich people to work the system, not for my brother and his mates though. I think about how I get asked that same question that all criminal barristers and lawyers get asked. Every fucking swanky, self-righteous dinner party I get asked, 'How do you act for someone you KNOW did it?' I reapply the mascara. This time I'm precise, not distracted. Apply red lipstick and fix my hair again. The truth is, only lawyers understand that, paradoxically, despite everyone thinking we have all the power, our job is not that grand. We don't have the right to KNOW our client is guilty or not. Like Adam says, 'Stand outside it, test the story'; our job is not to KNOW, it's to NOT know. Try explaining that to someone though. (They look at you as if, 'But you DO know, you must know.') If barristers go about prejudging their clients, then the system would not be able to work properly. Sure, behind the scenes we have an opinion, but the job is to put that aside and play our role. And our role is to make sure we tell the best version of our client's story.

And the prosecutor's role is to tell the best version of the police's story, so that the court hears everything that is possible to be heard, and the justice system can do its job.

We don't take responsibility. We are just mouthpieces who also advise clients if their story does not work. Storytellers. No more, no less. It's the jury who decides, and the judge who sentences the clients. Not us. Anyway, as people we all *think* we know the truth of our lives, but we all make mistakes. We would all swear we left our keys there but find them somewhere else. Think we wore a blue dress to a dinner, only to be shown a photo of ourselves on the night in a red one. People are fallible and their version of a story must be tested. Even if I think I know what my client has or hasn't done, they still have the right to have their story before the court, the right to be heard. The minute you start judging your client, you're fucked. You've lost your standing. The legal system is lost. You are lost.

I stop thinking about work, one last glance in the mirror before I hear Alice calling out. When I leave the bathroom, I see her by the lifts, and we leave.

CHAPTER 10

Cabs are impossible in the evening near chambers, so we walk. A hot and balmy London summer's night. Still light. We chat a bit walking across the bridge to Southbank. I look up and see the clear night sky. This is what it means to live in London, and I never take it for granted. The greatest city in the world and I live here.

When we arrive at the bar, I pull Alice close as I make my way over to a table of barristers. Some of them are old faces I know from law school, others through the courts. Julian is there, he's already downed a few, but he's in good shape. There is music and someone has a tray of tequila shots. Everyone's suit jackets are flung on the backs of chairs; hair down; ready for a proper night out. It's a cliché that criminal barristers are party animals, but it's also true—and we play it up a bit when we can. After two rounds of double tequila shots, I throw my hands in the air, shout out to everyone.

Everyone up. Dancing!

Not everyone gets up, but moving with the music feels freeing. I'm at home here with my tribe, with my colleagues. I just want to forget the night back at home, so I am hitting back a few more shots, which makes me lose any remnant of shyness. Alice is watching me from another part of the bar; I gesture to her to join me but she's deep in conversation with a senior barrister who mentored her. Julian gets up, he's dancing close to me, a few others up now too. We're all a bit tanked. We dance to a song by the Clash, an old song that is a favorite, something about fighting the law but the law winning. It seems that generations of barristers have loved this song. We scream out the lyrics.

I toss my hair around. Julian is up close to me; he puts his hands on my hips and pulls me in close. I like it, but I'm also aware of where we are. I look over to Alice again and she indicates with her eyes a young male barrister watching Julian and me dance. Robin. He is assisting me in a large matter, and he is staring at us. She's right, I don't need him seeing me like this.

I whisper to Julian:

>Hey, hey. Everyone is watching us.

He doesn't care, he's so confident. I flick his hands away and he gives me a look. A challenge. I laugh. A song comes on and he leans in and kisses the back of my neck. I feel electricity rush down my back, but again I turn to him and flick him away. We laugh. It's nice to feel sexy, to feel wanted. I'm used to dating apps and this feels different. Still, there is no way I would ever go home with him. It's Julian. From work.

Alice catches my eye and we both roll our eyes at each other. My head is in a delicious carefree haze but I know I have a case tomorrow, so I won't stay. Another man cuts in and tries to dance with me; Julian shrugs but stays put. The new guy asks me:

>What do you lot all do then?

He's talking to me, so I respond rather than Julian.

>Criminal defense barristers.

>Right. So you spend your days in court then?

>Yep.

I side-eye Jules. Speak back to the interloper:

>We believe in justice; we believe in the law.

I'm yelling above the music, but I'm still dancing. I'm aware that some of my words are a little slurred. The guy on the dance floor tries to toy with me:

>Yeah but you fight for criminals, don't ya?

That old line, usually I would ignore it from a stranger, but I'm feeling tipsy and I like the flirtation of being playfully combative. I wag my finger at him.

>No. No. Criminal barristers are about fighting for those
>>who need you. It's about human rights.

I am taken with my own line, and I shout out as the music fires up.

>HUMAN RIGHTS.

My hands are in the air, I am now dancing in a manner I assume is quite sexy. But in reality, it is no doubt a stiff version of my mum's dancing style, with strange shoulder movements shrugging this way and that. Mia has laughed at me before. Apparently, there's such a disparity between what I think I look like and how I appear. The guy is talking again:

The prosecutors are the ones fighting for rights!

I fake a horrified look.

No, they're fighting for jail time.

I mime someone behind bars looking miserable. Then I laugh and back myself:

Prosecutors work for the police!

The guy is laughing and has no idea what I am talking about. He reaches for my waist, but I turn. There's Julian, looking amused. He touches my hair. I see Alice again at the other side of the bar, she points at her watch. I look at mine. It's way after one a.m. Jesus, time to get the hell out of here. I grab my jacket from behind the chair, give Julian a flirty look.

See you tomorrow.

He shrugs. The other guy is calling out.

Don't leave. Hey? What's your name?

I stumble over to Alice, who leads the way out of the bar. I spy Phoebe being touched up by some older guy. He has her against the wall, her head seems to be lolling. His hands are groping her trousers. I move over to her, grab on to her. Address the man.

Hey, she's out of it, mate. What are you doing?

What's it to you?

I take hold of Phoebe, who lets me lead her out of the bar. The man is swearing at me, but Phoebe's had way too much to drink, her eyes are closed. I hear the guy mutter.

She's a cock teaser.

I look back and look him up and down with utter repulsion. He moves away. It's home time for all of us. Phoebe ends up in an Uber with Alice, who does not look too chuffed about having to drop floppy Phoebe home. I hop into my Uber and wind the window down, feeling the cool night air slap my face as the car makes its way to my flat. The lights of London all about me, the noises and beat of the early hours of the streets. I still feel delightfully carefree, yet now looking forward to a night of sleep.

CHAPTER II

By eight the next morning, after two soy lattes, I am back in chambers.

I have a hangover, there's no doubt about it, though I'm sure I am not alone. As I move through chambers toward my room, I take out my morning sausage roll but can't even think about eating. Back in my satchel. I feel strange walking in after last night. Can't quite recollect how many people saw Julian's hands on me. I know Alice did, so I brace myself and head to her room. Partly I want to control the narrative, bring things back to normal; perhaps I don't want Adam to hear about it. Not sure why, but I feel embarrassed in front of Adam somehow. Then I fleetingly see Julian at the other end of chambers; he waves, I wave back and make my way quickly through the hallway. I barge into Alice's room and Phoebe is already there, slumped in the pink velvet chair in the corner. Alice's room always manages to look so uncomfortable, so neat, so middle class. She has a trendy teapot on her desk, matching teacups, and a mat underneath she picked up on one of her trips to somewhere abroad. She takes one look at me and pours me a tea with raised eyebrows. Of course, it's her usual green tea, which I will never get used to, served up in dainty mugs like in some sort of tea ceremony. Phoebe has one in front of her but isn't drinking hers either. I realize that being hungover helps me dismiss the night before.

My head!

Alice smiles, thin lips.

I have no doubt.

She looks from Phoebe to me and back again. Mumbles something about learning to have a water between drinks like she does. Then she hits me.

So, you and Julian, hey?

Her voice a confusing mix of accusation and curiosity. Phoebe perks up, she didn't know. Her face screams, 'What the fuck?' I'm on my guard.

> No, it was just dancing. Too many tequila shots and good
>   music.

Alice smiles knowingly, and I hate it. I try to change the subject, but she won't have it.

> You looked like you were thoroughly enjoying yourself.

I brush it off, glance over at the neatly stacked files on her desk.

> We were just flirting.

Alice looks at me, laughing. Then her face changes. She's serious now.

> He's a really nice guy, I'm happy for you.

I'm not sure what to say. She's been single for a bit, but so have we all. This job is not one where it's easy to have long-term relationships; the workload, the hours in chambers, the need to do the work now so we can all get to the top as quickly as possible, not be left behind. I feel stronger without a boyfriend in this world; it's easier not to let my guard down, and there's no shortage of Tinder hookups if I want them. I'd never talk to Alice about this, there's things I can only share with Mia and Cheryl.

Phoebe leaves to grab a coffee. Alice changes the subject and I'm grateful.

> What do you have on next week?

I think over the busy week ahead. So many cases, I do a quick mental calculation—three hearings at least.

> I have a break-and-enter on Monday, then two sex assaults.

Alice looks at her desk and tries to wipe a pen mark from the surface.

> Tough.

I sense something coming, but not sure what. I find it hard to read Alice at times. I respond:

> I'll get them off. The break-and-enter only has unreliable
>   eyewitnesses. And of the two sex cases, one has PTSD
>   from Afghanistan, so if he goes down, I'll milk that to
>   make sure he isn't potted.

Silence. I think she is considering how I will keep the PTSD client out of prison. I am running it through my head too. Chances are he won't even go down so I might not have to address it. But that is not Alice's thought. She looks up after her nails have scrubbed off the pen mark. Her beautifully manicured nails that she is now checking for damage. Then it comes.

You're doing a lot of sex assault these days.

I shrug. I'm thinking, 'So, what's your point?' I consider this a middle-class way of making me feel guilty for having more work than she does. I know I have something I can send her way, a boring matter that she will jump on.

But then she gives me a look. I realize she is pointing out not just that I am doing more work than she is, but specifically that my prac-tice is taking on more sex assault defense matters. I feel betrayed. She's smart, and she's acted in sex cases herself. We all have. It's part of the job, you don't suddenly decide that some crimes are outside the rules. This is not a dinner party, she knows the rules, why is she saying this to me? She meets my eyes, waiting for a response. When I hear my voice, it is challenging, sharp.

Cab rank rule.

She nods. I continue.

I don't choose them, they choose me.

It hangs in the air. It is the rule that makes sure everyone gets fair representation in court. Alice has a strange look about her.

What's going on, Alice?

Just thinking I might not want to take sexual assault cases
    anymore.

Well, as a barrister, you don't get to choose; otherwise some
    defendants would never have representation.

Inside I am burning up, she is challenging this rule and she is a bar-rister. I wait to hear what she says next. She is computing, and it feels dangerous somehow.

A barrister's diary is run by their clerk, and if there is a gap and someone calls to hire you for a brief in your area of law, then they are entitled to take that slot. My specialty is criminal law, so if my clerk gets a brief in crime, then like all barristers, I must take it. It's like at the airport, or a taxi rank. Cabbies can't pick and choose the ride they want. They get what they get. It's been known by the 'cab rank rule' forever in the law, we all know it, and we all live by it. Why is she asking me this? She finally speaks.

I know the rule, Tessa. But there are always ways around it.

Come on! I'm a feminist, Alice, but if you work in crime
you don't get to pick your defendants.

I think that sexual assault defendants are choosing women
for their cases because it looks better in court to have a
woman defend a sexual assault or rape case.

I don't take my eyes off her.

That might be true, but if we are briefed by a client, we cannot
refuse them. They are allowed to brief us. That's fair.

My voice careful, I state the rule again.

Cab rank is cab rank.

But she doesn't let it go. She's looking genuinely troubled.

I just think a lot of barristers hide behind the rule.

I feel my hand tighten around this precious teacup of boring green
tea. I don't like her saying this. She's referring to what people think
barristers do—that if they really don't want to do a case, they have
their clerk call back and be on 'holidays' or have a 'family occasion.'
But this is wrong, and she knows it, and clerks are not supposed to
let that happen. I put the cup down. Eye to eye. This is important.

No, Alice. We play by the rules.

I know. Sorry. It's just . . . Nothing. God, Tess, I'm sorry.

She lets it go. Eyes back on the file on her desk. I think on how she
has lost her last four hearings. She knows it's not good. Even as we all
wave it away with a dramatic flourish of dismissal, she knows we're
all terrified of the same fate. She's so anxious about work, and the
briefs are not flowing as they once did. She picks up her file, which is
barrister talk for 'I have to work now.' But I don't move.

I can flick you some of my matters this week?

A moment while she thinks about it. She has to pretend she has
other work to juggle.

Also probably next week, I'm overbooked.

She finally nods, grateful, I know, but embarrassed. We sit in silence
as I consider how glad I am not to be her right now. I couldn't afford
it for one; chambers is expensive, and while I am sure Alice's family
would help her out—they have before—I also know she hates having to ask. It's a strange job, running your own practice, and always
thinking your current brief could be your last.

Mia tells me it is exactly how an actor feels. I mentally remember to call and to wish her luck on her last night of her Glasgow play. I had traveled up to see it at the Tron on press night as her guest, and she was magnificent. A play by Dennis Kelly, she says he is her favorite playwright. Afterward she made a big fuss of me to her actor friends. Most of them from Scotland, one of them could imitate anyone from anywhere, including my own accent. Mia kept telling them that I would be a judge one day, that I was a brilliant mind and had what it takes. While I dismissed this as her being too good a friend, I'm also tickled that someone whose grandfather was a judge would say this. Perhaps she knows more than I do about what it takes. A judge is so far out of my league though, my main aim is to take silk one day. If I win at the Chambers' Bar Awards, I would be on my way to being noticed, start to move forward.

But I hate it when I get ahead of myself; my mum would say when I was young that it was exactly this getting ahead of oneself that brings with it something we don't see. That we needed to be happy for what we already have. I'm so happy for what I have. It sometimes feels like a miracle that I made it here.

Adam stops by and asks me whether he can run something past me. I'm flattered and also glad to have a reason to leave Alice's room. When I reach Adam's room, Julian is in there too. Relief mixed with a strange awkwardness now that I am here with Julian. Adam outlines his knife case while Julian chips in with some ideas. It's complex and there's many angles.

> Looks like you could go with self-defense, but he shouldn't
> have had the knife on him in the first place. Does he
> have a legitimate reason?

Adam's internal phone rings, and Hailey is suddenly on speaker asking whether I'm with him. I tell her I am.

> Well, there's a client in reception to see you.

I'm confused. I don't have any clients today. Hailey signs off and the boys both look at me; I make it clear I have no idea about a 'client.' Julian turns to me.

> One of your 'walk-ins,' then?

He's referring to the occasional walk-in I have for a criminal matter.

Someone who has looked up where I work when they knew I was acting for them and walked on in before I could set up a meeting time. There's a slight flirtation to Julian's look. I need to swat it away so that Adam doesn't pick up on it, so I address Adam while clearly making a point about Julian.

My clients are real. Julian's are all scrubbed up, Daddy's
    friends with issues!

Adam looks briefly shocked that I am so direct about something we have spoken about before. I realize I have done the opposite of throwing him off the scent. Julian jumps in good-naturedly.

Touché.

I'm still challenging myself when I arrive in reception. There's a man in old jeans and a T-shirt standing by Hailey's desk and she clearly doesn't like him hovering. Hailey picks up the phone and tries to talk privately. I am jarred when I realize it is Johnny standing there. My two worlds in the same room. A jolt of catastrophe is my first instinct.

Is Mum okay?

He nods. And then I remember the last time I saw him we were fighting. But also that he's about to be a dad and that's his news to tell me.

What are you doing here?

I was just in town picking up something for Cheryl.

This feels like a lie. He looks so uncomfortable and it makes me see the marble fireplace, the antique chair in the reception. I hate that he sees me in here like this, but I have no idea why I hate it so much. He must know because he jumps in confidently.

Can we go somewhere?

Hailey jolts as she sees me take his arm and lead him outside. We walk in silence toward the river. There's a strange politeness in the quiet, it is not like us at all. I stop and order two coffees at a tiny takeaway place, and when I ask him how he likes his coffee he doesn't know. Asks for tea. We find a spot by the Thames; the sun is out, and he looks at me as he sips his tea. I can't wait.

Can't believe you're going to be a dad!

He bursts out laughing. And in that moment, we are back to being Johnny and Tess. It lights up something inside of me, something warm and familiar. Something that also feels sad. Johnny speaks.

It's weird, right.

I can see his twelve-year-old face right there in that moment. My big brother, before he failed school, before the tattoos, before the troubles. His big eyes carrying hope while barely daring to show it. I put my head against his arm.

> Congratulations. I'm so happy for you, for Cheryl. It's
> awesome news.

Johnny looks uncertain.

> You're really happy?
> Of course.

There's a pause. Something unsaid. We both know, but if asked we couldn't say what it was. Then Johnny broaches it.

> I'll do a lot better than he did.
> Course you will.

Johnny looks out across the river.

> The other night, what you said. You really think I'd ever hit
> ya?

Tears prick my eyes. He looks wounded.

> No, no.

My voice is a little shaky. I take a moment.

> I'm sorry. I'm really sorry.

A flash of Johnny's face getting swiped by my father's hand. I try to block it out.

The truth is that I remember so little about our father other than the horror moments, I can't miss him the way Johnny sometimes does. The only time I shared Johnny's loss of a father was the time he finally got a bike and then got chased by some of the bullies up the road. I remember watching anxiously as he tried to ride away, the bike braking suddenly, and Johnny flying over the handlebars onto the hard pavement. His bike was stomped on, and Johnny lying there in a crumpled mess. I ran over before they took off, only about seven, my anger already outranking the fear. They laughed at me, kicked Johnny, then his bike again for good measure. When Johnny looked up at me and asked me whether he'd broken his teeth, all I could see was a mouthful of blood. Even at seven I knew my reaction would determine how bad it was to him. I was terrified not only by my brother's broken teeth, changed face and bike, but by the vulnerability I saw, his eyes beseeching me to tell him he didn't look ugly. I wanted someone to find those boys and hurt them. I wanted our father to be here and do it for his son.

I suddenly saw how alone Johnny was in this world of men and I hated my father for abandoning him. For being the sort of father who couldn't be with him, for showing such little love for Johnny that he would have to harden up big-time to survive. I didn't care for myself though; I've only ever cared for Johnny's sake, and Mum's. For the violence that seemed to belt upon them both, making them both so shy of feeling worth more.

I was only three years younger than Johnny, but he left before he hit me.

Johnny tells me the house-painting job is over. But tells me he has a new job lined up. I'm overjoyed for him. It's in scaffolding. I don't know whether I've inherited the sense of doom from living in a house of violence, or whether it is just me being overprotective of my brother, but I instantly fear a work-related accident. Johnny must read my ambivalence but thinks it's because I don't know how he got the job so quickly. He explains how, and his great ambitions with it all, probably thinking he is reassuring me.

These Polish guys are showing me the ropes, and then I can
        get a loan, buy a truck—have my own business.

I can't help myself, perhaps it is the legal training, but more likely it's the anxiety about what might happen to Johnny; my first question is not one he is expecting.

These guys, are they insured?

Johnny makes a face.

I dunno. Probably not.

He laughs.

Don't think they'd get it even if they wanted to pay for
        insurance.

This does not reassure me at all.

What about you? Can I help get you insured?

I cringe as soon as I've said it. Johnny hates it when I indicate I can pay for something for him. If ever I do it has to be done without him knowing. His face creases in a frown. Then he softens.

Nah. It's their business. I'm just getting cash.

My heart sinks further.

'Kay.

Johnny's face lightens.

Cheryl made flyers.

I love Cheryl, she believes in him. What's my fucking problem? 'Show some enthusiasm,' I chastise myself.

That's great!

Johnny gives me a strange look. He's grinning beneath it.

What?

You want to see them?

Sure.

I want to suggest I'll send it around my workplace. But I know I can't. I feel a wave of pity, I know that Johnny and his Polish mates are not the sort of risk that wealthy renovating barristers take, they hire architects and designers who contract with builders who decide who does the scaffolding. I'm glad he can't detect any pity from me— it would enrage him, make him feel small. My voice is flat without intention.

Why don't you email the flyer to me?

Johnny doesn't hear my tone, becomes his old enthusiastic self for a moment.

I've got some printed. Hang on.

He rummages through his backpack and pulls out a photocopied flyer. Hands me one proudly.

I make all the right noises. I feel badly that I can't take a bunch of flyers and put them in the pigeonholes in chambers like all the other barristers do for their family and friends who run businesses that we might all require sometime. When I first understood that people with money do things differently, it took a long time for it to sink in, I couldn't grasp it. That most people don't hire workmen or -women just because there is a leak, a broken door, or the house falling apart, but for the purpose of redesigning and refurbishing something that already works, was a revelation.

It's not just that I am out of home and living in London that separates Johnny and me, it is that I have exposure now to how the world works for other people. I have listened hard and kept my questions to myself until I could work out what others take for granted. There are always gaps, and I am always catching up; my new life comes with a loneliness that I can't even talk about to anyone other than Mia, and sometimes not even to her either. The gaps aren't there for people born into this way of life, but for Johnny and me they were always there, only now I know what they are. I am left in that in-between space. I can't be them—and I don't want to be—but I also can't go back to not knowing. The place where I didn't realize how powerless I was. Before I went to university, I didn't know that people like Alice and Julian, people like Phoebe, really existed—that they somehow did not know how people like me, and Johnny and Mum, lived. Really lived.

I remember how I felt at the bar when people would comment on my accent, the Souse one I brought to Luton with me when Mum moved us from Liverpool. At university I didn't care, and Mia was always 'never lose your accent, it's real.' I realize I have lost a little of it, well, a lot. In court it somehow magically disappears. Like the Scottish barrister I chat with in the foyer sometimes. Thick accent, speaks fast, we laugh that we find each other hard to understand. Then in court, speaking at a 'court' pace, slow, carefully. Using legal language, she has no trace of an accent. People tell us both this, think we are putting it on in court; truth is if we are, we don't even realize it. She has no shame in her accent and thanks to Mia I mostly like mine, but it does expose you. And for me it's more than just a regional accent, it's also my class. My use of words. I admit I have picked up that this isn't helpful, dropped the words that really stood out by the time I left Cambridge. Still, I wonder whether I mask my actual accent itself, or whether it just softens automatically. When I'm back home it's as if I never left, my accent straight back to normal, although Johnny always teases me if I say a single word that he notes is not from 'round here.' If I have a vowel that ever sounds posh.

Johnny is showing me his flyers with great enthusiasm, he gives me one to keep. I tell him I'm proud of him. Both for getting the job and for working hard toward being a good father. There's a moment of tenderness that both of us feel but don't know how to respond to. Why can't we do it, I wonder, before automatically moving away. I shove the flyer he gave me in my bag. This is the measure of the chasm that opened up between the life I grew up with and the life I now have. The weight of knowledge. The isolating understanding of how things really work that has nothing to do with fairness or working hard. Not really. I fight through the layers of unsaid things, latch on to something safe.

    Mum's going to be so thrilled to have a grandkid.

    Yeah, well, someone had to help her out on that front.

    You're sure not!

I laugh. We both do. Then more quietly now, Johnny leans in.

    It's a girl. Cheryl told Mum we're going to name her after
    Mum.

I feel the prick of tears again. Too much feeling. Banter is our 'go-to' relief.

    What, June Junior?

I'm laughing, and he looks at me fondly.

    We're going to call her Junie.

I'm nodding. I hug him, smell the sweat of him, the rawness of my brother, then pull away. A new little girl in all our lives. It makes family feel real again. A pull toward the girl I was perhaps. A sense of pride in where I came from despite all the pain attached to it.

CHAPTER 12

THEN

When we arrive at Inner Temple I don't see any of my bar school friends. This is the day when we are all going to be called to the bar. It's a big deal, and I know they will all be here. Across the way I can see a guy who is also on a merit-based scholarship. We were both dragged out to talk to the fundraiser a month ago as examples of how the scholarships help. It was sobering to realize that there was no hiding from the fact that we are not like the others. Jacob is from the Sudan, came to Britain as a refugee. He coined our secret mantra: Once a scholarship law student always a scholarship law student.

Mum and Johnny are dressed up, Mum has new shoes that I know are a big deal. I also bought her a smart jacket, in navy. She actually looks great. Johnny has a suit he borrowed from a friend that is a little too big. For the first time in his life he is wearing a shirt and tie. A gift from me, paired and purchased by myself, using the skills I gained at M&S. No matter, Johnny always looks scruffy.

Mum frets when she sees another woman wearing a hat, but I tell her it's not necessary.

We stand around after taking photos on Johnny's phone. Some photos of Mum and me; then Johnny and me; one of Johnny and Mum alone. When Jacob comes over to introduce his dad, Mum is a little on edge. I ask Jacob to take a photo of Mum, Johnny, and me; and while she's thrilled to have a photo of 'the whole family dressed proper,' she's quite stiff. When Jacob and his dad move on, Johnny scans the families about us. We are off to the side and have a great view of all the large families, one with two members in their bar gear. I am wearing a borrowed gown and wig for today, only because I have not yet saved enough to buy my own and did not have a family set handed down to me.

Mum is surveying the other families.

>It's all very well-to-do, isn't it?

I say, for the hundredth time today:

>You look great, Mum.

I know she is nervous. Johnny jumps in.

>You look as la-de-da as the best of them.

He turns to me as he lights up a cigarette.

>So, who is it then? Who is going to 'call you to the bar'
>then?
>I don't know, maybe the Master of the Bench.
>The master of the fucking bench no less, hey?

He realizes he sounds a bit off.

>Fucking awesome, Tess. You're gonna be my posh little
>sister.

I roll my eyes. He grabs me in a headlock, joking with me in the only way he really knows how.

>Careful, my wig.

Johnny taps my wig. He continues smoking. I relent.

>Give me a drag, okay.

He does. I take it.

>I'm so fucking nervous.

He looks at me, this is where he comes into his own.

>Why? You're a fucking bullet.

He scans the space, this ancient place. He can't think of anything to say. I know he finds it intimidating. He turns his attention to the people about us. A group of upper-class barristers walk past; one fans away the cigarette smoke irritably, without even looking at Johnny. It gives him the ammunition he needs.

>You shit all over this lot, okay? Just keep your eye on the
>game; don't even think about them, you play the game
>your way.

He grabs my face with his hand.

>You got it?

It's annoying. I look him in the face. Move his hand with mine.

I got it. Yes. Take your hands off my face, I'm not twelve,
    Johnny.
All the other new calls to the bar start to move their way into the
temple for the ceremony. We are sitting separately from our guests.
Johnny grabs me by the shoulders, turns me in the right direction.
    Get in there, Mum 'n' I will be in the crowd cheering when
        they say your name.
I'm horrified.
    Mum!
Mum shakes her head. Johnny winks at me. I join the line and look
back when I hear my name. Mia has arrived, dressed like Mia, but
still fitting in of course. She waves at me and lands on Mum and
Johnny. I feel a wash of relief. She'll make sure they find their seats,
and that they know what to do. As I enter the temple, I breathe in the
smell, the years of antiquity, all those barristers who have walked this
way in before me, taken these seats before me. I breathe in the smell
of new gowns, aftershave and perfume, deodorant and hair spray,
and the slightly damp smell of hundreds of years of law. While the
whole 'call to the bar' is steeped in history, I do have a feeling that I
am part of it. For the first time ever, I know I have earned this. I am
allowed to belong.

CHAPTER 13

Catch the tube home, get off at Westbourne Park, and walk down the Harrow Road, dodging kids on scooters weaving their way around pedestrians. I stop and buy some noodles at the co-op; I like this area. Just north of where so many barristers live in West London I have a lovely flat in the middle of an area of London that feels part of a community. There's the canal that divides the Harrow Road from Notting Hill and North Kensington, but the world on this side feels right to me. A mix of public housing and renovated apartments and houses, it somehow catches me and lets me belong. To the north is Queens Park and the Bakerloo line that I catch into chambers every morning, but at night the Hammersmith and City line home gives me my daily walk along the Harrow Road; says I am back where I live.

Mum always feels comfortable shopping in all the smaller family grocer stores here when she visits, and there's green pockets and the walk via the canal on these warm nights. During summer the whole place, like most of London, feels like a celebration, but more so here, where kids still play on the streets, and family groups gather on their stoops. There are old people still about, they haven't been moved on to make way for the expensively dressed, and it feels like this area will always challenge that pretentious ideal. Through the front reception door, then walk up the stairs to my flat. It's been a big day. Exhausted, I perch on the edge of my sofa and eat my takeaway noodles. Pull a brief from my bag, throw it to the floor. Grab the remote and channel surf while the noodles go down. I roll down into the sofa and find myself mindlessly catching snippets of reality shows and dramas on free to air that I have already seen. I love my flat. It's renovated in mostly whites and earthy colors, and comfortable, two bedrooms and a great aspect. It feels like home, and while most of my colleagues live closer to the action, I'm in no hurry yet. The people in the flats downstairs all work on various airlines so they're often away, but when they are back we sometimes gather for drinks in the garden of the ground-floor flat. I hear of all their trips and adventures; they ask about my cases. At the moment there is no one downstairs so I Bluetooth my phone to the speaker and turn the music up loud, even though the TV is still going. It takes a bit for me to settle. When I'm done with the noodles, I close my eyes, turn off the TV, and just lie there for a bit.

I call Mum but she doesn't pick up. Her voicemail message is so stilted and strangely formal. I don't leave a message. Text her to say, 'Saw Johnny today, everything is good with us. Love you.' Always easy to say 'love you' in a text. Not possible to do it in person.

I call Mia. She picks up right away. I tell her about Johnny and Cheryl having a baby; she is delighted but distracted. Makes sense, she already has five nieces and nephews. Mia has news, the show playing in Scotland is going to Australia. She's a bit tipsy so they must have been celebrating. She's always wanted to go to Australia, she wants to see strange animals and spend time on the beaches, but she's going soon, and I remind her that it is winter down there. She doesn't care, the producers have organized a tour, she will be there not only for winter but for summer too. There's a festival in Sydney and down in South Australia and the company has been asked to fill a last-minute slot where there was a show that had to pull out. I'm thrilled for Mia, she's good and she has managed this all on her own, no help from her family. I respect that, I admire her for not leaning into her family contacts. She always tells me, 'Not yet I haven't. But there will be a day when I need them, and I will lean in big time. You don't look a gift horse in the mouth.' She's pragmatic, when need be, she always tells me. She is all excited and I laugh with her on the phone. She leaves next week because they are going to all spend time traveling through Southeast Asia on the way down south. Spontaneous decision by the cast, one of whom it appears Mia is sleeping with. She gives me details, lots of details, I pour myself a glass of sauvignon blanc, open the door to my Georgian-style balcony, light up a cigarette, and, looking over a view of West London, ask questions, legs on the balcony rail and leaning back in the outdoor furniture. She's full of news, and stories.

I listen to the sexual details of her affair, and how she feels about Leonard, this new guy. He sounds like her sort of fella, sensitive, creative, talented, a little self-indulgent—but this one has a healthy side of family dysfunction and is not boring like the last actor she dated. I sip my wine, hear the children from next door laugh, listen to my best friend talk.

She finally asks about my sex life, and while there isn't much to report, I mention that a guy at work is showing interest. And Mia, being Mia, picks up straightaway that it is something more than just a passing vibe. She cross-examines me better than most barristers do. She knows me well enough to read the subtext in my voice and accuses me of crushing on Julian. I'm quick with the denial, but there's something delicious in imagining the version of myself in a couple that Mia is reveling in. She's asking me to describe him, and I tell her how he's so good-looking but nothing like what I go for. She laughs and we talk about my boyfriend from home who came up to Cambridge in first year to visit me.

Jason was a great specimen of maleness but completely out of the world of Cambridge. I thought kindly about him making the journey to see me, only to be judged by Mia and our mates as not good enough for me. They were wrong in so many ways; he might never have read a book or had any education, but he was so easy to be around, and a great lover. I was too shy then to tell Mia that, but I tell her now. She's not surprised.

> Well, he had to have something going for him and it sure
> wasn't his great conversational skills.

I'm briefly outraged for Jason before Mia reminds me that he left me for one of the nurses who cared for him when he broke his shoulder on a plumbing job. I tell her that it was a relief that he did, my loyalty to him far outweighed my feelings of anything else, and where I come from loyalty to those from your area is everything.

When I return to answering questions about Julian, she is more circumspect.

> Those sorts of men can break your heart, so don't fall too
> deep until he does.

I tell her there is no chance of me falling for him. She laughs, tells me she knows these privately educated boys, especially the ones from the expensive school Julian went to. Says they're used to country estates, servants, and trust funds. I'm laughing but clear.

> Well, he works hard and is super ambitious, so it's not a
>   trust-fund thing.

She's relieved, I'm a little drunk now, I start to speak melancholically about her leaving for such a long time. She tells me to fly in and join them in Asia or Australia. It's a dream, and I entertain the idea, knowing that I could never do it with all the cases I have scheduled, and with the mortgage to pay, chambers fees due.

Before we sign off, Mia confides in me. She has had a crisis of confidence despite the play touring, she feels she should have already done so much more by now. It's a hard profession to get ahead in without using the contacts her parents have in theater and film. We both know she could easily get a head start if she did. And yet, I feel she is asking my permission to network with them all and push her way forward.

> You still need talent; contacts will only get you so far.

But we both know I am only saying that to make her feel better about herself. She appreciates it nevertheless and it takes us some time to get off the phone, there's always one more thing.

I remember to tell her a story of running into the guy from our first-ever law school induction—Benedict—at a law function.

> He's working as a solicitor in banking and finance!

Mia and I both laugh at how we predicted this, at how his life is exactly what he expected it to be. Mia reminds me of the 'one in three who won't make it.' She considers that she is the one in three who didn't get through. I reassure her.

> Deciding to dump the law is not the same as failing!

Then I tell her.

> Oh, and just so you know, Benedict had no idea who the
>   hell I was! But he remembered you, of course. I told him
>   you were a famous actor now.

We piss ourselves laughing. We end the call.

Then I am back in my flat alone, thinking about work.

CHAPTER 14

It's after nine the next night and I'm still in chambers finalizing some advice work. I lean back in my chair and survey my desk. Four undrunk cups of tea in mugs—which need returning to the kitchen before someone comes looking for them—a few half-empty paper coffee cups. Papers everywhere and yet somehow the chaos is completely methodical for me. I know what everything is and why it is placed where it is placed. Books of legislation facedown at a page I am reviewing, a few cases open on my computer, and my shelves are bursting with white binders and knickknacks. I have accumulated so much stuff, and yet there is so little of me in this room—no photos other than the shot of me, Johnny, and Mum when I was called to the bar.

Chambers are so empty that I can hear the air-conditioning whirring. I glance out my window. Night is beginning to fall, and I momentarily consider going home—but there is still more to do, and besides, I'm not tired yet. I stretch my back out and then return to hovering over my laptop. Continue highlighting parts of the brief to assist with a big break-and-enter cross-examination I have coming up. I'm absorbed when I hear a male voice. I nearly leap in the air. Julian's face at my door.

  Hey?
  Fuck, you scared me; I thought I was the only one here.
  You, me; and . . . and old Harrison is still here.
He smiles right at me, scans my desk, sees I am deeply in my work.
  You look busy?
  No, nearly done, just working through a cross-
    examination.
A moment of silence. Then he makes a face. Quizzical, inviting.

Can I . . . Can I run the brief for my GBH trial past you? Grievous bodily harm. It's a serious indictable matter. We've both found ourselves doing quite high-profile and serious criminal matters. It's a bonding moment. I lean back in my chair, relishing his desire for me to help him. I grin at him.

I thought a hotshot like you only ever asked for Adam's
    advice?
Julian laughs, a sweet, unpretentious laugh.

You've also been nominated for the Chambers' Awards now!
It's disarming, and flattering—and I don't want to get ahead of myself. There's no fake modesty in my response, because it's too big an award to believe I will ever actually win it.

I'm only nominated because Adam won last year.
But it has worked, he has won me over. I'm thrilled that he thinks I'm a brain to trust, that I'm as smart as he and Adam. I am a year behind him in my bar call, and I know how highly Julian thinks of himself. It feels like something major has shifted.
I smile at him.

I'll be there in a moment; I'll just finish up here and I'm
    yours.
His eyes widen flirtatiously. I blush. But he is gone before I can think of a way of reframing it. I finish my notes and pack up my things. Put them away and consider it quicker to go straight to court in the morning, so I roll up my gown, shoving it roughly into my barrister bag with my wig on top. I put on some deodorant. Glance in the small mirror on the shelf and fix up my hair, quickly fix some lip gloss on, looking over my shoulder to make sure Julian hasn't returned in the meantime.
I feel the thrill of being invited to be alone with Julian in his room. With this guy whose father is a King's Counsel, whose family is legal aristocracy itself. His father's father and his father's father's father all barristers. Am I so pathetic that I need their stamp of approval that I'm smart enough? I can't be satisfied that I am already? How many tests will I put myself through before I believe I truly can relax here? I root about and find a small perfume bottle. I consider spraying it, but then change my mind. Deodorant is enough. I remember Julian's touch on the dance floor—gentle, irresistibly

confident. His body knew how to move, and in spite of myself I liked him touching me.

I walk into Julian's room like it is an everyday event. Not that it is after nine at night, not that it is one of the most expensive-looking interiors possible. Yes, it is a small room, but the way he has put it together gives it a real edge. I take it all in, the built-in book-shelves, the red modern sofa in the corner, just the right size for the space, the rug on the ground laid out like it was thrown there, but which was clearly carefully considered. His desk is small to fit the room, yet made of some expensive dark timber, and his chair is leather. There's a small coffee table in front of the sofa and on it laid out neatly is a white binder, some notes next to it with handwrit-ten pages beside that. Julian's handwriting, all privately educated curves and readability. I'm intrigued.

He points to the brief, and I sit and flick through it. Julian pulls down a panel on the bookcase and there's a table for pouring drinks. He takes out glasses and a vodka bottle and comes and sits by me on the sofa. I can feel he is watching me. His aftershave or men's cologne reaches my nostrils and I breathe it in. He takes off his jacket, rolls up his white shirtsleeves, revealing suntanned forearms. Julian is completely unaware that I am having a moment of distraction. He asks me a legal question and leans in, flicking through the file to show where he is having some issues.

As he leans in, I feel heady, slightly intoxicated, and it is not just the vodka. I look over the pages and become absorbed, all traces of attraction pushed aside. Everything else drops away and the legal machinery in my mind takes over. Crunching story with legal doc-trine. Comparing snippets of evidence with legislative clauses. I tell Julian that the case looks bad for his client. He grimly agrees with me.

I'm feeling a bit desperate to find something, anything; but

I'm stuck. Should I plead it out for a lesser sentence?

Julian is in the zone, that zone that we all find ourselves in from time to time. Where someone's life is truly in our hands. Where a deci-sion about strategy decides what risk to take or not take. I ask Julian about his client.

Does he have a record?

Julian sighs and pours us more vodka.

　　Yes, he has a past. And all similar types of violent offenses.
Our eyes meet, we both know that if he pleads guilty, he will definitely do time if he has a record, probably a lot. But at least that time
would be discounted compared to the sentence he'll get if he goes
down at trial. It's intense, and we both talk through the police statements and evidence. There is a chance that the facts don't work for the
police, but it's a knife's edge to know what way Julian should advise.
I pore over the evidence neatly provided in the brief. Silence in the
room, I can feel Julian is hoping I will find something, anything. I
can feel him looking at me, his eyes all over me, and I daren't look
up. I scan everything on the page. And then—I spot something.
Flick back to a previous page, I see an inconsistency. Triumphant, I
point it out to Julian.

　　Look, the informant police officer says this, but here,
　　　　reading between the lines, here it hints at the opposite.
　　Looks like they fixed it to cover any doubts.
Julian looks, his face lights up.

　　Fuck. That's great.
An inconsistency opens the gates to cross-examine and show that
someone is lying, or someone has stitched it up. It's a great feeling. I
ask Julian about the case.

　　Who's the alleged victim?
Julian is still peering down at the statements. I pick up the Scene of
Crime Officer photos. Julian responds.

　　Just some deadbeat at the pub. Too much rum in both of
　　　　them.
I ask more.

　　Your guy talk?
　　Yeah, made a statement but he's no cleanskin so he didn't
　　　　give much away.
I suddenly get excited; I have spotted something in the photos.

　　Julian, did the brief include any CCTV footage?
Julian's following my finger.

　　No.
And there above the toilets is a CCTV camera with a light on it to
show it is working. I'm excited.

Here we go!
Julian leans right in.

Fuck. Camera. And no footage in the brief. Right, it's been
'accidentally damaged,' no doubt.
He looks up at me. I shrug. We both smile.

Who knows!
He's still looking at me.

Well spotted. It gives me something to start with.
I sit back, satisfied, relieved, vodka swimming in my veins. Look at
Julian's tousled hair falling down toward his brief, absorbed, note
the brand of his shirt. It's what I expected. Back of his neck is sleek,
warm, tanned. I feel the heat of him beside me and I move my arm
slightly away. I know I've had too much vodka perhaps, but I look
over and see that the door to his room is closed. I hadn't noticed
that before. Still looking down, he turns his head to the side, hand
holding up his hair to his forehead, and he gives me a breathtakingly
slow smile. His eyes are upon me, and I am transfixed. He sits up and
moves closer, his arm touching mine, and a rush of electricity spikes
through my body. His arm is leaning against mine and the weave of
his shirt is up close. I find myself kissing Julian. The entire mood has
shifted, there is no brief, just vodka pumping through me, the sofa,
his face up close to mine and our lips merged. He's more gentle than
I thought he would be, boyish, sheepish. Jules! Who'd have thought
it. All his boisterous, bantering ways, all his football talk and brash
front yet beneath it all, there is this. He's not at all a look that I
would normally go for. As I'm kissing him, I briefly flash to Mia and
our conversation recently. Mia would say he is definitely not the type
I usually find attractive at all; he's all clean and well pampered, and
expensive. But right now, in this moment, on this sofa he is exactly
what I want.

We are kissing as clothing is shed and there are no words. The corner
sofa is plush, and we fuck like experts. It's awesome; when I find my
way on top of him, he looks longingly over my body, it's empower-
ing, and sexy. It emboldens me and I watch him as he touches my
body, kisses it. I feel assertive and tell him what feels right, giving
him signals when he nails it. We end up in a tangle as we fuck on the

sofa, and as I start to climax, he tells me to quieten down. I realize I have been loud, and that Harrison is still next door. After we both cum we lie there still hot, sweaty, and attached, and he looks into my face. Pupils wide, mouth hungry, sweat through his eyebrows.

He talks before I laugh.

You're amazing.

He's sincere, dreamy. He strokes my face, my neck as he gazes at me. I need to break this.

We're such a freaking cliché, barristers doing it in chambers.

I'm relieved when he laughs, the old Julian back again. But then he pulls my face to his and kisses me deeply. It takes my breath away. When the kiss is done, he still looks at me. He is both the old Julian and this new Julian. He is serious for a moment.

I never thought I had a chance.

I am shocked by this.

Really?

I start to recalibrate. How the fuck did I become the sort of girl, the sort of woman, whom Julian Brookes thought he wouldn't have a chance with. I am suddenly very aware of my nakedness, embarrassed at my physical confidence. I start to pull my clothes back on. Julian doesn't know what came over me, but he notices it.

Hey?

It's all too intimate, this soft voice of his. I have my underwear and shirt back on. He starts to pull on his. My mind is clouded, not with regret, although perhaps that will come; but right now I'm trying to catch up on what just happened. He's still shirtless and his torso now strangely familiar. He is looking at me, is he upset? Is he confused? What's going on? I try to contextualize.

I don't come from your world, Julian.

He's puzzled. I don't know why I even said that. I am no less than he is. Surely, I believe that by now. Fuck. I must look like I want to explain because he holds on to me, smiles at me kindly.

Where do you come from?

I pull away and pull up my suit trousers. My mind is racing, I need to make light of my last declaration. I flash him the cheekiest look I can manage.

But I can do private school better even than private-school
     girls.
Quizzical, he looks at me, and I do the best imitation of a private-
school girl walk and flick of the hair. I even look up when I walk the
way they do, the way I have tried to emulate walking. The truth is I
have studied these girls, including even Mia, for years. I have watched
how they carry themselves, don't hide away, speak with confidence,
have a sense of safety. I have admired it and been intimidated by it,
that is the truth; however, I realized as a lawyer that so much of what I
do in court is performative, and the best way to feel that I am measuring up is to copy how they do it, copy that way of walking, of taking
their time to speak because they expect people will listen to them.
I have watched them in robing rooms, watched how they feel they
belong, listened to them talk of their families and lives. Copied their
hairstyles, studied their suits, their shoes especially, marveled at how
they just know what to wear and how to stand. I am showing Julian
that I am not one of them, just a copycat, I am doing it as a joke for
him, to show him something of myself but also to insist on not being
intimidated by my class status. He doesn't quite get it but partly does,
and my sassy way of making fun of the ones I learned from is me
telling him 'I don't care,' but I did care. Because once you have been
relegated to less than, even in casual comments about class, once you
have recognized that you don't have the status of others, the chip on
your shoulder, the one fed by shame and embarrassment, is a deep
cut that rarely goes away. I consider that this impersonation might be
considered by Julian as me mocking him and his people, because of
course it is. But my intention was merely to escape the moment, not
to mock him, and besides, I have longed to be those women for so
long. Julian does not take offense, instead he laughs good-naturedly,
and I feel compelled to offer more context.

     Thing is, I was just making the point that you're not
          my usual type . . . I mean you have Eton and Oxford
          ingrained in your cells.
Julian responds quickly.
     It's embarrassing.
Which is not at all what I expected. Surely there was a quick, witty
comeback to put me in my place. I want to backtrack, I am not the

sort of person who ever wants to make people feel uncomfortable, much less embarrassed.

What? Why?

I am legitimately confounded, desperate for the answer, or is it a trick? But Jules is serious, honest, takes a moment.

Because the truth is, if it wasn't for my dad—I wonder if I would ever have made it.

I meet his eyes, he is raw and exposed, I am at a loss. I desperately search my brain for what I said the other night to Mia about being talented and giving her an out from her privilege guilt. But he jumps in.

I mean, brains, sure . . .

I smile, there he is, the old Julian. He's right too, he's smart, super smart. He continues.

But the rest . . .

The silence between us is not unnerving, it feels that something real has just happened. I look at Julian, beautiful Jules. I look at him and I see something that I haven't seen before. An openness, an admission; he trusts me. I ask him what his mother does.

She's a professor of modern languages at the University of London.

I consider this and realize that 'of course she is,' I guessed as much. Makes sense it would be something like that. There's so much security, such a safety net beneath him. Without even thinking, I just say what comes first.

I envy you.

We are both surprised. I because I said it; he because he doesn't understand exactly what I envy. He looks into me, wondering.

What does your father do?

I try the joke.

Well, he is not a King's Counsel, that's for sure.

But it falls flat. We have established something honest, and he is holding that space, waiting for me to offer some part of me. I feel a need to tell him, this man who is no longer Julian Brookes, this man who has just had sex with me, who has just kissed me deeply in his chambers room.

I don't know what he does.

not sure what to do next. I don't want to leave Julian asleep in his room in case he'd still be there when everyone comes in tomorrow and they'd ask questions. I put on my shoes and socks, then gently wake him.

Julian. Jules. Are you awake?

It takes a bit, but he wakes up and looks at me. I pick up my jacket.

I have to go home. It's three a.m. and I'm in a big case tomorrow.

He's slightly adorable all sleepy but he moves around, apologizing.

Do you need to go home?

I've just said I do, but I feel like he wants a reason, so I invent one.

I have to feed my cat.

Oh God, cat? I just made up a cat. He's awake now and putting on items of clothing that are missing. He's scuffling around.

Sure. Sorry. I'm nearly ready.

I take out my phone and call an Uber. Plugging in the address. When he is dressed, we leave chambers. It's awkward, he holds my hand, but I take my hand away, then feel badly and show him I need to check my phone. He nods, smiles.

When we are outside chambers we stand together. I'm not sure whether he is being chivalrous and will return to chambers when I am gone or will hail a black cab. It's still dark outside, but I know the sun comes up early these days, and I don't want to be here when daylight starts. I have my barrister bag with all my gear and my satchel with my brief. Julian is scratching his head when the Uber arrives; I kiss him on the cheek and open the front door. I normally wouldn't do this, but Julian is right by the back door of the car. As I jump into the front seat, greeting the driver, I notice that Julian has opened the back door and is moving to get in. I'm confused, not sure what this means.

Oh? You're coming?

Julian looks embarrassed and pulls out of the car, still with the door open in his hand. The driver turns to peer at him, and Julian leans into me.

Or, I could . . . NOT . . . if you prefer?

There's an awkward silence, I'm not sure what he thought. That he

There's a pause. Then I offer half-heartedly:

Prison, probably.

Julian's eyes widen with interest. I feel I have gone t[o]
outside what he expected. I reel in the comment.

Joking. He left when I was six.

I never wanted to tell him so much but there it is. A [
crosses my face, he must have seen it, because Julian [
hand gently and puts it against his cheek. It is such a[
gesture that as we stand there I lean into him as he as[
question.

Your mum?

I am tired, and there is no place to hide. I put my head a[
The facade is undone. It's late, and there is nothing to [
more.

She's a cleaner.

I can hear his heartbeat, it's steady and reassuring. He [
anything, but he kisses the top of my head. Then I hear hi[
with care.

That's a tough job.

Blood pumping through his heart, in my ear. I think to my[
you have no idea.' And I say nothing more. He holds me to [
I give way to the tiredness. I rest. Then I hear him snoring s[
I know he is asleep.

I carefully take myself away, look around his office. I wal[
desk and look at an array of photographs. His parents, a bro[
good-looking, smiling, with arms about each other, a massiv[
try house in the background. Another of him and his father, [
their legal gowns and wigs, a book nearby that his father has [
about defamation law. I pick it up and flick through it, there'[
erence to Julian at the back, and to what must be Julian's moth[
brother—Araminta and Rupert. I look over to Julian on th[
and then choose a case law book from his collection on the [
No one reads bound copies anymore, all the cases are online, b[
collection must have been a gift from his father, as I see they[
his name in light pen when I open the book. Strangely, I settle [
and read a case in the book, then another. It's absorbing, but [

would come home with me? To mine? What's going on? I try to rescue the situation.

It's just . . . I need to sleep.

Julian nods, he closes the door, then moves toward me in the front
seat, the front door still open. I think he is going to lean in and kiss
me. But he speaks.

Can we, um, perhaps, do something later this week?

I realize that Julian is nervous. Oh my God, Julian Brookes is nervous. I'm amazed. He's nervous about asking me out. I cannot think
of an answer, mostly because I am so flabbergasted that he is so nervous, but also because I don't know what to say. The driver waits
patiently, eyes ahead. Julian speaks up again.

I mean, if you . . . ?

I am charmed. Julian is nervous. So nervous. The driver must feel
it too, he winces a little as they both wait for me to respond. Julian
speaks again.

We don't have to if you feel . . . weird.

He looks so small, so delicate. I do feel weird. Our rooms are in the
same chambers. What if people find out? I look over at him.

I don't even know my own answer before it comes out of my mouth.

I'd like that.

There appears to be relief all around. Julian beams, returns and kisses
my cheek, then closes the car door, waving me off; the driver lets
out a held-back breath and relaxes into his seat; I look ahead at the
London streets, deserted and unfamiliar in this quiet mode, and feel
a delicious sense that something is happening in my love life.

CHAPTER 15

I'm in chambers and Cheryl screams out, 'Was the sex hot?' I turn the volume down, it's a few days after the night with Julian and we are FaceTiming. She's been up early with morning sickness and I'm in extra early before a long walk into court today. I panic.

Cheryl. I'm at work, you're on speaker!

Then as she leans into the camera and repeats her question as a whisper, I know my face gives it away. She squeals in delight. Then peers at me.

Oh my God, you're blushing.

Bloody hell.

You like him, don't you.

No.

Cheryl clocks the inconsistency and teases me in a singsong voice.

Tess and Julian. Julian and Tess. Tessa and Julian. Jules and
    Tess.

I'm interrupting her.

Shhh. He works here too. Please, Cheryl . . .

She stops and studies me. Serious now.

Are you falling for him? OMG you are!

I'm ending the call. Bye. Bye.

I hit 'end call' and sit there; a text comes through from Cheryl right away. 'Tessa and Julian' with a red heart emoji. I haven't seen Julian since the night in chambers, and I have felt a little paranoid about him telling anyone. Adam? I can't bear to imagine him telling Adam. I think I'm worried what Adam might think, or that it will interfere with the connection we have around work. He's an ally, a person I trust. Perhaps Adam will consider this as a strange choice for me. Oh stop. Why do I care what anyone else thinks? Especially Adam, he's my friend too, not just Julian's. I just prefer to conduct any sexual nights outside of work is all, to avoid any crossover. Done now though. I find myself thinking of funny things that Jules has said, it's endearing me further to him.

Phoebe waltzes in, wearing trainers like I am. We decided to walk to court, talk about the case I'm running, and factor in some steps along the way. We walk down Chancery Lane; I need to pick up a barrister collar I ordered. We've all been to Ede and Ravenscroft; it's been there forever. Since barristers began, this is the major retailer for barristers' wigs, gowns, and collars. They also sell expensive business shirts, men's socks, and judge's attire. The black and gold wig tins that everyone is given as a 'called to the bar' gift are only sold here. They are stamped with the name of the shop, and the initials of the barrister are printed or engraved on it.

Ede and Ravenscroft is an institution, which connects us all to barristers immemorial. KC wigs and judge's wigs are also made here, the strange symbols of hierarchy and mystique that keep the profession so elite, so expensive, so staged. Up on the shelves, lining the highest points of the walls, are the large wig tins—the largest of all, tins that housed the big wigs, the judge's wigs.

One of them has the name of Lord Denning on it. I always look up for it when I enter the store. So many judgments I read at law school had his name in them, and yet here I can be so close to something he would have touched. Although, truth be told, those old judges had people to dress them, protect and prepare their judicial robes and wigs (and place them on the revered man). There are only a few women who know the patented way of making an E&R wig. The workshop studio below the shop is where they labor, threading and plaiting the hair from horse tails until magically a new headpiece for a barrister or judge emerges. No one knows their secret design, or the methodology of these older women who have inherited the protocol through the ages. The law is so much about inheritance, yet this one slightly delights me.

I remember Johnny, when he and Mum came with me to be fitted and I told him about the women downstairs making all the wigs, he was joking about whether the women got their revenge on barristers and judges by spitting in the wigs of those they didn't like. While it wasn't Johnny's intent, I found this subversion of the patriarchy, and all it represents to those women downstairs slaving over horse tails, to be intoxicating.

And yet of course there I was, lining up for my own wig.

CHAPTER 16

THEN

Johnny and Mum have come with me to my world. When they saw me called to the bar, I had borrowed a wig and gown from the family of an older barrister who had put it aside to be used by 'those less fortunate' after he retired. The rule was that I could use it until I could afford to buy my own. The old barrister mustn't have been very tall because while the gown was long on me, no one commented on it, but his head must have been big—'bursting with brains, I guess,' Johnny laughed at the time—because it was certainly big on my head. The wig would often slip off my head, sometimes at the worst possible moments. For the months that I wore it in court I was constantly aware that it could slide off. It also had a strange smell about it, which I became accustomed to as I wore it, but sometimes on a weekend I could smell it around me and feared that my own hair had somehow absorbed it.

Johnny is making me nervous, touching things and whistling at the prices of shirts.

Blimey, I could service my car for the price of this one alone.

I can see Tommy smiling behind his hand, he winks at me. Tommy's one of the sales guys, tall, handsome, Scouse accent. He met me when I was measured up by a short posh man in the store, and we chatted while the short, stocky posh man—Mr. Powell, he introduced himself as—tut-tutted that I was talking to staff. Eye roll. Mr. Powell was so bad tempered, and he is here again. Measuring up an older man, I realize this barrister has just taken silk, and the deference shown to him stands in stark contrast to the way Mr. Powell glances at my family.

Mum and Johnny don't notice.

Tommy is serving someone, so we wait for Mr. Powell to finish. There's a chair, but sitting down in a shop is not something that feels right to Mum. It's not a large shop, and a strange mix of modern digital payment machines and seventeenth-century Britain. I look up to find Lord Denning's wig tin, an antiquated huge thing with his name blazoned on it. A big judge's wig would have been stored in there. He might even have stood here where I am standing.

When our time comes, Mr. Powell fetches my order and treats each piece like I am being gifted something precious. No mention of the fact that I'm paying substantial sums for the getup. He fusses about me when I rush to put the gown on, insisting that I do it right. He then places methodically a woman's collar on my neck. I have been wearing the one that the men wear until now, which I actually like, despite having spilled coffee on it a few times, and I am not sure I want this special female collar, but I'm too shy to say so.

I mentally calculate how much more it will cost and chastise myself for not speaking out. Mr. Powell asks Johnny to 'not touch the shelves, please.' His voice is the sickly pretentious voice that well-spoken people use with children, and we all clock it. It makes Mum fade; Johnny jumps away.

When Mr. Powell is delicately taking out my new wig, it is a moment he assumes my family are beholding as sacred; instead, Johnny looks at me and subtly does a middle-finger birdie at Mr. Powell. Perhaps this is when I first loved Tommy. As I turn to see whether anyone else saw, there is no mistaking that Tommy had. His mouth is wide open in a silent roar of a laugh that he is trying to suppress. It makes me proud for a moment, that this act of subterfuge happened. Why should we all feel so stiffly inappropriate in this place—I am buying a significant purchase and I am a barrister. Surely Mr. Powell does not get to treat me like this? The wig is placed upon my head like a crown. There is a moment when I look in the mirror, this brand-new gown, this white collar previously unworn, this brand-new wig made especially for me, or so I am deciding to tell myself. I stand there and I am not in the room with Mr. Powell anymore, I am looking at myself in the wig I shall wear for years and years, that I will have my own name written inside, that is mine. Earned. In the next second I realize I look like a kid in a new school uniform, all pressed and new, fitted and proper.

Tommy appears in the mirror in the background. He is smiling gently. I turn and ask him whether I look okay.

Smashing!

He's taking the piss. Mum looks gobsmacked and a little fearful, Johnny goes to ruffle my hair but his fingers ruffle my wig.

Look at you, horse head!

Before it is all packaged up, Mr. Powell looks to Johnny and Mum.

It's often customary that the family consider ordering an Ede and Ravenscroft initialed wig tin to keep the wig in its best form.

I shake my head.

As Mum and Johnny reach the end of the street, they stop at the lights. They seem so vulnerable here in London. Have I not proven myself enough just to get here, can I not just do what Johnny just did—give it the middle finger and race out? Because there is no doubt as I lose sight of those two that I feel lonely without them, and yet I am horrified to recognize that I sometimes feel lonely when I am with them. Where I once belonged, and where I now am desperate to belong, are now both places where I must pretend. Both of them. I have educated myself out of my world, but it takes more than brains to belong in this new world; this world that I carry the costume to fit into in a large bag with an impressive name on the front.

A memory from last week haunts me. Among peers chatting about school holidays, I mentioned the one time my family took a trip. Mum had taken us to the Lake District for two days. We were older, Johnny and I, but it was like we were in another country. I didn't labor it, but without thinking talked about how beautiful, how extraordinarily different it was. Vanessa, one of those in my bar call, was among the group, and someone turned to her and asked her curiously, not to make a point, whether her family still had their country house up there. Vanessa responded without any sense of pride or status.

I'm not sure, I think so, but we have the place in Southern

France now and mostly when we get together as a family,
we go there.

Vanessa's nonchalance, her failed attempt at recall, was without men-
ace or provocation. She simply had to think about it. That everyone
else didn't exclaim, that they didn't think this was the most extraordinary thing they had heard was how I was shamed. The people talking
about me were not comparing me to them, just talking facts. They
weren't shaming me, but I felt my background and it didn't feel good.
I didn't feel proud as I should have or could have. I felt drenched in
embarrassment. Shamed by myself, for not being vigilant about what
I disclose. Shamed by my own lack of knowing what I don't know.

I learned something. Not only that I didn't belong, but that I didn't
even know the ways I didn't. That completely harmless disclosures
can make you stand out, and not in a way you want to. I knew
from previous experiences that despite no one mentioning my background, it was always noted, the shift was tangible. It was enough to
be a woman at the bar, I didn't need this as well.

Later that day, Danielle approached me at the court lunchroom and
sat with me. Her father is a solicitor, she knows this world, but being
a Black woman, she understands what it is to feel different to everyone else, and knows how hard it is to find one's place. Danielle was
on the panel that decided whether I would be offered pupillage at
my chambers. She knew I was a scholarship student, about my background, yet she had no doubt been one of the voices who spoke up
for me. When I broach this with her, she stills me with a sharpness
in her voice.

Never thank me, your university marks, your advocacy in
court, and your ability gave you that place.

I will always be so grateful for her comment.

CHAPTER 17

Phoebe and I enter Ede and Ravenscroft as a small bell chimes on the door. Tommy is upon us, dressed in a morning suit. He is pushing sixty now and still here. While we chat and banter, Phoebe looks on; it occurs to me that Tommy is part of my network, the people who I have befriended, and who secretly have power behind the scenes. Tommy pulls out my collar and tells me that there is a stock shortage, but he held one back for me.

I glance at Phoebe triumphantly. She stands meekly beside me.

I introduce her to Tommy, who is polite but keen to tell me a funny story about a silk being fitted for a full-bottomed wig because they are allowed to wear one for ceremonial occasions. Laughing subdues and Tommy asks me in all earnestness:

When do you think you might become a King's Counsel?

It's not that I haven't thought about it, or even planned for it, but no one ever really talks about it at the bar. Tommy asking me outright is confronting, especially in front of Phoebe. I laugh it off, but not so much that I rule it out. Phoebe looks at me curiously. She's still a pupil, a baby barrister (this is not the official title, but we all use it). She's a baby barrister and I am becoming a senior junior. A baby barrister progresses into a junior junior, then a senior junior. You are only senior counsel when you are anointed King's Counsel.

When you 'take silk' and become a KC, it's because you are invited to. You might put yourself forward, but the process is unknowable. Not the meritocracy it projects at all.

Phoebe and I leave E&R, grab some takeaway lattes, and continue our walk. Through the Houses of Parliament gardens and all those sculptures of men, across the bridge and onward to the London Inner Court.

Phoebe brings up the cab rank rule. She has been thinking about it. She has been told that if she needs to, she can make herself 'unavailable' if she can't deliver. I jump in quickly.

> Phoebe, it's against the law, otherwise barristers would
> dump the legal aid cases they've agreed to in order to
> pick up well-paid private cases. And then who would do
> the cases for those without money and power?

Phoebe knows this through ethics training but needs to be sure about when something can be sent back. I've been asked this before by many baby barristers.

You can send the brief back ONLY if you think the work is outside your area of expertise and you wouldn't be able to do a good job for your client because it is not a practice area you are familiar with. I start to sweat and after all this cab rank talk, I suggest we cab it the rest of the way. The air-conditioning is a welcome relief. I tell the driver:

> Inner London Court, please.

We strap our seat belts on and then out of nowhere Phoebe shocks me.

> My dad was arrested once.

I do a double take. This is unexpected. She continues.

> I was thirteen.

I'm not shocked that a family member was arrested, just that it is Phoebe's family. I feel a wave of kindred connection. She's brave for telling me. The bar gossip is rampant. I know this is an act of trust.

> Can I ask what he was arrested for?

I realize this is strange territory. Usually even clients don't tell their jail buddies what they are in for. Phoebe quickly responds.

> Nothing sexual!

I feel badly that she has to reassure me of that, I hadn't even considered it.

> He was arrested for financial fraud.

It sits in the air between us. White-collar crime. She continues.

> It was brutal.

I nod in sympathy. I wonder whether powerful people have the same terror at being arrested as my brother did the first time. Phoebe fires up.

> He didn't do it.

A moment of silence, then, to underline this.

He got off.

We both know this doesn't mean he didn't do it. She sighs.

But he had a massive breakdown.

The car starts winding its way up to court. I feel for her, I know beneath these simple sentences is so much trauma.

God, Phoebe, I'm so sorry.

She turns and looks me in the eye.

I know he didn't do it. He was innocent.

I want to reassure her.

Being arrested doesn't make you guilty.

I feel protective of her, wonder how many people know this story. It would have hit the press when her father was arrested, no doubt. She looks vulnerable.

Court case was . . . awful.

But pulls herself up, and her familiar fury emerges.

I'll never work for the prosecution.

We are about to pull up in court and I'm taken aback. I think about how I used to say I would never work for the prosecution until one day they briefed me. That's when the cab rank rule makes you do things you say you would never do. That's when you discover that the rules are there to protect you from yourself. To remind you that as a barrister you are just a voice for hire, that you are just a spokesperson offering a version of a story to the court; it's the jury, the community, who decide which is the best version. When I respond to Phoebe, I try to do it in a wry, ironic manner.

Unless the prosecution decides to brief you! Then you DO work for them.

I feel her grimace, but the cab pulls up and we are tapping cards and moving toward court together. An unusual new bond has formed. Even if we never speak of it again; even if it was white collar for her father, and street violence for my brother; we have both known the fear of the law coming down on our family. The difference is her father was found not guilty. Yet, even so, their records each have permanent notations of crime.

As we hit security, we both must take out our water bottles and take a sip. A very lo-fi way to prove that we are not carrying flammable liquid or explosives, but no doubt effective. I chat to Lionel at security, ask him about his dog and his face lights up. Phoebe looks on in amusement. I notice.

What?

You know everyone.

I think on this and realize that in some ways I do. I know those whom Phoebe and Alice and Julian don't. I like this; I turn and wave to Lionel, who tips his imaginary hat at me.

We arrive at the women's robing room. A few senior juniors are hard at work on laptops crowded around a small table. We nod, strangely familiar with one another's work rather than the ins and outs of our lives. I like the women's robing room, although I used to feel so out of place. I remember the first year I was fascinated by the sorts of shoes the women seemed to know to buy. The same expensive, understated designer, comfortable yet stylish, similar colors too.

When I first went looking for the brand to copy it, I was stunned at the price tag. Why would anyone pay that amount for such boring shoes, shoes that people didn't even notice, shoes that looked almost orthopedic, when they could buy much nicer-looking ones for a quarter the price. I dared to ask Alice once.

She laughed as if it was obvious.

　　Better to have shoes no one notices in court and that you
　　　can stand up in all day.

They were something of a badge or uniform, the secrets that women knew at the bar that kept you included in a sort of unspoken gang.

When I had my first massively well-paid, big private brief, I found myself wearing the very brand I'd laughed at. Told myself the price tag was worth it, but if I am being truthful, it was never about the arch support.

As I pack away my trainers and look over at Phoebe, I realize she must have had the memo on shoes before she even came to the bar. Hers have a bit of pizazz.

Phoebe pulls out her wig tin and whips out her newish wig. She had apparently been offered her uncle's hand-me-down. She had refused, and in keeping with her eating habits ordered a vegan wig. I laughed when I first heard of vegan wigs, made from hemp, but I admire her for bucking the system and staying true to herself. She's daring and turns her back on the status thing.

Perhaps it's easier when you have the status of a legal family; or perhaps it is an act of rebellion from within the system as a means of expressing her rage on behalf of her dad's arrest and trial.

I know for me the subversive acts were more subtle and have become less so as I have gained years at the bar. All women at the bar conduct certain acts of subterfuge. An uncollared shirt with one's suit, colored tights, or fabulous earrings. With women having been excluded for so long, having been so low in numbers in the legal profession, having for years watched male barristers and judges assume their superior intellect without any heed to the exclusion of women, of people of color, of those from working-class backgrounds, it is a welcome relief that there is some secret act of women's expression. The ultimate thrill is seeing one of our own on the bench; it's a quiet exchange of pride, as are the secretly exchanged glances of support when a male judge hammers down on one of us.

I take out my trusty Tupperware stolen from Mum's all those years ago. I used it for my borrowed wig and have used it ever since. Someone suggested they were going to buy me a wig tin last year, they were sick of seeing me 'slum it' with a Tupperware. It was a joke, but my response was one I didn't expect.

> This reminds me of where I am from, what sets me apart,
> and how to stay grounded.

The look I received was a startled glance, an acknowledgment that they might have lacked insight. I liked the owning of my life, of my mum's kitchen plastics. Phoebe has already tucked her tin back in her barrister bag and smiles at my Tupperware. I no longer whip it in and out quickly.

A barrister I know, Vanessa, is in the robing room; she's addressing me.

> I'm being led in for the Crown Prosecution Services today,
> are you still acting alone on your sex assault?

I put on my wig.

Sure am. I also have our pupil with me, this is Phoebe.
She cuts in.
Yes, I know Phoebe.
She nods at Phoebe, who calls out.
Hiya.
As we walk out of the robing room toward the meeting room to take further instructions from my client, Phoebe notes:
So, how come you're running the case yourself whereas she
is being led by a KC? You're both at the same level, right?
I brush it aside. Competition is everywhere at the bar, you have to ignore it, or you start to feel paranoid.
In this case today, the Crown only has two witnesses, one is the alleged victim and the other is her sister. I've read the statements by her and her sister. Phoebe is excited.
Can't wait to see you do this.
My client is upon us. We move into a small room to have a quick meeting. I ask him the usual questions about being clear why I am not calling him as a witness. He's very happy about it. He's not a pleasant man, and he knows that I know he has a record for domestic violence. He is adamant he didn't rape the complainant and has pleaded not guilty.
Phoebe is polite to him. She hasn't done a rape case before. He clearly likes impressing Phoebe, as he glances at her for her response when he answers my questions. He insists that the complainant agreed to have sex with him, that they had a big night out and that he ended up at her place.
I take as many details as I need for the cross-examination of the complainant. My mind is computing, and my notes are extensive. It's a standard case, but I want to give Phoebe a good showing. When the client has gone to meet his family, I remind Phoebe of the way Adam does a sex-assault cross.
Don't go in for the kill, just test the case.
She remembers the talk in chambers. Adam's tactic.
Yes. Exactly. If their evidence has holes, just point them
out.
As we walk to court I continue with tips.
Stay calm, just appear that you are checking information,

and then show the complainant at the end that the
evidence doesn't add up. It's not as hard as you would
expect.
Right.
I find that the more sympathetic I am, the more they'll
offer information.
But does your client worry you are not going in hard
enough.
I smile at her.
The client's opinion isn't the point, it's about bringing the
jury onside, so you win the case.
I wave at a barrister I know, our robes swishing as we move quickly
through the corridor.
The trick is to convey, 'I don't want to hurt this woman.' To
somehow let the jury know that you believe she deserves
her day in court, but that you do have to point out that
she is mistaken. And you do this in a way that shows you
are finding it hard to do because she is probably not a
liar, just mistaken in this instance.
Phoebe considers this.
What if she is a liar?
Same tactic. Rise above it, resist the urge to destroy her,
that's my way of doing it. The story rarely adds up—
I'm not saying they are all lying, but the legal truth is
something else. And that is all we are there to find. The
legal truth. And you work with that to try to stop your
client from going to jail.
Phoebe tells me she saw a rape trial when she was at university, and
the guy cross-examining the alleged victim held up in court the
underwear she wore, telling her that wearing lacy undies proved she
was expecting someone to see her underwear. We all know these stories, it doesn't happen anymore. I don't know any barristers who
would be so stupid as to do that in front of a jury even if they could.
I tell Phoebe it's difficult:
As a defense counsel you must do whatever you think
will get your client over the line and propose doubt.
That's your job. But you work within the rules, and

therefore if bringing certain evidence, or using a certain cross-examination technique is allowed, then you must consider if it will help your client. Adam and I both agree that it can be counterproductive to go in too strong.

Phoebe is nodding, then says:

> I think your strategy is great, makes me believe that I can do these cases. Because in a way, the woman on the stand is lucky it's you, or someone like you, trying to get to the truth without bullying her.

She understands.

I want Alice to ask Phoebe's opinion of me in court today. I'm still smarting at her mention of me doing sexual assault cases. It is legal lore that a great barrister can act for anyone, regardless of the crime. A great defense barrister serves the system of law, getting it right at the first instance.

When we approach the courtroom, I see a media scrum. Among the many male reporters are the women court artists, they're always women. I see Rachel Myers, who reports for the *Times*. She's also legally trained, apparently, so knows what she is writing about.

For a moment I think they are all coming to our court, but apparently there is a well-known rugby player next door, accused of drug dealing. They all disappear and Phoebe and I take our seats in the court my client has been allocated. Court officer greets me, I introduce Phoebe. We take our seats and set up our papers and files. Phoebe has lugged the evidence act with her; I already know what I need but she wants to pore over any section mentioned in court.

The Crown prosecution arrives with the barrister from the robing room, and the KC on the case. This is unusual and gives me pause. Must be on my toes. Still, I like the challenge. Makes the win if it happens all that sweeter. The KC carries himself with a weary aloofness. Most of the older ones do this. It works. Makes us all stand aside when they arrive. The rule is that they take precedence in court, so we are expected to behave as such; younger silks are not as formal around it all. The KC is a prosecutor favorite, he does a lot of their trials. I look up and see my client behind glass in the dock, his family in the gallery above him. They can't see him, but I see them both. A strange family resemblance leaps out. On the other side of the gallery are two women in their thirties. They're probably friends of the complainant. I tell Phoebe to stop staring at them. She thinks she knows one of them but then realizes she doesn't.

The jury arrive and are seated, and the prosecution case continues. The police facts are not contested. My client said nothing incriminating. I guess that with his domestic violence conviction he has learned not to speak.

The prosecution calls the complainant. She states her name and I write it on my notes: Jenna Quinn. When she takes her place in the witness box, she glances around at who is in court, smiles warmly up at her friends—or are they sisters? She rests her eyes on me, not realizing at first that I am acting for the defendant. I nod benignly. She's not what I expected; an intelligent face, carefully groomed, and not dressed in a suit that usually the prosecutor calls for. She is just herself in a bright dress. Jenna gives her evidence without tears, without fuss. I am studiously writing down what she says on one side of my page—the other side will be what I intend to say in cross. I rise and interject respectfully from time to time.

Your Honor, I'm so sorry to rise, but my learned friend has gone beyond what the evidence expresses.

I win some submissions, lose others. Mainly I am making them so that Phoebe is entertained and that my client and his people recognize I am doing my job. The judge seems to perceive this and is slightly intolerant of me standing. I smile and try to make a connection for the jury. I know the whole case rests upon my cross-examination. I have made copious notes throughout the evidence in chief, discovered all the holes that need to be exposed, seen where the prosecution's frustrations are. Now I just need to point them out in the cross-examination. Put on my most sympathetic face and encourage the witness to feel comfortable with me, not too comfortable but just enough to confuse her. It's not what she expects. Jenna is in her thirties, a teacher at primary school. She met my client at a bar and agreed to go out with him on a date. I know my client is in his forties, divorced, has his own business in some sort of sporting company. The prosecution is not allowed to bring up his previous convictions unless I bring up his 'good character,' which of course, knowing his criminal history in domestic violence, is the last thing I want the jury to hear. I have researched the details and it was around smashing a door open when the locks had been changed. I've seen much worse than that, to be honest.

I look over at Jenna before I stand; she is looking right at me, waiting. Phoebe next to me is also looking at me. I stand slowly, clear my throat, and use the voice I know is helpful in these matters. I speak to Jenna sympathetically because I genuinely do feel sympathetic that she must be here and go through something that's so invasive of her privacy. I also recognize that a man's liberty is at stake. If he is found guilty, he will go to jail, that is certain.

I speak to Jenna:

> I'm so sorry, Ms. Quinn, you understand I must ask you a
>   few questions about the night you spent with my client?

Jenna nods, then speaks. Strong, clear voice.

> Yes, I understand.

I launch right into it:

> You said in your evidence that you helped remove your
>   outfit yourself?
> Yes.

Moderating my voice.

> We know you had been drinking at the club that night,
>   would you agree with me that you had two glasses of gin
>   and tonic, a vodka lime, and two or three glasses of wine?
> I think so.

I take note of her not being sure. Then continue in my most modulated voice.

> Would it be correct to assume that they were all, at least . . .

I look at my notes.

> Standard-size drinks?

Jenna doesn't flinch.

> Yes.

> Then you invited my client to your home, and together
>   there you both consumed more alcohol? Two tequila
>   shots each and a bottle of wine between you?

Jenna doesn't look at me.

Yes, that's right.

I look up from my notes. Glance at the jury; they are glued. Then to Jenna, and ask with sincerity despite knowing the answer:

Is it possible you were intoxicated?

A pause, a small snicker from someone in court, I ignore it. Phoebe is writing furiously next to me. Jenna responds.

Yes, I was somewhat. But I . . .

She doesn't finish. So I jump in.

That's a yes that you were intoxicated.

Yes.

I don't labor it, instead move on quickly with the next question.

And while you were intoxicated, you would agree that the
     events of the evening were a bit . . .

I look at my notes.

'Blurry,' as you stated in your evidence in chief?

I wait patiently for her answer. The judge coughs, I can feel the KC about to leap up, but he doesn't.

Yes. As I said.

My heart is beating fast but my voice must be quiet, modulated. I ask my next question.

So, I suggest to you that when you took off your own
     clothing you were not saying NO?

She jumps to answer too quickly. She has been waiting for this question.

No. I remember I didn't want to have sex with him.

This means nothing in evidence, and it's a gateway to my next question. Carefully, with sympathy.

And I suggest to you that even if you had reconsidered as
     you said you might have, you didn't say this at any stage?

She's clear in her response, but it feels rehearsed, coached somehow.

No. I asked him to leave. I said no.

And with my next question I go gently. I don't want to get the jury offside; I don't want to destroy the witness, but I must point out where the mistakes are.

I'm confused then because didn't you say it wasn't until
     your sister asked you about the date 'a few nights later'

that you first indicated . . . and these are your words,

  Ms. Quinn . . . 'that it *might* have been sexual assault'?

She's stuck and I am waiting. Jenna speaks.

  Well . . .

I pretend to flick through pages, waiting for the jury to see where we are. Then I jump in.

  Oh, I see it was three days, in fact? Is that correct?

  Yes.

I stand completely still. Look right at her, say a single word with the intonation of a question.

  Might?

In the pause that follows I am making the biggest point: the alleged victim wasn't even sure it was a sexual assault, she said so herself. There was at least a reasonable doubt. A conviction cannot be made when she isn't sure. I wait for Jenna to speak.

She doesn't, so I speak quietly:

  Is that what you said, Jenna?

Everyone, including me, is slightly shocked that I just used her first name. I was being kind and careful but it's too personable, and I know it. I jump in again.

  That's what you said, isn't it, Ms. Quinn, and your
    sister confirmed it in court today—that it might have
    happened, which means you 'weren't sure'?

She is upset.

  I'm sure. I just . . .

She says nothing else. I tell the court I have no further questions. It is a slam dunk; Phoebe is giving me eyes that say 'wow,' but it was easy. The jury shift uncomfortably in their chairs as the court officer moves to walk Jenna away. Before she leaves, she leans forward, looks directly at me, speaks softly but just loud enough to be heard by everyone in court.

  I am not getting anything out of testifying. I don't want to
    be here. I'm just doing this to protect other women from
    this man. I want you to know that.

She is making eye contact with me, and it's like she is talking to me, not as a barrister but woman to woman. I'm not usually thrown by something so simple, but it is so significant.

I stand there, unmoving, frozen. The judge is expecting me to make a no-case submission, but I'm stuck. Finally, the judge jumps in.

Thank you for your time, Ms. Quinn, you are free to go now.

My eyes are on her as she walks to the door, strong, poised, and graceful, and never looking back. Does she hate me? I'm sure she does. Then, abruptly, she loses her composure completely. Lets out a choked sob and then seems to fold in two. A murmur from the jury. The court officer helps Jenna up and out. I don't take my eyes off her.

When the case is over, we sit outside in the warmth of this summer's day. I turn my phone on. Phoebe is not leaving my side. She's energized and buzzing.

That was amazing.

I light up a cigarette. Then flatly:

Everyone thinks they remember.

Phoebe has no idea where I am heading.

Yeah.

She turns her thoughts to the case.

But you got him off, you won. It was the best cross.

I nod. She thinks I'm being nonchalant about my win; the truth is it was much easier than I expected. Everyone in the courtroom would have known it, but Phoebe has already rewritten it as me being heroic.

We see my client emerge from the courthouse with his family, celebrating. I had already done a perfunctory debrief with him inside and don't feel like talking to him again. Phoebe waves and he starts to head over to us. I stub out my cigarette. Phoebe turns to me conspiratorially.

Do you think he did it? That he was guilty?

I shrug. She's studying me carefully. I feel my body sigh.

Come on, Phoebe, you know that's not the question.

Well, if he was guilty, there wasn't enough evidence, was there?

She smiles.

I've got to go, but if you want to ask him, go for it?

She laughs and walks with me, checking her phone, until she bumps into a friend. They chat and I move onward. A small internal voice echoes Phoebe's question: 'What if he did it and I got him off?' But I shake it away. The reality is you can't lock someone up without proper evidence. I replay Jenna leaving the courtroom; her shoes were like the ones I used to wear before now. I remind myself that the guy was an asshole, but perhaps not a rapist. That's the responsibility of this job, you have to trust the system to work it all out. Have faith in the system finding the truth.

I look back at Phoebe chatting away. My phone buzzes. Another text from Julian. 'Can I take you to dinner on Friday night, 8 p.m.? That new Japanese place everyone's talking about? Xxx J.' Three kisses. I feel my breath quicken, quickly send him a thumbs-up. It seems measly so I follow up with 'Sounds perfect!' I know he has a trial all week off circuit, and I still have a few days of work to finish before Friday. I call Mum, hang up, call again so she knows it's me—

she will pick up if she's at work. She's breathless when she does, missed the bus home despite running for it. She asks me how I'm doing, and I ask about Johnny, Cheryl, and life at home. She knows Johnny came to talk to me, and chats excessively about Johnny planning to start up his own business soon and how proud she is. I know she is overplaying it because she doesn't want any friction between Johnny and me. She says Cheryl went for another ultrasound.

I'm alert now.

    Why? Is everything okay?
    Yes, of course, why do you jump to such conclusions?
    Cheryl needed to do a scheduled check; the baby is
    growing nicely. And guess what?
    What?
    It's a girl.

I pretend I don't know. I'm surprised that Johnny told me before he told Mum. I tell her I will come by in the next fortnight and we can do a dinner? She's not committing. I take a moment.

    Mum, I'm sorry about last time. I shouldn't have . . .
But she's already off the phone, her bus has arrived.

The rest of the week I'm busy, with matters in court each day. The first is a private, high-paying brief for some city guy, and the other is a complex legal aid matter. On Friday my matter is adjourned, and on the way back to chambers I do some shopping. I'm thinking about dinner with Julian. I quickly find a fabulous dress; I try it on, and it looks so sexy that I fall in love with it. I already have shoes that match and it's silky and body hugging.

I need new underwear and find myself in Bravissimo in Soho. The woman serving me is intimidating at first, but completely unfussed as I reveal more and more of my body to her. I try on a few sets of bras and undies, and a gorgeous black silky set goes seamlessly under my new dress. I feel very grown-up in this moment. I've never done this before. This feels so very luxurious; I run my hand on the fabric, touch the lace delicately stitched in place as the long mirror in the dressing room reflects to me the woman I would like to be. I think of an article I read about underwear making successful women feel more confident. It sounds like bollocks, but there's something decadent and secretly sexy about knowing you're wearing matching, sexy gear without anyone else knowing it.

I have two expensive-looking bags swinging from my arms as I cab it back to chambers. Alighting at Lincoln's Inn, I walk through the posh gardens that once felt so unwelcome—all those 'Please keep off the grass' signs, felt like there were menacing eyes about. Now I just see it as a strange old-fashioned garden, and I love walking through it. I dare to consider the night ahead, Julian and me, what might it be. I linger on some of the sexual details of our last encounter, and my blood moves faster. I realize I like him, as in really like him. I laugh out loud. As I come to the exit, weighed down by my satchel and barrister bag, swinging my new purchases in their posh bags, I almost run into Mr. Hugh Dalton KC. He's startled, then recovers.

> Ms. Ensler, just the person I was trying to reach. I've just
> come from your chambers.

Confusion, slight fear. Why would Dalton want to see me? My face must show my anxiety because he smiles warmly, continues quickly.

> I have a proposition, let's step this way, shall we.

He moves to the side of the path. Respectfully I follow him, the gravel crunching beneath our shoes. Dalton speaks in his mellifluous tones.

I'll cut right to the point, Ms. Ensler, our chambers has
a room available and we are looking for a competitive
young candidate to join our group. We'd like that to be
you.

He knows he is offering me something huge. He smiles kindly, happy
with himself to be the bearer of such an exciting offer. I'm flabbergasted. Is this really happening?

I'm flattered.

Dalton looks at me expectantly then.

I'm sure you understand that this is confidential at this
stage.

I nod furiously. He says more.

It hasn't escaped our attention, indeed mine specifically,
that you have won some complex matters of late, and it
appears been nominated for a prestigious award.

He pauses and I compose a response but don't speak. He continues.

We think that welcoming you to our chambers would be
mutually beneficial.

Finally, I find my voice.

That's very kind, sir.

Inwardly, I am computing, this is top chambers. They charge so much
more for their rooms, way out of my price range. Dalton doesn't stop
there, he shifts his weight to his other foot, makes a gesture with his
hands.

Perhaps you could come by and have coffee next week?

I'm stunned. I hear a voice chastise me. It's my own internal voice:
'Nod, for God's sake, say thank you.'

Thank you so much, Mr. Dalton.

He reaches into his pocket and takes out a card with his details on it.
I reach up to accept it and Dalton's attention is taken by my shopping
bags. I look down and blush. One bag has 'Intimate Apparel' written
in a sexy bedroom-type font. He's not taking it in, but I try to hide it
behind another bag. Dalton is smiling again.

I look forward to hearing from you.

And he's off. Through Lincoln's Inn gardens again. These are the public gardens, the ones where you *can* step on the grass. Like a child, I do

a leap onto the forbidden green area. I'm stunned but thrilled, I can hear myself thinking it over.

I mean if things go well with Julian, then maybe I will actually have to move, won't I? A couple couldn't possibly manage in the same chambers, and he's been there longer than me? STOP. Fuck, you're not even a couple! And besides, you could never afford it or justify paying what they charge.

I almost skip back to chambers, but of course there's no one I can tell. The barristers in Dalton's chambers do such exciting human rights work, and highly complex international matters. It's all so flattering, but as I return to my chambers, I know it's not feasible on what I earn currently. I don't want to work even harder than I do now, just to support the fees; I'd be so stressed about ever taking leave again. Plus, their rooms are enormous. I would get lost in one; I like my room, it's my home at the bar. I make a mental note not to mention it to anyone for fear of people thinking I'm considering moving.

CHAPTER 18

There's no long mirror in chambers, and in my room only a small handheld. I pull the tags off the lingerie and strip off my suit, shirt, and old grayed-out underwear. The straps on the new bra were adjusted by the woman in the shop so they slide into place perfectly with a slight snap. I am trying to check out the lingerie before I slip the dress over it. Someone knocks at my door, and I quickly yell out.

Hang on, getting changed.

Alice's voice.

Only me.

The dress goes on fast, and I tell her to come on in, embarrassed that she will see me, all dressed up for a date. Alice is not expecting it.

Oh wow. Do you have a function?

I nod. She's disarmed.

You look awesome, never thought you would scrub up so
well.

I am slightly peeved that she couldn't have expected it, but to be fair I wouldn't have either. So used to suits and a sort of manufactured nonchalance that I've copied from other women barristers, I saved all my sexy gear for Tinder dates or clubbing with Mia. Alice tells me she's heading off, but that she needs a book on torts she'd lent me. It's right where she left it, so easily found in my messy room; I hand it back and she takes in my dress again. It dawns on her.

Or is this a date?

I roll my eyes.

No, of course not.

I don't know why I deny it. I don't have to tell her it's Jules. But I also know he's Alice's mate, and she has been lamenting all her friends are marrying and having children, and she is anxiously hoping to find someone for herself. I also just can't tell her right now. It would

involve a whole conversation. I also know that she likes to think of herself as more ahead in the dating game than I am. I don't know why I give that image oxygen, probably because it is true. This whole excitement over tonight is completely out of character for me.
She lingers.
    What's the function?
I quickly fire back.
    Gallery thing.
She is briefly confused; I have never mentioned galleries to her ever before. I try to sound annoyed.
    I told you about my friend's exhibition.
She feigns remembering. For a second I think she is going to ask to come with me. But she doesn't.

When Alice is gone, I slip on my shoes and make my way to the toilets. I stand on a toilet seat to check out what the bottom of my dress looks like, check the time, and open my makeup bag. I feel good. There seems to be a strange mix of barrister Tess and let-loose Tess coming together. It feels buzzy. I put on makeup, fix up my hair, then expertly slide on red lipstick. Grab some loo roll to blot, then another coat. Black mascara and I stand back. I like what I see. I relax and take a selfie. Email it to Mia. 'Date night!' I know she won't get it for a bit, but I like the photo.
Spray on some musk cologne, push up the short sleeves of the dress, and roll on deodorant. I pull up the front of my dress and gaze down at my bra.

I walk out of chambers without seeing anyone. Hailey at reception has long gone home, and most of them are probably out for Friday night drinks (or in Adam's case home with his wife and daughter). The shoes I brought from home I've only worn once; I can feel the slight pinching at the heel. I walk slowly in them, but in this dress, and feeling as I do, the brief amble to the new Japanese place gives me time to feel confident.
When I turn the corner and see the entrance to the Japanese place, Julian has already seen me. Was that a double take? He smiles at me, mouths 'fuck,' and makes his way over.

You look fucking hot.

I hover with this for a bit.

Thank you.

It comes out sultry without me even intending it. I watch his eyes follow the shape of the dress. This moment, when you are completely in your power, where even the likes of Julian with all his confidence can be rendered nervous, struck him dumb.

Finally, he speaks.

My God.

He leans in, eyes flirting with me, lower teeth over his lower lip.

I have a booking.

Great.

He lets me walk in ahead of him, I know he is checking me out, eyes grazing my body. I like it. It's strange for a woman, sometimes all it takes is a killer outfit, and some sexy makeup, high shoes, and you feel like you could do anything. It comes together and you know it is fleeting, that you have caught hold of something that can't be held. Not just that it is impermanent, but that it's a coming together of elements you have no control over, how your skin glows or doesn't, whether you're bloated pre-period or not, an inner energy that you can't describe, so many factors coming together that you take and run with. Amazed, excited. Holding on to it lightly. It's the same feeling I have in court when I know I have the precision and the timing to take the case. The savoring of the moment, the slow win. It's a strange feeling of power, of holding all the power and someone else knows it. Right now, Julian is in awe, and I am relishing it. I want to savor this feeling. I almost tell him about Dalton but know better. We are competitive, in a way that I love. He's older than I am by a few years, and more experienced, but I'm catching up. I like that he is not intimidated by smart women, he grows in my estimation on that front.

Julian scans the restaurant and declares there is no one we know in the place. We order sake straight up, there are loads of different types, which is news to me. But Julian, of course, negotiates with expertise. It makes me consider that he might well have been here before. On a date? A wave of something; curiosity? No, jealousy. Wow.

Julian is talking and I am not taking it in. We are seated close to each other across a small table made of heavy timber. He pours sake for me when it arrives and gestures for me to do the same for him. A Japanese tradition. He's warm and chatty with the waitress and she takes in all that is Julian. He manages to drop into the short conversation that we are both barristers and have had a heavy week. She's small and fair, glances at me as she places the menu down. I smile at her. In her eyes we are a couple. I see her compute it, which makes for a slight furrow of her brow when Julian smiles at her. I catch what she saw; he's warm but there is something else in his smile: a sense of expectation, of arrogant generosity toward her. Is he attempting to prove to me that he is embracing of those in the service industry, or is he flirting with her? A small strain in her neck, an almost imperceptible glance at me. I know what he is trying to do, he's showing me he is immune from the classist assumptions I have made about him. Showing me he is a nice guy.

A tiny pinprick of recoil before I feel the warmth of the sake not just in my mouth but smoothly gliding down my throat, and Julian and I are in sync. He asks me about my day, I give him the rundown in the most entertaining way possible, offer some in-jokes about other barristers I saw in the court foyer. Jules is patient, intrigued when appropriate, and leans toward me. All his attention, focused, is intense. Without the sake I would be self-conscious, but I'm liking it right now.

Just before the food arrives, he rests his hand on my forearm and a current rushes through me. That same electricity: I inwardly gasp, move my forearm as a reflex action, make a big fuss of the food as it is placed on the table between us. Sushi and sashimi, more sake, spiced beans, plate after plate of vegetables, fish, and meat. Small dishes designed to look spectacular. Julian picks up his chopsticks and handles them like a pro. I know I will embarrass myself and ask the waitress for a fork. I wait for Julian to tease me, but he is a different man over dinner.

He has spent the last week in a trial off circuit, outside of London. A murder case with interesting elements of eyewitness identification. I'm listening, engrossed.

The sake is going down between us fast, and I like the mellow warmth, the syrupy flow down my throat. I hear myself laughing and see Julian beam at the response he is getting when he details a part of the case that went seriously wrong for the prosecution. He picks something up with the chopsticks and offers it to me. Wordlessly I open my mouth and he feeds me with large pupils and lips aching to kiss me. I swallow whatever it was. I'm feeling his leg move up close to me under the table.

The waitress returns, in my mouth the next delicacy placed by Julian. I can't say anything, and Julian ignores her entirely. She hurries away before speaking. I'm suddenly alerted to how public the restaurant is. We are separated from other diners by a muslin screen. I peep around it and don't recognize anyone. The moment is broken, my mouth empty, but his leg is pressing up against mine.

I see Julian wordlessly gesture to the waitress for more sake.

I tell him about an exercise I was asked to do at a conference. All the lawyers watched footage of a street crime. Twice. Of course, being lawyers, we knew that they would test us on what we had seen. So, we knew that was coming. Questionnaires were then handed out— we could not compare notes.

Julian cottons on:

>Ah, like being a witness in court. You can't talk to the other
>>witnesses.

>Exactly. So, we complete the forms. I'm adamant about
>>lots of the answers, a few I'm a bit scratchy on but upon
>>reflection can recall what I saw.

More sake. Julian jumps in:

>And you nailed it.

>No. That's just it.

He laughs.

>Oh, what, the brilliant Tessa Ensler made a mistake?

'Brilliant.' I swoon a little, I know I shall revisit this moment in days to follow. Julian Brookes, more senior to me at the bar, father a KC, said I was 'brilliant.'

>No, Julian. The shock was that none of us had more than
>>forty percent of the questions right.

Julian is truly surprised.

>What's the twist?

>No twist. They were making the point that all ID evidence
>>is faulty. That even lawyers who *know* they are going to
>>be tested on what they see, and know they are going to
>>be asked to relay the scene immediately after witnessing
>>it cannot remember clearly. All of us sat there, and even

though we knew that ID evidence was unreliable, we all
never thought for a moment that we, who were trained
to work with evidence, could be so unreliable in recall.

Julian grins at me, shakes his head.

No way! They rigged it.

I'm overly emphatic, and I'm not sure why because it doesn't put me
in a good light.

We self-corrected our answers. I didn't even get the color of
the car right. It was confronting!

He waves it away.

I don't know. I think I'd remember it all.

My mouth is gaping. I'm joking with him as I swipe him gently on
the forearm.

What, you think you would be a better eyewitness than any
of the barristers or lawyers at the conference?

He pours me more sake and nods. Laughing. Tells me another story
about a client he had. As he talks, he occasionally runs his hand
through his hair, eyes flirting. The pressure of his leg still against mine,
and yet his tone is completely professional, with the occasional eye
roll or embellishment. We clink our pottery sake cups together before
sipping. I feel a wave of something I haven't felt in a bit. The excitement of what might be happening, and the warmth of knowing I am
on safe ground in the conversation. I like talking law with Julian more
than I expected. It's usually Adam I talk over cases with; there is the
unsaid politics behind the cases that we both know well, that informs
the context of the client in question. It's strangely and enjoyably different to chat with Jules and see the humor from his perspective, see
the eye roll inherent in his retelling, see his darkly comic timing, his
self-knowledge that the client is a million worlds away from where he
stands. I start to consider that Julian is more complex than I have previously thought. Having sex together in chambers showed me some
of his softer, more vulnerable side. This is not what is on display now,
but I am sensing an insight that I assumed was not there: his understanding of his place in society; and I'm finding it attractive that he
isn't someone pretending he doesn't have it.

I am looking at Jules, listening to Jules, and it strikes me that his
lack of sentimentality in the narrative is a relief, a sophistication, an

entertainment. Not every case has to be loaded with despair, perhaps not every context is worthy of my emotional engagement.

I like that he can separate from the story, can make it sing a little. I could learn from this; I could carry my work more lightly and be less intense. I need to depersonalize more.

Maybe Julian is teaching me that.

Maybe it's the sake.

My blood races. Julian has described the day, the setting, the difficult judge. A smattering of detail that makes me laugh. A woman with a toddler outside the courtroom who almost vomits on him. I imagine Julian horrified that his designer suit would sport a projectile vomit. I want to laugh with him, but I think about Cheryl and how I could imagine her outside a courtroom one day with a vomiting toddler awaiting the result of Johnny's run-in with the law. How she would be afraid of someone like Julian being angry with her, how she would be nervous about people seeing what happened, how she would fear to lose standing if ever she even had any in that room. More sake. Julian is continuing with his story, buoyed by my early laughter.

He draws me in.

> Client's family are waiting for me when I come back up
>   from the cells. They are beside themselves. Dad's a pastor
>   or something, a full-on Christian type, Pentecostal faith.
>   Whole family are. I'm standing there surrounded by
>   them all. Mother's crying; daughter too. Apparently,
>   there are another five siblings and an uncle in the foyer.
>   The daughter, she's very pretty.

I give him a foul look.

He laughs.

> She's in her twenties, tries to hold on to my sleeve. I'm
>   not used to all this emotion. And I'm cursing Adam for
>   flicking me a matter that's so intense.

Was it Adam's to start with?

Yes. The day his wife went into labor.

I nod. Sounds like one of Adam's cases.

As if Julian reads my mind, he continues:

> I mean Adam and his legal aid matters! Save me! Turns out this
>   one was some legal center for the church that have latched

on to his bleeding heart. So, the father is praying and telling me what a great kid the accused is. 'My son would never ever do this,' blah-blah-blah. His wife is bawling all over my gown, and the sister hanging on to me. Police statement said there were three of them in the bank robbery. Police raided my guy's house, and they find trainers there that match the footprints they had on the floor of the bank.

I nod, waiting for the twist.

I read Adam's notes. Adam's clear on the defense, it's all laid out. The trainers, and of course Adam has the documentation to prove this, are the highest-selling brand, style, color in the UK; everyone has them. So not good evidence. Every boy in the kid's street has them. Adam's notes go into detail about police targeting Black kids in the same area the kid was in. He even provides some comment that a judge made in court about it. You know Ad?

I smile.

Julian continues:

So, I go see the client in the cells—he's bail-refused on the facts. The kid's only just eighteen. He looks scared, staring at me, eyes begging me to save him. He's basically still got cuts on his chin from shaving badly. I mean, he looks fifteen. I tell him if he is found guilty, he goes to prison, but if he pleads guilty, he will get less time. He tears up. I then tell him 'don't worry,' we have a case, and I would suggest we run it. I do the usual, tell him I'd be running it for him, and unless he has anything he wants to say I am going forward with the matter. His eyes, like a puppy dog, he just nods at me. Over and over, 'I didn't do it; I didn't do it,' pleading with me, 'why are they saying I did?'

Julian picks up a small piece of sashimi with his chopsticks, moves it toward my mouth. Our eyes meet. The sashimi slides down my throat.

Kid's as innocent as the day. Helps his mum around the house, his dad in the church of whatever it is. Loves his family. And I suddenly think to myself, 'Fuck this, I'm going to destroy the prosecution case.' It's as clear as the light of day that this kid is not involved.

He pauses for effect. It tickles me.

> So, I call to the father outside the court, tell him I'm going
> to fight hard for his kid. The father is this older man,
> face wrinkled with worry. The whole family, all those
> kids, staring at me like I am going to do something
> magical. I feel the weight of the legal system on my
> shoulder. I feel like Adam. I fucking feel like YOU.

He flashes me a flirtatious look. I am in the moment and loving it.

> I start the case. Jury sworn in. I'm on fire during the early
> procedural directions. Fire in my belly. Been a while
> since I felt that.

The waitress appears, asks us whether we have enjoyed the meal. I rave
a little, Jules asks her for the bill. She is more anxious, less warm about
us now. Nervous? She has the bill with her and puts it in front of Jules.
In one quick movement he has whipped out his credit card, placed it
in the leather payment pouch without even checking the bill. As he
hands it back to the waitress, he grazes her hand with his fingers.

Make sure you add a good thirty percent tip for yourself.
He must be trying to impress with a very high tip. Or is he just prov-
ing his status? The waitress looks uncomfortable but is gone quickly.
I feel drunk but my legal mind is keen to hear the end of the story.

Go on, what happened?

Julian sips the last of his sake.

> Prosecutor suddenly has some evidence arrive, apparently
> the CCTV footage from the bank has arrived despite
> the head teller assuming the camera wasn't switched
> on. They say it's date stamped. I'm handed a copy.
> Adjournment. I watch it on my computer in the robing
> room. And fuck me. There he is virtually waving at the
> camera, goddamn knife in his hand.

He goes on.

> Tessa, I race back down to the cells, show him the footage,
> watch his face as he studies it. He doesn't move an inch.
> Still the baby face, still the innocent puppy dog eyes. He
> doesn't miss a beat. Turns to me when the footage is over,
> and he says . . . no word of a lie . . . 'but that guy on the
> film has a goatee.' I groan in sympathy. I lose my shit. I

tell him you want me to go into that courtroom and tell
that jury, that judge, that the person in that footage isn't
you? He just looks at me, right in the eye. I have to go
further. 'Mate, I'm on your team and even I can see it's
you.' He's still thinking it over. I stand up. 'Fucking hell,
you have a shaving sore! People know that a goatee can
be shaved off.' He sighs. It's been a total act.
I laugh. We've all been there. It's a shock to see them go from 'I'm so
innocent' to 'Game's up.' I say to Julian:
　　He must have shat himself.
Julian's voice is slightly highly pitched. He is outraged.
　　No. NO. He says, calm as day, new voice, dropped the act:
　　　'Guess it's a good time to plead guilty then.' I mean, the
　　　kid was a cleanskin, but fuck he was totally playing me.
　　　Obviously despite no record, he was totally seasoned.
I laugh at Julian's outrage. I love that the kid got the best of him. It's
a hard one to floor a criminal barrister who has been around as long
as my group. We've done years of it, and every now and then, we feel
the outrage of a human rights violation and it gets us all fired up. We
see ourselves as warriors for those targeted, tortured, wrongly accused.
But when someone totally shocks us, someone we believed, it is always
a strangely humbling experience. Reminds us that we are, of course,
only spokespersons, that we are not there to judge. And the truth is
when we think someone might truly be properly innocent and part
of a systemic bias, a racial profiling, a jumping to conclusions by the
police or prosecution, we are excited to go into the fight. It makes us
feel valuable. This is what movies are made of, what heroes are made
of, and we secretly all want the test case, the trial, the matter that
shows we changed the world. All our cynicism belies the need to be
the one who shows that the law is indeed a tool for good.

An older criminal barrister once told me, when I was starting out, that
when she is convinced her client is innocent is when she is most afraid
in court. I understand it now. So often it's about showing doubt, and
holding the system to account, providing due process for a client so
that they have had their day in court. We don't ponder whether they
did it or not, rather we serve our purpose, let the court decide.

But if the client has gotten under our skin, when they have convinced us completely of their innocence, when we are all that they have between freedom and incarceration—it's terrifying.

Everyone has a case they lost that haunts them. Even if later we mollify ourselves that perhaps the client DID do it. We know we should have gotten them off. If we were convinced that they didn't do it, it's calamitous. It wakes you at three a.m. It makes you hate the prosecutors for taking it to court. You relive the evidence and your role, over and over. It takes another barrister to attempt to unstick you from it. You suggest appeals and even before you are told, you know that someone else must run it, that you are overly invested and need to let it go. For all our 'objective' storytelling, for all our 'I am a tool of the court,' for all our strangely egocentric 'I am not that important, just the storyteller,' we are also human beings with starkly unpredictable emotional reactions when we drop our guard. There is not really any rhythm or reason that a particular client manages to get so far under one's skin, and it is dangerous when they do. Not just for the lawyer, but for the client, because when any barrister is too attached to a client's narrative, they stop seeing the case for the prosecution, they lose the composure required to argue effectively. Ironically, it is in denying your emotional investment that you do the best job.

There is a reason lawyers hang out together. We all understand this strange straitjacket we are legally starched into. It's hard to have to respond to someone who has read an article in the *Telegraph* that blames us working against safe streets. It makes one's blood boil at first, now more of a sinking feeling in the gut, and you smile benignly at a family friend, at the mate from uni who studied worthy science or languages, and answer back, 'It's actually a bit more complicated than that,' before changing the subject and setting aside your seething disrespect for the question. The rhetoric around law and order is bandied about the country during any election time, the outrage about the criminals on our street. But most of the people in court are in the criminal justice system because they are poor, disadvantaged, discriminated against, and powerless. Sure, it can't always be explained away, but make other things equal before you start to holler about 'criminals.' Not all crime stems from poverty. There are plenty of second chances.

Not all my clients are like poor old Tony, not all of them are like my brother. It's not easy when things are not absolute. Everyone wants yes-or-no answers, they want guilty or not guilty, they want us and them. But it's more confusing when the 'us' *is* 'them.'

I'm more drunk than I realize, but as Julian helps me to my feet, he glances around and groans, not at me.

Fuck, there's three from upstairs at chambers. Anderson, Mossop, and the other one they hang out with.

I know the panic. None of us ever wants KCs from work to see us out and a bit too drunk. But I giggle and lean into Julian. He giggles too. We both stumble, and I see the table in the distance with three serious men dining. Cramped on the small wooden stools, strangely awkward so close on the timber table. Ties still on, glasses, all look the same to the untrained eye. But we have watched these men over and over in court, can recognize their nuances even if they happened to have no idea who we are. The waitress materializes, thanking us. I guess the tip was significant.

We duck our heads as we make it to the door. Julian makes a comment and I almost collapse laughing. Once outside he kisses me. It's hot and passionate. I feel his body ripple close to mine. I hear my own voice, slightly drunk, but deep, suggestive.

We should go somewhere.

We kiss again. He gently, so gently, moves my hair off my face.

Let's Uber it to yours?

I wasn't expecting my place. I nod in agreement but then as I am kissing him, my mind casts back to the mess I have left at home. Clothes on the floor, kitchen stacked with dishes, nothing in the fridge. I have an idea.

Let's get some gelato from the posh place.

The next kiss takes my breath away. My hands are reaching for him, but he wraps his arm around me, and we walk to the gelato place nearby.

Inside, the lights are bright. I'm keen to get out quickly, but Julian is taking his time choosing exotic flavors. I steady myself. I'm relaxed and nicely mellow. I touch the back of Julian's shirt as he talks to the server, tracing his spine, enjoying the slight shudder it creates. I fast-forward things to the next day, realize that Julian is going to be at my place, and we can walk to Notting Hill and have breakfast. He'd like the cafés there, and the markets will be on.

His back shudders again, and a picture of the two of us eating eggs and drinking coffee in the morning floods my mind. What is happening to me—I really like him. Maybe this is how people find each other? At work, having a laugh, things in common? Tess and Julian. I reach my hand up to the back of his neck. His own hand clasps over the top of mine.

After the gelato place, Julian picks up two bottles of expensive red wine from the off-license and asks me for my address. Next thing we get into a silver Prius, the Uber driver gently laughing at how funny we are, before scooting west through London streets. I'm still adjusting my seat belt when Julian is kissing me in the backseat. There's an expertise in his kissing that surprises me, but then perhaps men like Julian learn that along with Latin and cricket. Someone makes sure they are all equipped to attract women and marry well. I'm jolted out of my cynicism so easily by flattery when he stops kissing me and looks into my face.

    You're a fucking great kisser.
I pull him back to me, no longer self-conscious. No longer thinking of anything other than the warm, sexy body pressed close to mine, lips locked.

I realize when I climb the stairs to my flat that I am more than tipsy, but as I open my front door—Julian attached to me from behind, holding my hips close to his—any concerns are chased away by the mess I'm faced with. There are takeaway containers by the door. I can see clothes and mess in the reception room. I tell Julian to stay outside while I clean up; he objects. I tell him to close his eyes and I will lead him to the kitchen. When he is there, I beg for a few minutes. I'm alert but not stable, I manage to kick all clothing under the sofa, move things around. I call out to Julian as I hear the cork pop on the wine.

    You're a Coldplay fan, aren't you?
I ask with a smile, expecting him to be embarrassed that I haven't forgotten his dancing to 'Yellow' at Inflation a few weeks ago. It's an

attempt at banter from me—'the posh guy is still into Coldplay'—
but he has no qualms.

He quips back:

>Sure am.

I take my phone, Bluetooth it to the speaker, then speak to it:

>Alexa, play Coldplay.

It magically comes on just as Julian appears with two glasses, an open
bottle of wine, two spoons, and the tub of gelato. I fling my phone
away somewhere. He pulls the coffee table closer to the sofa, places the
wineglasses on it, and pours. The gelato tub is one with flavors I don't
recognize. It's a large and luxurious sofa, a truly decadent purchase that
I love about my flat. I sit down and he doesn't hesitate, sinks in close
beside me, running his fingertips up and down my legs. I suddenly
have to catch up. Julian is in my flat, on my sofa. It's us, but we are
not at work, we are at my place. He looks different here, and I can't
quite place it. He stops, opens the gelato box, and starts to feed me
and himself icy-cold gelato. The gelato slips in our mouths, my lips
icy cold. We eat all of it, take a long sip of wine, and then kiss. The
cold pistachio and mango gelati and the warm, smooth red make the
kiss deliciously intimate. When we pour more of the wine, Jules is not
saying much. I try to start the chat up again.

>Tell me something about you that will surprise me?

>Like what?

My voice is flirtatious, eyes all over him.

>Something that will impress me.

Julian thinks on this a bit.

>Well, after our pro bono chat in chambers the other day,
>>I put my name down to do some work for a homeless
>>shelter.

I feel myself swoon.

>I love that!

I swoon again in exaggeration. He laughs.

>Don't get too excited, it's only a case a month.

I like this new Julian; it intrigues me that he would do this and not
mention it before. It's like he is changing, and all the changes are
toward things I admire. We drink the rest of the bottle and Jules goes
into the kitchen, bringing back the other red. I am so into him right

now that my eyes are undressing him. He pours wine and before I can drink it, he lifts me, places me so that I am facing him on the sofa. He's strong, and it's sexy how easily he does it.

Someone's been working out?

He doesn't respond but his lips are kissing my neck, my lips, my ears. His hands are inside my dress. I take a breath, break away from him, and go to pour more wine. I ask him some questions about his family, his dad's practice. I then ask him about his past relationships. He's distracted, breathing heavily, nonchalant about the women he has been with. There's been a few. I'm surprised how many—short-term girlfriends, long-term relationships, lovers here and there. I have only had one longish-term one, and mostly casual sex with the occasional one kicking into a short-term thing. I don't go into much detail, but he nods as if he expects me to have had a lot of sex. I'm not confused by this and subconsciously alerted to the fact that he has thought about it.

We talk a bit more over the second bottle of wine, and then we are on the sofa writhing. Jules stops for a moment and takes off his shirt, unzips himself, and there is no turning back. I pull him toward me. In a few moments, without me even realizing, Julian has expertly removed my dress, and I look down as he cups my breast to his lips; he has also removed my bra. Our hands are everywhere. It's wilder than in chambers, not as gentle, and it feels exciting. As we kiss, I feel dizzy but in a nice way.

Is it the kiss or the red wine?

I don't know how Julian knows where my bedroom is, but the flat is not huge and he manages to steer me there as if he has been here before. We are on my bed. I'm not even aware that it is unmade, I don't care anymore. It's hot and urgent, and we fall into having sex. He's confident and really into my body.

My eyes are closed as we fuck.

We are both wasted afterward and there is no talk, just a tangled sleep on a bed with barely a sheet left on it.

We must have dozed off, but I am woken at around two a.m. by his hands urgently probing my body. I turn toward him, and he kisses me hard—he's so awake. I touch him and move toward his. We are in sync. It's nice. I want this, my body is talking to his. Then suddenly I have an overwhelming urge to . . . vomit. I move away, almost fall off the bed, and run, stagger to the loo. I vomit my guts out. I feel everything. The dank smell of the toilet bowl. My throat feels raw and my head is thumping. I look down at myself.

Oh my God I am completely naked.

I am squatting on the floor.

And Julian is in my bed hearing me vomit.

He calls out:

> Are you okay?

I try desperately to sound like I am, willing myself to sound normal, but aware that I am failing.

> Yep. Yep, I'm fine, just the red wine . . .

The thought of the red wine makes me retch like a dying elephant. I try to hold the noise in but it makes it worse.

I attempt to continue what I was saying:

> Just the red wine and gelato mixed together!

Even thinking about the weird pistachio gelato and the red wine together starts me off again, retching dryly, every noise amplified by the mini amphitheater of the ceramic bowl.

I flush the vomit down by reaching up to the button without leaving the floor. The effort is great, and the water gushing down sounds loud. I close my eyes. This is mortifying.

I slump on the floor. The tiles are cool, and my thumping head is soothed by it. I am infused with relief that Julian hasn't ventured in, enormously grateful that there is some chance that I cannot be revealed in all my mess. All I know is that I feel like crap, and I can't move from this position. From where I lie, I can see the underside of the toilet roll holder—it's a different color from below, which is odd. I spend a bizarre amount of time considering this and I don't understand why they didn't just keep it all a uniform color. Even though no one would ever see it. Except me. Lying on the ground.

I must have been there for . . . a while. Maybe I had closed my eyes and slept a little. I don't know. Then I feel strong arms lift me up from the floor. It's Julian; he puts my arms about his neck and carefully carries me back to bed. I am mortified at how I must look. I keep my face away from his. I must smell dreadful.

Julian whispers in my ear:

Are you okay?

Still trying to normalize things, I nevertheless don't open my eyes.

Yep. Yep. Just a bit . . . yuck.

Understatement. I am so relieved at the softness of the bed and the coolness of the pillowcase. I know I am still naked and try to lie on my front. I think I fall partly asleep but am roused by Julian rolling me over and kissing my cheek. I scramble to move.

I have to brush my teeth.

He strokes my naked body, continues to kiss me. I pull away, hand pats around for a sheet, something to cover myself with. I'm still dozy. He scuppers in close, holds my waist on either side, and tries to kiss me again. I try to move away.

I say:

I can't kiss like this.

I still feel ill, drunk, dizzy. He licks my face.

I feel gross.

My eyes are shut, because I don't want to be in this moment, want to sleep off the mess, put my head into a pillow and stop it spinning around.

When he tries to kiss me again, I say it again.

Not now, I feel gross.

I can smell him up close; the muskiness is too much for my senses and I'm scared of the wave of nausea that comes up. Julian keeps kissing my face, he's saying something in a voice I don't recognize as his. Telling me I'm beautiful. But it feels like he is impatient. He is kissing me in a different way than before. I move my face; his hands are all over me. I still feel sick. I feel him press his naked, aroused body up close to me.

Somewhere in the corners of my mind I hear his voice:

Just lie there and let me make love to you.

No, no, I can't.

I squirm again, but this time his hands and legs are pushing against me, restricting me. A flash of fear, and I am suddenly very much awake. He's on top of me but he is not kissing my face anymore.

Hang on, hang on, this is all too . . . No. Julian, I can't
   breathe.
The weight on my chest is heavy, hard.
   Julian, STOP. I, I . . . I need to brush my teeth.
I am not computing what is happening. He is not hearing me, not
listening. He is writhing against me.
   Julian, Julian! Stop. No.
I hear my own voice, desperate, confused. I can't breathe properly. I
push him hard with my hands, and he puts his own hand on my face,
over my mouth. Over my nose. He's in a different place, and I am not
there with him. He doesn't seem to know. He doesn't seem to care. Or
is he a completely different person? How can he not know I don't want
this? How can he not know? My hands are suddenly over my head, and
he is leaning on the hand on my face. I can't breathe. My mind is trying to figure it out. Could he not hear me? Of course he could. I start
to panic. My arms ache, they are both pulled up hard above my head.
I can't do anything, his thighs are holding my legs down. My brain
slowly catches up to what is happening, but not entirely. Fear, fury.
Eyes about the room, darting from one thing to another, trying to find
a way out. The picture on the wall I bought with my first pay, its red
lines upside down from here, the lampshade with tassels in the corner, a
handle on my cupboard, silver, sleek. Nothing of any meaning, nothing
that can help me. I'm panicking, trying to move. What can I grab on
to? Nothing. I hear Julian grunt and then there's a searing pain inside
of me. My whole body feels the shock of it. I try to move but I can't. A
heavy thigh bearing down on each of mine. I want to vomit again. I am
in both disbelief and terror that this is happening. The hand over my
mouth pushes harder. The same hand I had *let* explore my body earlier
in the night. I try to bite it, but there's no way. My nose is so squashed
that I think it might break. I try again to move, to bite, but nothing.
I feel useless. He pushes himself inside me further. I hear him groan.
His face is far above mine somehow, I am just this thing beneath him.
I am trapped. There is pain, unbearable pain inside me. He moves with
a thrusting, a roughness, further inside me. Every muscle in my body
is taut. In my mind I am begging some un-believed-in greater power to
help me. The desperate fight for anyone, anything to intervene. Mia,
Adam. Johnny. Help me.

But there is no way out. My eyes get stuck on the ceiling as it goes on and on. My eyes glaze over. The room is silent for me now. Nothing can get through.

This is how it happens.

This is how I get raped.

It's a strange, otherworldly moment. I am outside my body. I feel my body slump, give in, freeze. It goes on and on and on. My body is being rocked with his thighs, moving without my moving it. My insides are screaming, 'Make it stop, make it stop.' But I can't. I can hear the bed banging up against the wall, and then everything goes silent. I am like a thing that is just there, this is being done to me, my body is no longer mine. I stare at the ceiling. It goes on forever and ever. I find myself wishing I could just leave my body, fly out of the window, leave my body here. The ceiling has a dirty mark to the left. I fixate on it. I can't breathe and I feel dizzy. Am I going to die? This is the last thing I will see, this incidental mark on the ceiling. The last thing I will ever feel is this hideous pain. Life feels so small. I feel so small. I am nothing right now, just a thing for someone to fuck. I start to feel guilty; if I die here, my mum will have to see me dead. I see her crying and trying to reach me. I see my lifeless body. I feel my lifeless body.

And then with a final weight, he is done. His body is heavier, but the movement has ended. I have heard nothing for a while, and time has changed. Now everything is still and without meaning. Is he still inside me?

His hand is gone from my mouth, but I am not speaking. My arms are free, but they are still above my head. My eyes still on the ceiling. About me is this strange denial, and his body just slumped on top of mine.

I am here but, I am not.

I can hear again. My breathing is desperate. Julian starts to softly snore; I am crying silently. Salty tears accumulating at the edge of my mouth. My brain still cannot catch up. I struggle to move out from under Julian as he sleeps. He's heavy, and my limbs are sore, achy. My tears fall hard when I manage to find my way to the floor. I do a glance for the sheet from my bed but can't see it. My nakedness upsets me, but I stagger to the bathroom again, lock the door. I move toward the loo, and I vomit and vomit and vomit. Then I brush my teeth. I look at my face in the vanity mirror. I don't see me, I see someone else. My mascara has run, my skin is blotchy.

I touch my face but I can't feel it.

My body feels him all about it, his sweat, his smell. I feel stuck, but somehow make it to the shower. I turn it on hard, then sit on the ground and scrub my body raw with the nail brush. I scrub my body until the skin is red raw. Then I sit in the shower. Huddled against one of the glass walls, staring at the mosaic tiles; I chose them, I tell myself. I chose the tiles for this bathroom. I have scrubbed so hard that there is some blood coming from my leg. I watch it swirl around near the plug hole, diluting into pink before it washes away. My vagina feels pain. A pain that I have never felt there before. A rising fury reaches my throat. I scream out but only in my own head. 'How dare you?'

I slump again and in my mind, I run the lines I have asked in court over and over again. I can hear my voice, but not my usual voice. My court voice, strong, sure, interrogating. I look up and the water is falling in huge lines, straight upon me. I close my eyes. I just want it all to go away.

But the court voice persists: the restaurant bill indicates that there was a lot of sake drunk by you both. Witnesses say you were giggling, yes? And there are two empty red wine bottles at your house, would you agree?

You'd agree you were intoxicated, wouldn't you?

In fact, you drank so much you vomited, is that right?

You took off most of your clothes, is that right?

You'd told people, friends, family that you were 'hooking up with him,' had you slept with the defendant before?

I sit in the shower. What do I do now? Should I call someone?

I get out of the shower, my skin red, red, red. I wrap it up in a towel and feel fear. Julian is still in my bedroom. I go to the spare room. Open the closet with all my out-of-season clothes. It's too hot for the winter stuff, but there's a green maxi dress I take on trips with me, and some flip-flops. It feels so out of place when I see myself in the reflection of the window.

I look over at my bedroom, I am not going back in there. I head to the living room, start to clean up, even though I should probably leave it. In case. God, in case? What am I going to do? I just want to hit rewind and . . . ? And what?

Julian is in my bed. Still there. And me? I see the life I have built, my career. Think carefully, Tessa, think carefully. My career.

How dare he?

What do I do now? Be a witness in my own courtroom? With Julian and his dad's brilliant contacts. Running his defense case past Adam. Calling witnesses. Mia about the email I sent, Alice, the Uber driver. Waitress at the restaurant, people who saw us laughing, kissing. Off-license guy? Gelato server? Because this is legal truth, this is how the law tries to understand. No. Nup. Can't do it. I don't know what to do. The living room is still messy, I can't believe last night on the sofa was merely last night, it feels like a lifetime ago. I look around at my speaker still switched on, remember my phone, and scrabble about until I find it. I want to walk into my room and scream, call the police, scare the shit out of him.

Instead, I leave my own place. I'm not sure why, or where to go? It's the still hours of the morning, dark. I walk and walk. Talking to myself, running it over in my mind. I walk. The Harrow Road is deserted as I move toward Ladbroke Grove. I walk and walk, past the big Sainsbury's, onward past the Ladbroke Grove tube station. I walk past all the houses and flats, all those homes with people sleeping in them. My head hurts but I barely acknowledge it. I am parched and thirsty but there is nowhere open to buy water. It feels strangely better to have a sore throat than to have to consider the other places I am feeling pain. I walk farther and turn left at the Notting Hill high street. There are joggers about, one runs past me, tall, angular, almost brushes my body, and I jump. His AirPods stop him from hearing my yelp, he just runs by. A few cyclists appear. Where are they going? By the time I reach Marble Arch and turn toward the West End, I am only thinking about my mum, about talking to her, getting to her. I take out my phone and pull up her name.

How do you tell your mother you've been raped? How do you say those words out loud? Put my phone in my pocket. Walk on. Feel numb, but over and over in my mind I tell myself that I have been raped.

I have been raped.

Julian just raped me.

I have been raped.

It feels ugly and pathetic. *I* feel ugly and pathetic. Stupidly gullible. Girls like me, who come from where I come from, how dare I think I could be with someone like Julian. I feel foolish, and humiliated. I told him so much about my family, did that make him think . . . ? I go over and over the way he flirted with the waitress, was that a sign? It felt uncomfortable at the time but . . . ?

I'm going mad. An anger roars through me that frightens me.

I have been raped and he will be able to walk out of there and never have to pay the price? I think to myself, am I going to let him get away with it? That's not who I am. I believe in fairness; is this what I think should happen to women? That they should stay silent? No. My legal mind starts reminding me, there is no point, you will lose, this is not something you will ever recover from if you take it to court, this will destroy you. Maybe you're mistaken. Maybe it didn't happen? Already my mind has taken flight, my truth is being ripped apart by my own self. I need to do something; I cannot hold on to this. Go to work as if it is normal that he did this to me. Am I so embarrassed to be the victim of a violent crime that I won't report it? What about justice? What about believing in the law to get it right? It starts to rain; I feel the droplets upon my face. Instinctively, like I did as a girl I turn my face skyward and open my mouth. The raindrops are real, they are there. I am still alive. Rain starts to fall more heavily. I am tired from walking; my body starts to ache. I am resolved, I want to go to my mum's place. I want her. I need to see her; I want to think. I need to get away from here. I will catch an early train. I walk on slightly faster, toward a taxi rank I know is nearby.

CHAPTER 19

When I reach the cab rank, I am wet through. I barely notice. I have been walking for hours and as I approach the taxi at the front of the queue, I am suddenly aware of how exhausted I am. I feel fragile, wet, lost. I want to find my way to Mum's place, it's all I can think about. I let myself in the black cab, glad for the shelter, glad for the familiarity of the cab.

Morning.

Morning.

The cabbie's eyes on me and I know I must look rough, my long dress saturated, sticking to my body, feet in rubber flip-flops. What I must look like on this morning, after everything I have been through? He is silent. I jump in. Trying to maintain as much of my dignity as possible.

St Pancras station, please.

He's quick in response.

Sorry, love, only taking proper rides this morning.

What?

His voice is singsong, speaking as if what he is proposing is entirely reasonable.

Love, I haven't sat here the past hour for the lousy ride.

It's not far, he's right, but I am burning with fury. My voice higher-pitched than usual. Accusatory.

You're at a cab rank!

A fact that is certainly not news to the driver. He doesn't like my tone.

And you're dripping wet all over my seat back there.

He's not addressing the issue and I sit tight. Quietly.

St Pancras station, please.

But he doesn't turn on his car. He's sticking to his guns.

I told you, I'm not taking you. There's a hotel full about to
    arrive heading to Heathrow.
Well, guess what, buddy, you don't get to choose.
It's my taxi!
You're at a taxi rank, you go where the ride goes, that's the
    rule.
He digs in:
    Not this time.
I'm only just holding it together. My voice defaults to my legal tone.
    You can be suspended for breaking the rule; if you don't
      take me, I will report you . . .
And then with fury:
    . . . and I will make sure you lose your licence.
It has the opposite effect.
    I want you to open the door and get out of my cab.
    No.
I look out the window. The rain is falling harder. He has lost all of
the genial civility he had when I first entered the car.
    If you don't get out, I'm calling the police.
I feel every fiber of my being start to break.
    That's not fair.
I hear my voice start to tremble. The cabbie must have heard it too
as he turns from the rearview mirror, where he has been conducting
most of the conversation, and looks at me through the Perspex shield
between us. I see the cabbie take me in and I lose my hold on everything. I am sobbing.
    It's not fair.
My voice is softer, pleading. All I can think of is my mum. I just want
to be home with her, wrap myself up against her on the old floral sofa.
Feel the rough heat of her. Silently, the cabbie hands me a tissue. I blow
my nose, ball up the tissue into a snotty, wet ball. This man doesn't
realize that he is seeing me at my most vulnerable. But when I see his
face, the expression he has, I think he knows something. This stranger,
this adversary, this man providing solace. He is suddenly so patient, so
quietly with me that it gives me a strange strength. I have never felt so
alone, so fearful for what might be ahead, and yet he is here.
    I'm not sure where to go.

His eyes are back in the rearview mirror, kind eyes now. Waiting. Waiting for me to decide. It's as if he is waiting for me to realize what I must do. The cabbie waits. I look at the car clock, it's 6:09 a.m. I can hear my breathing is labored. Legal instinct tells me that this is a losing case. But I must do something. I can't not. I have to believe that the system I have given my life to will do the right thing. The legal system gave me the life I have, gave me a chance to rise to the top. I have to rely on it. Maybe the system will work. It has to. This crime happened, and it happened to me, so I know it is the truth. And I'm scared that if I lock it away forever all that I have believed in will be for nothing. Another voice in my head is rationally telling me to sit tight and think it over. But if I go now, if I do it now, then it is done. I don't know whether I am being naive or just trying to survive. But this rage will eat me alive. I have come all this way, so far, and all the way through I have believed the system works the way it is supposed to work, that it can find justice, so now let it show me that it does. I look up at the cabbie and I ask:

Can you take me to the nearest police station, please?

AFTER

Seven hundred
and eighty-two
days later.

CHAPTER 20

NOW

This is me. Watching myself. London's Old Bailey Court. I walk in, no longer do I know the security guards. All my old familiars are not on today or have moved to other courts. These new ones I haven't reached out to, so today I am just another unknown walking through the doors. Sound of my heels on the floor. Moving through the security system. Detached. Objective. This time, no barrister bag with my wig poking out the top; no gown inside waiting to unfurl. This time, no one at the security belt recognizes me. No barrister's ID, no easy pass.

I walk through the metal detector. An alarm rings. Take off my shoes, walk through again, alarm rings again. I'm swiped by the handheld metal detecting wand, arms out wide, staring ahead. My bottle of water is passed to me, and without asking I unscrew it and sip. Security guard nods at me. I wait for my handbag, no books. Just a notepad, pen, and folded papers. I slip my shoes back on, straighten out my skirt. So much thought went into what I would wear. Mia popped over and went through my wardrobe with me, found the only skirt suit I own, tucked away at the back of my closet, navy. This outfit, this costume, this suit is all for show, is all for the role I am expected to play. 'A skirt and heels if you have, professional, not casual; smart and not revealing.'

I have never acted for alleged victims in sexual assault. I haven't prosecuted in this area. I didn't realize there was a 'look,' but of course it makes sense. Do whatever you can to influence the jury. I draw the line at wearing a string of pearls as one of the older police suggested. Everything is different these days. Even my hair is cut shorter. I consider whether everything I have done is to make myself more manageable. Dismiss this as a thought that doesn't feel comfortable. My eyes involuntarily glance across. Robes swishing, horsehair wigs leaning into each other. A group of barristers, papers, folders, confident chatter. A wave of longing. Did one of them see me? Oh God. Head down. I collect my bag and mobile from the belt. The person behind me is taking off their shoes. This is me walking to the lifts with a woman allocated to show me to the witness rooms. I don't bother to tell her I know where they are. I'm glad for the company even if we don't chat, even though Mia and Mum had both offered to accompany me in and I had adamantly refused both. I didn't want to draw any unnecessary attention to myself. It's enough that the profession is so interested in my case. Enough that it has been listed at the Bailey, where only rarely do they list a sexual assault case. The Bailey where I have loved appearing, loved the majesty of the place. The thrill of a courtroom where ancient cases have been heard; famous cases: this court has been the criminal court of history. All through my studies, I leaned into cases heard at the Old Bailey; my first wander through was intimidating, exciting. The first case I ran there, walking through as a barrister, eyes floating to the beautifully painted ceiling, like being in a living museum. The privilege, the aura, the smell, the mere fact that I was allowed to work here. I wanted so much to belong here, then I did. Yet now. Listed as a witness rather than running a case. Like in so many moments in the 782 days between the night Julian raped me and today, I am doubting whether I can get through this.

This trial.

This day.

Two barristers, both of us as witnesses in a criminal trial, a serious matter. One of us on either side, one alleged perpetrator and one alleged victim: accused and complainant. Each of our stories represented by other barristers. I know if, before this day, I had heard about colleagues as litigants rather than as counsel appearing, I would have been alerted, and super keen to hear the details. As I stand waiting for the lift, I feel the sharp pain in my wrists. Thumb and fingernails on opposite wrists. My own nails dig deeply into my flesh, grabbing my attention, neatly changing the focus from anxiety to physical pain.

I walk through the lift doors. Stand to the side, look at the floor. Doors shut. Ding. Solicitors, barristers, police. Exit, enter, exit.

Ding. My level. I see the court list on the wall and instinctively cast my eyes over it.

There, in ordinary font, right before me: "The King v. Julian Brookes." I am just a witness for the King! Breathe. It's happening. I tell myself, 'Keep walking and hold my head up. I'm being subtly steered by the witness support worker toward the witness meeting room area. I have been here before, but only to speak to clients. I've swanned in and out, and have never really looked properly at the place before now. The walls in the common area are of fading gray paint. There is a child's abacus carelessly thrown to the side, a blue train upright nearby. The sofas in the common are someone's old nineties castoffs. Behind the scenes of this magnificent building, this intimidating notable building of history, are old, cramped spaces, bureaucratic paint, and no decor or charm. Those of us who see behind the imposing courtrooms, the painted ceiling, the hallways, and court foyers are used to the familiarity of the space that barristers see, but I imagine that the usual visitors to this part of the court would be shocked, or possibly relieved, by how ordinary it looks.

The witness support lady has a badge saying 'witness support'; it occurs to me that she is probably a volunteer and I scan everything about her, dark hair and skin, neat bun, older face, warm smile. For the first time in my career, I think about these people who make up the role of witness support. I have never wondered what inspires them to take up this role. To give up days of their own lives to stand by a witness and make them feel human. When do they decide this is what they would like to volunteer for, and what inspires it? Have they been witnesses? In crimes? Victims or defendants, accused of something and been found not guilty, or seen a loved one go through the criminal justice system in some form, or read a newspaper story of someone's experience? I'm grateful to her for making such little fuss. Do they teach the volunteers to read the witness, just like they teach barristers to? Yet they are taught to make the witness feel comfortable, go with what they seem to need or want. A barrister has their own script that must be coaxed from all the witness elements in court. I hear a sob from one of the rooms and stiffen. I am shown the room allocated to me, and after some small talk the witness support person leaves. She shuts the door after flashing me a sympathetic smile. And this is me. Tessa Ensler. Sitting in a small windowless room. White plastic tabletop.

Waiting.

Waiting. I have been waiting for 782 days. I think about how many times on each of those days I have wondered about facing this day. This trial.

I scan back over the years to the times I could have easily dropped out. What barrister in their right mind does what I have done, shown the profession my vulnerability? There are solicitors who will never brief me again; people have had to choose sides, people are questioning my judgment, my decision to go forward.

I am not privy to the conversations that are no doubt whispered in the halls of various chambers, but I am aware of those people who avoid me, who have not reached out. It's political to support someone accusing one of our own, but even more disturbing when it is a barrister herself pointing the finger. It has made me wonder what they think I should have done? Ignored that I was raped? I see how that would save me the humiliation, save my reputation. But that enrages me. Why must I have my reputation in question when I have done nothing wrong? A woman from my bar call told me flat out that everyone knows I was 'into Julian' and couldn't understand why I would do this to him? I jabbed back quickly.

Have you ever wondered why he would do this to me?

Then:

But don't you see it is hurting your standing in your career?

The very people who back Julian are the people who

decide if you ever get silk.

Of course, I knew this. But to hear it spoken out loud was alarming. I wasn't so much taken aback as frightened. What was I doing? I needed to explain. Mia understood, Cheryl understood; but is it strategic to do something like this? I know I am seen as a curiosity, not so much brave as impulsive. As someone about whom people want to say, 'I don't know her well,' even as they decide to avoid me. 'I'm not taking sides' became a way of supporting Julian; and I realize that not getting Julian, his KC father, his father's KC friends offside was the main aim. To stand back from anything that might jeopardize their career. I feel sick that a single night led to something that has divided every aspect of my life to before and after.

And yet. I am here, and I am going to see this to the end. Because the law is the thing that gave me everything. Gave me choice, and an opportunity to fight for justice. I need to prove that the law definitely finds justice, or how else can I trust? If I am silent in the face of Julian and his people, then I am selling out more than this case, selling out more than my peace of mind, my devastation, my truth. I am giving up on the one passion I believe in, that which I have been trained to do, what I have passionately argued: the system is bigger than just whoever has the money and power.

It's hard for me as a defense barrister to be a witness for the prosecution. But I have to believe that the system of law works for both true victims and for those wrongly accused. I have to know that if we take a crime to court, that if all that has been done has been done correctly, by the book, then the law will find the truth. That justice will be served. Because otherwise how do I continue to argue so close to the line? If I can't do it, then who will?

If I didn't decide to be a witness in this trial, to hold Julian to account, then what would become of me? I have a voice. I am a barrister. I know courts.

Being raped has damaged me. I am not the person I was.

I am scared, terrorized by a man walking out of the supermarket at the same time as myself.

I cannot trust people anymore, especially men.

I won't work late into the night because I don't know who else is in chambers and someone might surprise and hurt me.

I cannot accept my body in the same way, I cannot think about intimacy as a good thing. I don't like the fear. The humiliation.

But as I run that night over and over in my head, I don't like the voice in my head that chastises me, that demands to know, 'What were you thinking?' and, 'How could you not know he was going to do that?' I can't bear to think over and over about what it felt like to not be able to breathe, to feel the pain and be trapped beneath someone. To not be able to escape. I feel weak and pathetic, I feel out of my body, and stupid for thinking I had any control. 'What

were you thinking, thinking you had a chance with Julian Brookes?'
'You got ahead of yourself, Tessa.' It makes me wild, but I know that
if I don't do this, I lose the very thing that I have protected: my sense
of fairness. The belief that when you do the right thing, have good
representation, and tell the truth, all the discrete moving parts of the
legal system will come together and justice will be served.

But I'm tired. Three years of university, one year of bar school, and
now over eight years of practice.

I have always believed I was doing the right thing. Now I need for
the law to do the right thing by me. I remind myself that if Julian
gets away with this, he will do it again, he will think he was in the
right. He will consider that he has the right to hold someone down
and ignore their 'no,' their pleas, that he has the right to what he
desires, when he wants it, and no matter whom he damages in the
process.

I found myself at my desk in chambers, crying as I reread a document
over and over. It was early on and a month after I moved chambers.
I thought I was silent but a gentle knock at my door and one of the
women, from the lunch rounds, popped her head in.

>   You all right?

Mortified, embarrassed. Nodding, I swivel my chair. I don't know
this woman, she's older, curly hair, a lot of eye makeup.

>   I know what happened, love.

Fuck. Does everyone know what happened to me? Even this total
stranger. I'm silent.

>   You know, it happens to a lot of women, and you must try
>   and forget it.

I stiffen. She must have noticed, she rushes in.

>   Best way through it is to just ignore it, put it behind
>   you. Men will be men, won't they; they don't always
>   understand!

I know she is being kind, but I feel a shuddering rejection of her and
everything that is about the class of women that I come from. You
can't beat it. This is what my mum and Cheryl have implied. Everyone just wants me back as I was, wants to skate over it. But I cannot.
I will break into little pieces if I do nothing. If I let Julian walk away

from this. Carry on as if this hasn't happened. The Tessa Ensler who fought her way through everything to get through school, to find her way to Cambridge, to keep her scholarship, to be called to the bar. I can't find her anymore and I need to.

The woman is gone when I turn back. The door snaps shut. I feel unsafe with my own fury, dig my nails into my thighs hard, causing deep rivets.

CHAPTER 21

The door opens and Richard appears. Richard Lawson, the KC running the case for the prosecution. Tall, lean, smart. Kind, professional, considerate. I'm lucky, he's well respected, knows the law. He's already in his silk robe, his wig. Ready to run the case.

He has had to manage me providing him with strategies and cases that I believe will help the case. But Richard does not represent *me*, he represents the prosecution case, the government, the King. The whole case might involve me, but I am 'a witness for the prosecution,' I don't get to decide what solicitor or barrister the Crown Prosecution Service chooses to brief or use for the matter, the choice is not mine. I am just so relieved they chose Richard. I know with Richard I have the best of the best. As long as my evidence stands up in court, as long as Richard is with me, I know I have a shot, a better chance than most, before the jury.

It was an unknown police liaison officer who comforted me, a few months in. I had asked to talk about how the case was progressing. Meeting with Richard was hard. He had the brief, and he sat with me and gave me the rundown. It wasn't an easy case to prove. He knew I knew the drill, but reiterated that there were low conviction rates with sexual assault. I looked him in the eye.

> But this really happened, there is no word of a lie in my statement.

He nodded; he believed me.

I continued:

> My only fear is that I am anxious about what I can lose by taking it forward.

He sighs.

> I don't have to tell you how serious sexual assault is, or that

rape is at the most serious end of the spectrum of what
sexual assault is—to be held down and have someone
force themselves inside your body.

I look away. It's hard to hear him talk to me like this. I know the law,
but he is telling me this as a victim-survivor. I feel very vulnerable.
Unexpectedly.

He continues gently:

If someone walked up to you in the streets, trapped you in
a headlock and started hitting you, there would be no
hesitation to take it to court, would there?

No.

I am a witness now, not a barrister. He continues:

And that isn't even as serious as someone you know, coming
to your home and violating you intimately, where there is
no one to help you, no one else to call the police for help.

I'm silent.

All I can tell you, Tessa, is that I will do the best I can
do for you but I need you to give evidence well. There
is no shame in this for you, the shame is for the man
who did this to wear. And right now, he isn't taking any
responsibility.

I'm silent but there is a fury in me. I look back at this officer. He
knows he is hitting a nerve.

It's your decision, I will respect whatever you decide, but
never be swayed from the fact that this is a serious crime.
And the Crown Prosecution Service have decided that
they will prosecute it if you give evidence in the trial.

Basically, he knows, and I know, I am the only real evidence. I feel
bolstered by what he is saying. It makes sense to me. I don't want to
feel this feeling. This shame. I'm angry that I am the one feeling it.
Angry with him, and yes, angry with myself for taking it on.

I think over all this and tell Richard that I will see it through. He
doesn't smile, he just nods.

Richard is addressing me. I was outside myself deep in memories. I
look up at him as he glances around the pokey room. He comments
about how unfortunate the rooms are. I laugh a little.

He opens his white binder of neatly tagged and collated documents, to run through the evidence and my statement with me one last time. I don't need to do this myself: I remember it like it was yesterday.

CHAPTER 22

THEN

Police station foyer, 6:40 a.m. Still waiting. I feel my body shiver. I'm wet, but the air-conditioning must be on. The seats are blue vinyl, uncomfortable. Each with a plastic armrest between it and the next. There's a young woman sitting almost upright, sound asleep. I glance around. I've not been to many police stations. Barristers do not normally represent clients in police interviews, solicitors do that for you, or a private solicitor. The matter only reaches us when there is a police brief and someone pleading not guilty. Or they have pleaded guilty and have a folder of references or other documents attesting to reasons for mitigation of sentence. These are the main occasions when a criminal barrister is involved. The solicitors do all the police station work, the client hard slog. I glance about the room, shivering, rest my eyes on a notice board of missing people. I can see the photocopies of faces that I can't imagine anyone would recognize. There's a sticker on the wall next to it that reads 'Be a Hero. Stop Crime Before It Happens.' I stare at it. Someone has tried to deface the sticker with a blue Biro, but the pen didn't work on the shiny sticker surface. I read it again and again. Tears prick my eyes, but I won't let them out. 'Should I have done something before the crime happened? What? Not had sex with him? Not gone for dinner? Not worn that stupid sexy dress? God, the underwear!' I tell myself 'stop it,' but it starts again. How could I have stopped it?

I jerk my head away to the opposite wall. There is a poster of a young woman, facing forward. Bruises on her face, an eye swollen. The text under the image reads 'This Is Not Love.' I stare at it for a long time. I know she must be an actor playing a role, but she looks so vulnerable. In my long-ago memory, I remember my mum with bruises. Fresh, not spoken about. Covered up with cheap makeup before she left the house.

I feel so defeated; all my life I swore I would never be someone waiting in a police station. The times as a child I sat with Johnny while Mum spoke to them about Dad and trying to get him out of the house. The time I was a teen and I sat with Mum, in one of these chairs, waiting for Johnny after he'd been arrested. We heard him scream out from the cells. Mum frightened. People whispering behind the desk, then looking at us, just sitting there, the family of the accused. Hours we were there. Just waiting. I had a test at school the next day but had left all my books at home. He wasn't free to come home with us until after two a.m. He raged all the way home in Mum's old car. I sat in the back, silent. Mum driving, not knowing what to say.

I don't feel that I have moved far from those days as I sit here in these clothes from the spare bedroom, wet hair from the rain. I stand up, feel pain in my vagina, my legs, walk over to a water cooler and take the last paper cup. I drink cup after cup of water. The taste in my mouth a mix of toothpaste, old vomit, and red wine.

An older police officer arrives, he's a big guy. I'm not expecting this. I don't know what I was expecting. He asks if I am Tessa Ensler. I nod, gulping a mouthful of water. He introduces himself, but I miss what he says. Indicates with a nod that I am to follow him. I do. He lurches forward and I follow. Heart thumping. He arrives at an interview room. I know these rooms because I have watched thousands of client's interviews in rooms just like this. They always look suffocating, but probably because the interview camera is only trained on the client and the wall behind them. I've sat back in chambers and watched these videos, feet on my desk at times, all my sass and outrage at the tactics and the tricks the police play. As I sit here though, there's quite a bit of room at the table, and the big officer takes his time sitting down opposite me. I'm cold and shivering, trying hard to stop moving. I panic. I want to ask for a woman officer, I need to. He must have read my mind.

Tells me I could come back another time.

When the sexual assault unit is on, or a woman is on duty?

But I know I must get it over with, there's no coming back at 'another time.' I tell him I want to do it now. He puts his coffee mug on the table, looks like he drinks it straight black. He scratches around and the questions start. He's asking me if I have any objection to the video recording. He waits for me to answer.

No.

He sets it up, then starts right away asking me all sorts of preliminary things. Easy, auto responses from me. He asks my name, I stare at him as I hear myself state my full name.

Tessa Jane Ensler.

Asks if I need some water.

Um, no. Thank you.

If I acknowledge I am being recorded.

Yes, I recognize I am being recorded.

I give him my date of birth and address. He asks me why I am there. My voice is shaky.

I wanted to report—

I can't finish. He repeats that I had told the front desk that I wanted to report a crime. I nod. He's waiting. I freeze. Then I stumble through some answers.

Because I think—

I try again.

Because I WAS . . .

Heart beating. Hands clenched. I try again.

Something happened to me.

The big officer nods. I try to breathe. Start again.

I was just—um.

There is a weight on my chest, it's cramping down. I hear my voice say:

Last night. This morning . . . I, I was assaulted.

Then.

I was sexually assaulted. Raped.

And it's there. In the room. I have said it. It is out there. Taking shape, catching me up. I feel the tears behind my eyes again, but I will not cry. That might be the only thing I can make myself do. Not cry. I am sitting there in this room, looking over at the big officer, his face has started to blur. My ears are hearing him ask questions, but he

feels so far away. I consider this a moment and hear his voice as if he
is far underwater. I prefer this somehow. The underwater voice asks
me questions. More and more questions. I hear them all and I answer
them all. There is a camera recording me saying all of this. I briefly
wonder what I look like, then back to the questions. I hear myself as
if I am listening to a client's interview, I focus in on what I am saying.

    Yes, he's known to me.

He asks me Julian's name.

    Julian Brookes.

If I had only just met him tonight.

    No, we work together.

    How long have you worked together for?

I have to think for the next answer.

    I don't know, about six years.

    Were you in a relationship?

I cringe at the question.

Mocking myself slightly.

    A relationship?

I roll up my sleeves. Not sure why but it gives me a moment. I think
I am sweating now. I fill in the space where an answer must be.

    Well, no . . . but tonight wasn't the first time we . . . but

        no, we weren't. We hadn't defined . . .

I hear another voice, the one in my head, this one is furious. 'You're
a fucking idiot. You bought a new dress, you bought new lingerie.'

I look around the room, but there is nothing other than a dip in the
wall.

    No. Not a relationship.

The next question is leading somewhere embarrassing. I answer it.

    Um, well, a few weeks, or last week, we had . . .

There's no point in laboring the point.

    We had sex.

Cringey few questions from the underwater voice while the big officer looks down at a notepad. I answer them clearly.

    At work. After hours. In his chambers, there's a sofa.

I sit in this moment. Glad the big officer is not looking at me. I'm not
so much embarrassed, more humiliated that I must tell this stranger,

an older man, about it. He asks whether I consented. My eyes dart, heart beats hard. I don't know why. He looks up at me. I look back.

Yes.

I want to differentiate that night from this morning. Distinctly. As the big officer looks down at his notes, he clears his throat. I wonder to myself why I don't take notes? I'm a lawyer, that's what I do. Isn't it? But the underwater voice interrupts my thoughts and starts firing questions. After the initial part of the night is outlined, I realize this is where I must talk about the rape. Describe it even. I watch his mouth as each question is asked, and I answer it without feeling. Just trying to get through it. I'm surprised when I look down and see my fingers are shaking. I seem to have lost control of my body, my connection to what I am doing. I pull my sleeves down again, put my fingers under the table. I don't want to be a victim. I want to be a survivor.

I hear my voice say, 'I tried to bite him.' I hear myself talk about being trapped. I feel the tears again, I don't want to feel any of it ever again. I don't want to talk about it, describe it. I'm afraid. The big officer asks if I want some water. I shake my head. I don't want a break either, I just want to get it over with and go home. The face of the big officer is either close or far away from me. I am answering questions, but I am not in my body. I have never felt this before. I have always been connected. I have to say where this leg was, where my hand was, which hand was over my mouth, how I felt. He asks me if I kicked him, pushed him away. Did I leave marks on his body? Did I try to fight? I feel consumed with guilt, did I? I remember the helplessness, the fear, and the pain. The pain being done to me. And I'm naked.

I tell the big officer:

I said no, I said no. I said stop. But he didn't. I tried to
        kick, to push him away. I couldn't breathe.

I'm shaking now and I don't care. The big officer looks down and asks me other questions about other body parts. Intimate body parts. I answer them as I rub my face. I feel desperate. I think about how I lay there as he raped me. Frozen. I am furious with myself, but it abates into feeling pathetic, feeling weak. I don't like this feeling at all. I am back at home hearing my dad rage at my mum and my brother, hiding in a bedroom. I am back at the corner shop near Mum's. I'm five watching other adults look at bruises my mother has. I feel the pity. I hate the pity. The big officer asks me another question. But I can't answer anymore. I feel cut open and splayed out before him. Humiliation.

I raise my voice.

> I don't know. I don't know.

I apologize. Silence as he thinks. I want to leave but I sit tight, trying to breathe, to calm down. In, out. In, out. Tessa, stay calm. I need this guy to be on my side. I breathe in and out over and over. He asks me:

> Can I have your phone to submit into evidence, please.

> No. Not my phone.

He's not happy about this. He stands and leaves the room. I sit. Waiting. Waiting. Returns. Takes his seat again. Again, about the phone.

> No.

He looks up. Is he irritated or surprised? Or is he angry with me? I try to explain without emotion.

> It's just my work, my friends, family . . . I'm sorry, I need
> it.

He quips back.

> I thought you wanted us to make a case.

> Yes, I do.

I hold my phone close. Wait. He sighs loudly for effect. Closes his notebook and turns off the recording. A wash of relief tingles through my body. It's over. But it's short-lived. He's matter-of-fact.

> We'll take you to the Havens, it's a sexual assault specialty
> clinic . . .

I know this.

> . . . and get a forensic medical examination done.

I freeze. Consider putting it off. My mind races with images from the rape. My foot taps uncontrollably. He looks down at it. I pull my foot into line. I can see the ceiling of my bedroom, remember staring at it. I think about the pain. I feel shaky. I try to buy time.

> It might not come up with much.

He looks at me. I inwardly groan and explain.

I . . . I had a shower, straight after.

My internal voice pipes up again: 'I'm a fucking idiot. I keep doing this. Cleaning up the living room, washing my body after.' I dig my nails into the palms of my hands.

I washed everything away.

I look over at the big officer, he is unwrapping a piece of gum now. He puts it in his mouth. I see him chew. It feels like the most wonderful thing to be able to think about gum right now. I envy him.

Thinking out loud, I address the big police officer:

What if he says we didn't have sex? How can I prove it now?

But I realize:

Oh, he'll agree that we had sex. He'll just say it was consensual . . . won't he?

The police officer leans back in his chair, hand behind his head.

Once he gets a bastard defense barrister, he could say anything!

Silence. My heart beating so hard I can feel it against my chest wall. I carefully watch his face as I speak.

Actually . . . Julian IS a defense barrister.

The big officer stops chewing, this is a roadblock. He looks at me. Like it's my fault. It's uncomfortable. I brace myself before I add in a small voice—I know he won't like this—

Actually . . . I am also a defense barrister.

He flashes me a look. Is it compassion? No. What is it?

Then the police officer speaks in a flat voice,

Now you need us though. Don't you?

CHAPTER 23

NOW

Richard asks how I'm holding up? I tell him I'm fine. Confident voice. I study a stain on the table, a watermark or coffee. Richard's voice continues, it's melodic but soon it blurs, starts to become the underwater voice. The one I hear so often these days. A long way away, indecipherable. I look up when he finishes.

Sorry, what was that?

He speaks carefully.

All we really have is your testimony. I mean, I know you
know this: when the rape kit is inconclusive it comes
down to who the jury believes.

I am not sure why he is saying this. I understand there was no evidence collected when I was examined for forensics. It's not unusual, any bleeding or bruising is hard to detect, and often isn't there to detect despite the awful pain. I don't know how he wants me to respond.

He repeats himself.

The jury are only asked to decide whether they think your
story has anything that they have a doubt about. You
know how these trials work as well as I do?

It's a rhetorical question. I consider whether he is giving me any subtextual hints, like barristers often do. You can't coach a witness, but you can give them hints that they may or may not pick up on. I look at Richard, thinking of what he may want from me. Richard speaks up.

I would be telling my client 'if you feel like crying then . . .'

I stop and I am super clear.

But I won't do it, Richard. Not if I can help it.

Richard responds with such serious gentleness that I consider I had his subtext all wrong.

> I believe you shouldn't have to cry to be believed on these
> matters, Tessa.

He sighs quietly and I can't help but be so pleased it is him I am talking to and not another barrister. He understands. Still, I feel a need to elaborate.

> I can't bear to let him see me cry.

Richard nods. I tell myself to breathe. And I do. Richard is formulating something to say, probably something along the same lines, but he stops himself.

> Just stick to the facts and stay strong.

His words roll around in my thoughts. 'Stick to the facts,' just 'stick to the facts.' But I want to get ahead of what I will be asked. I turn my mind to what Julian's instructions to his counsel might be. What does he say? What does he tell himself? How has he managed to explain himself to others? 'Think, Tess,' I tell myself, racking my mind so that I know what his defense is. But he doesn't really have to have a defense; he just has to pick holes in my story. Richard's talking.

> Hold tight in the cross. Barristers on the stand always think
> they can handle cross-examination; that they've seen it
> done every day. But Tessa, it's rare that a barrister is in
> the witness box and it's harder than you think.

I nod. Consider this. It's rarely occurred to me what is happening in the witness box for others, when I'm in court cross-examining them. I want to be meticulous in the box. I have asked before but this time I know Richard will know the answer.

> Is Julian considering giving evidence himself?
> No.

He's quick to move that option out so I don't linger on it. Possibly, he thinks I'm shocked, but I'm a defense barrister; I would most certainly not advise he submit himself to cross-examination. Richard continues:

> And Tessa, I don't have to tell you this, I know, but just to
> remind you that there's a very low rate of convictions in
> these matters. It's not your fault if he walks.

I don't like Richard saying this. I know it's true, so low, not even two percent, but I am telling the truth and I know what I'm doing up there in the witness box. I want him to tell me that a truth like mine, with a good barrister like him and an excellent witness like me, has good odds.

I tell him honestly:

> I just want the law to work, Richard. To be fair.
>
> Are you sure about refusing to have a screen? I could still ask for it. Or if you'd prefer to do video evidence, we could still ask for it.

I'm sure.

> Yep. I want to look Julian right in the eye.

He nods, looks at me, then stands.

> I'm heading into court for the jury empanelment. You're going to do great, Tessa.

It's a sweet comment, but as he says it, he puts his hand out and touches my shoulder. I flinch. We both notice it; he withdraws his hand quickly. In my mind I am telling him, 'I'm sorry. Sorry. It's not you.' But I don't say anything, I try to pretend nothing happened. I look at the tabletop, white plastic turning dirty cream. Richard asks me if there is anyone coming to be with me, and I respond.

> Uh-huh.

I can't elaborate, too afraid I might tear up. Richard speaks before he leaves.

> We're in courtroom one.

I know this already. I think he had to say it out loud to us both. So that I could acclimatize as much as he has about where we are about to play out this trial. I consider the last time I was in courtroom one. It's hard to imagine being anywhere else in there other than where the barristers sit.

I'm strangely glad that Mum insisted on being at the meeting room with me and to go into court with me. It feels right that she is here with me, I need something from her, I am not sure what. Possibly her fortification, her sense of 'always being there for me.' Mia's fine about it, a text arrived from her earlier. She's going to wait for Johnny, Cheryl, and Junie to arrive. I've begged her to remember to remind

Cheryl under-fourteens are not allowed in court, only the foyer. I also don't want Junie in the witness room to see me talk about it, I don't want her to hear the words. She's right on two years old, and I don't know if she would remember or not. I won't risk it.

The arrival of Junie has been the one joy of the last two years, laced also with a newfound vulnerability on behalf of someone else. I feel an urge to protect her, feel the fragility of a girl-child in the world. It gives me another reason to be strong enough and see the trial through. I want the world to be safe from men who do this to women. I want accountability to be demanded. I never want to think that this could happen to Junie when she's growing up, or ever.

Little Junie, she has breathed life into our family. Made it pulse and return a heartbeat. She has been a uniting element between Johnny and me. And for Mum, it's like the sun comes out whenever she sees her granddaughter. A small girl named for her, reaching out for her, eyes lighting up when Nan is in her sights. A precious newness that makes me ache at times, not just with love but with fear. My family has always felt to me to be unbearably exposed to the whims of the world.

CHAPTER 24

THEN

The Havens sexual assault unit. I've read about that place in briefs, pored over the results of various pathology tests. Never considered for a moment I would ever be there. It's around nine a.m. when I am taken to the Havens after being offered some breakfast at the police station. The thought of food is hideous, but the cup of tea I sipped in the blue seats of the reception made me feel vaguely human. I note the young woman sleeping on the seat is no longer there, replaced by a man who jumps up between short bursts of chat at the police desk, then returns to his seat. He returned home from a trip to find his bike had been stolen He's steaming. How I wish I was there because of a stolen bike. It feels so simple, so straightforward, so inherently painless by comparison.

When I arrive with the big officer, I see that the Havens' reception is staffed entirely by women. They pass me a warm blanket and a rose-bud hospital gown. The big officer leaves for 'a walk.' I'm not sure whether I will see him again and feel badly that I haven't thanked him. A woman with an empathetic face comes by with a clipboard and asks me my name and details. She explains what is ahead, what to expect, but I hardly listen. I don't even care at this point, I feel that I am just handing my body over as evidence, that I am no longer attached to it.

I'm called in and despite all the kindness, all the women about me, all the care taken, every moment is awful. Surreal. My name is asked a few times, I feel robotic.

Tessa Jane Ensler.

I give them other details that I know they already have on the form

I completed. It occurs to me that they are asking me these things to keep me talking. They are preparing the bed, the awful gynecologist examination setup. A nurse with a perfectly professional yet empathetic voice speaks as my legs are moved down the bed.

Anytime you feel uncomfortable, let me know and I will
stop the examination.

I know I will just grit my teeth and get through it. But I acknowledge the autonomy she is providing me. It must be a protocol, I think dimly to myself.

Okay.

She is clear in her instructions.

If you could just let your legs both flop outward.

I do. It's awful. My body opened to the world to peer into and see what damage was done. I close my eyes, clutching my phone. I try not to think about what they are looking at. I try not to think about what happened to me, the pain, the terror. The long walk, the police station. All at once I feel a searing vulnerability. I feel my face grimace as the probing begins. The nurse is telling me what she is doing, but I don't want to know. She speaks again, this time with instructions.

Can you just wiggle your bottom down to the end of the
bed there, Tessa, so we can get a photograph.

I do as I am told, feel strange metal instruments inside me. I just endure it. No noise from me. I hear photographs taken; I think of how I took a photo of the dress I was wearing in the mirror at chambers just last night. Emailed it to Mia.

Mia.

I think about how I will probably have to tell people. Pain. Bright lights through my eyelids. Someone is taking photographs of my vagina. Outside. Inside. Pictures made of places deep inside me. I open my eyes and stare at the bright lights. I'm told that swabs are being taken. Suddenly my phone pings. A text. I'm briefly glad for the distraction until I realize with a slap that it is Julian texting me. "Where are you? J xx." I feel instantly clammy, the phone feels contaminated, and I'm consumed with an explosive anger. I delete the message with force. I then turn the anger at myself. 'Great, why don't you delete more evidence, you fucking idiot.' I lament to myself out loud:

What's wrong with me?

The nurse stops what she is doing.

Tessa, would you like us to stop?

I wonder silently if they are trained to humanize me at every point by using my first name.

No. I want you to finish it.

I go cold. I think of Julian still at my flat. I overcome an urge to throw my phone to the ground, smash it to bits. It pings again. Another text. It's Julian again. 'PS I hope you're ok after everything? I'm heading off home.' It confuses me, 'after everything,' then question mark. Thoughts rush through my mind: 'Is he worried about himself? About what he did?' He knows, but he's playing it cool. This time I'm smart, I don't delete the text; I even screenshot it. It's 9:30 a.m. and there's a woman with gloves on examining my vagina and the man who did this is still inside my flat? Is he taking a shower in my bathroom, looking through my fridge? I feel stupid as I reflect on just yesterday. I had imagined, hoped that we might be eating breakfast together this morning, strolling through the Portobello markets. I feel defeated, embarrassed.

I speak out to the nurse.

I'm not sure I want to do this anymore.

She nods as if not surprised.

We're done at this end; you can relax your legs now. We just need some photos of your hands and some quick swabs under your nails, from your mouth.

I lay there passively as she does it. A tear forms in one of my eyes. The nurse says something kind. I don't register it, but she's done. I can get up now. I hear her ask me in a hushed voice:

Do you have someone with you, Tessa?

I shake my head.

Do you have somewhere to go, Tessa?

I don't know, but I tell her.

Yes.

She can tell I'm lying.

Would you like to see a social worker?

No.

I just want to get out of here. I feel out of control, I'm in a hospital, swabs have been taken. I just received casual texts from my rapist. What if I'm overreacting? I'm not. But what if I am? I know Julian, I've known him for years. My mind is split between the rape and the way he has effectively erased it with his text. I feel crazy. I have a flash of the poster at the police station. The woman beaten up. The text reading 'This Is Not Love.' I rest on that sentiment a moment. What happened last night was real. It doesn't just go away because he decides it does. I'm glad I have reported it now, even if I don't go forward. I feel shocked that I am keeping my options open. The text message has bumped me back to my regular life. I wonder if it is possible to just erase, forget what happened. But I know it's not. Already I feel changed, different, and yes, broken. I hate it but I know it is there. I can't think about what to ask next. The nurse fills the space.

I know you can't imagine it right now, but things will get
    better.

She hasn't said my name this time. It feels more spontaneous. But it makes me feel that I must be showing my terror, my anxiety, grief on my face. She knows. I turn to this woman who has this job. A life of weeping women in shock.

Are they going to arrest him?

She shrugs. Leads me into the cubicles to change. Tells me the big officer is outside waiting for me. When I'm dressed again in my own clothes that are now warm and dry, I find my way out to reception. There is the big officer, standing by a phone charging station. I briefly consider how uncomfortable it would be for him, standing here among women, knowing that as a man you are probably the one stranger they definitely don't want to see right now. I see a young woman dressed up for clubbing, sobbing into another woman's shoulder. The sister or friend looking fearful and running her fingers through the woman's hair. Others waiting to go in, trying to hide in their rosebud gowns. Another woman is older and sitting far away in the corner, staring ahead. The big officer should see this, all men should see this. I turn to the officer.

Can I go?

I have a desperation to be out of here. He looks like he does too.

I just have to sign some forms, so we have a clear chain of
    evidence.

Right.

We both pause.

What happens next?

He takes me literally.

A junior police officer, a woman, is on her way over now.

She will drive you home.

I protest. No new people. And I am not sure I even want to go home. I have work to do for Monday's court case, thinking on that makes me calmer. I dare to ask the question I'm not even sure I want an answer to.

Will you arrest him?

He looks at me.

Do you want us to?

I'm stuck for words. This is the fork in the road, right here. I need to think. He explains the conditions.

Will you be prepared to give evidence in court?

I stand there, mute. He fills the space with statistics.

Only one in ten women who are sexually assaulted report it to the police.

I don't know what that means. I wait.

He continues.

And they don't all move forward.

I've never thought about this statistic before. I can see why one wouldn't report it, I can see why one would just try to bury the incident. I have so many conflicting thoughts. I have to admit my hesitancy. I have made the report, but I need to think about the next step.

I'll be honest with you, there's a lot at stake—my privacy for a start. And . . . my career.

There's a tiny knot in my voice when I say 'career.' I see his face assume it is a no. He has done his job and taken my statements, brought me here. I guess he is now moving forward with what his next job is. I don't want him to give up on me pushing for justice. Not yet. But he knows my career, he knows Julian is powerful. I think about the fact that everyone will know. Will know this happened to me. But then . . . I tell the officer.

But if I don't, and he does this to someone else . . . ?

He flashes me a look: 'Exactly.' He hesitates.

>Of course, we also must run it past the Crown Prosecution
>Services to see if it has a good chance of success. We can't
>call it. You no doubt understand all of that already.

I do understand but I feel it like a punch. I don't get to decide whether Julian gets arrested or not. Someone in a department somewhere will pore over the details of what happened to me, what I said in my statement, whether I am believable. That person will then speak of all those details in a meeting where somehow they will decide whether it is worth the time they will spend putting the case together. Is there a good enough chance of success? I know this intellectually, legally, professionally. It feels like, once again, I am at the mercy of another man somewhere, who will consider if my voice is worth hearing, who will decide if it sounds like I am speaking truth or not. I feel determined to not be held back, I want them to believe what happened to me, because it happened. Because I was raped.

The officer notices something,

>Here's my colleague.

A very young police constable, a bright-eyed, clear-skinned young woman, materializes. I can feel the big officer's relief at knowing someone else can deal with me from here on. The young woman is carrying two hot drinks in a takeaway tray; she speaks with a warm northern accent.

>Hi, I'm Kate. I'm so sorry for what happened.

She hands me a drink, telling me it is a 'hot chocolate.'

>I thought you might like it.

I smile at her. The big officer wishes me luck and tells me he is available if I need anything else, but that Constable Kate Palmer will take it from here. I thank him and he is gone. I have been handed over. Kate digs into her pocket, brings up a card, and hands it over to me.

>I'll be your police liaison officer going forward. You can call
>me anytime, there's a mobile number on the card.

I study Kate, she's so young, so hopeful. Her uniform is new. I remember my first week at Cambridge, new sweater, new world. I was brave, tough. Look to your left, look to your right, who's not going to make it? That Tessa fought and fought to be seen, to be heard. Do I let her down? Do I stop the fight? Because if I do that, I could lose her completely. For all time. I finger my phone, thinking, thinking. I look back at Kate.

> The other officer, the man who just left, he asked for my phone. Said if I wanted to go forward, they would need it, so they have as much evidence as possible. I want to make sure I do everything I can. All I ask is that you process it as quickly as you can, and I can get it back soon?

I hold out my phone. She puts her hand over the phone in my hand. Kate doesn't take her eyes from mine.

> I promise you will have it back within twenty-four hours. I will do it all myself today.

I'm shocked but I believe her. This never happens but I'm buoyed by her desire to make it easier for me. She takes my phone. Kate looks questioningly.

> Does this mean you want us to take it forward?
> Yes.

I'm nodding. She tells me she will return it tomorrow, so I have it for the week going forward. She will let me know whether and when they plan to arrest Julian after the CPS respond. She still wants to drive me home.

> I have the squad car.

But I need to be alone, to find my own way back. I need to just be for a bit.

CHAPTER 25

NOW

I hear my mum's voice at the door to witness support staff.

June Ensler. I'm here for my daughter.

When she opens the door, I take in everything about her. She isn't wearing her usual attire; no uniform, none of the clothes she changes into after work or weekends. She has bought something for court. Sensible trousers, sensible top. Her shoes I recognize. She enters the room and I see she has brought with her an oversized straw bag.

Mum, is that the bag I gave you for your birthday?

She nods.

I said it was a beach bag.

When do I have time to go to the beach?

Loudly in my head I hear my own voice. Fail!

Mum has a sense that she has said the wrong thing. She rushes in.

It's too good for the beach!

She looks around anxiously, she's breathing more quickly than usual. I know she's nervous. Is she afraid? I realize this court must seem overwhelming, she's only ever been to magistrate courts with Johnny. This is big, serious, terrifying in comparison. She looks so old now. I have given her all this worry. She's only here because of me. Everything feels like my fault these days. For 782 days everything has felt like my fault. I could not stop all the voices in my head.

You fucked a guy on a sofa at work.

You bring him home to your bed, you're so drunk you even vomit.

You didn't scream or kick enough.

You froze, in the middle of it all, you just froze—what's wrong with you?

You're pathetic—you let him sleep in your bed after he had done that to you, while you just cried in the shower.

Julian is a friend, isn't he, surely he wouldn't do this knowingly?

What if he really thought you were consenting?

It's as if I can't believe this could happen at all. And yet it did. It happened to me.

I dig into my thighs with my nails again, try to make myself feel the pain. Trying to remind myself, trying to . . .

Come on, Tess, remember! The law says, it says, you can't do this to a woman. Can't hold her down, ignore her, keep her trapped while you push . . . while you, you, push yourself inside of her. You can't rape and then pretend it was consensual. Can you?

CHAPTER 26

THEN

Saturday morning. This day. So much of my life has changed for all time. I know it but I am denying it at the same time. I wander up to the Thames and grab a cheap umbrella as I do. The Havens have given me a generic zip-up hoody to put on. The hood up makes me feel invisible, which is not something I often want to feel, but right now . . . I sit by the river, but nothing feels normal. The Thames in the rain is hardly cheery, but I'm actually grateful that it reflects my mood. The rain is not heavy, but it's constant. I consider catching the train home to Mum's, but I'm too exhausted to think about dealing with anyone else's reaction to what happened. I keep telling myself that I'm okay. Because to everyone else around me I must look normal, I must look okay. But I'm not.

For a long hour I refuse to think about what happened. I just sit and think about other things, mostly just watching vessels on the river. I avoid catching the eye of any passerby, and when I find my mind wandering back to early this morning, I slide my sharpest nail down the inside of my lower arm. An alert? A discipline? I have been in the company of complete strangers throughout the process of reporting the rape; I wonder to myself whether I could just spring back to who I was if I refuse to tell anyone else. I know it is magical thinking. I know it doesn't change anything. I also know that I will tell someone eventually, but I can't form the words in my mouth, I cannot make the sentences required.

I have never had to say to anyone in my life, 'I was raped.' I was tough, streetwise, I was a fighter. I was not going to be a victim. I had made that decision for myself early, and assumed by making it I was somehow protecting myself, creating a shield. Everything else I said I would

do, I have managed to work toward and achieve. But not this. I have
not protected myself. I feel a deep sense of failure overcome me. I hear
a voice repeating words I have always heard but never listened to.
You got too big for your boots; who do you think you are?
I was so lucky to get through my childhood, my teen years without
any sexual assault incident, so how does it happen now? How does
it happen when I am finally in a place I only dreamed of? Living in
London, working in one of the most prestigious professions possible.

My mind floats back to a party when I was a sixteen-year-old. New
Year's Eve party, at a friend of a friend's house. So much alcohol, drugs,
dancing. Boys trying to kiss me. I see him arrive: Steven. A few of
my girlfriends point him out. I have crushed on Steven forever. He
is eighteen, blond, tall. I have thought about him over and over, have
improvised a personality for someone I don't even yet know. Diana has
met him before; she's kissed his best mate in the past. She's seen my
pencil case at school, his name with small hearts written over it.
Diana leads him over to me and introduces us. I am dumbstruck.
He dances with the group. All the girls giggling at me, trying to do it
surreptitiously but it is so obvious. I know I'm blushing but glad it's
so dark that no one can point it out. I feel ridiculous, leave, head to
a corner where we have a tequila bottle stashed.
I take too many gulps and then Steven is behind me. His quiet per-
sona, the one I had imagined was philosophical, ironic, is not on
display right now, he is babbling, drunk. But he puts his arm about
my waist, and I am in heaven. I can't hear what he says, but he sits
down and pulls me onto his knee. I can't look at my girlfriends, I am
imagining a future with Steven.
After some madly flustered kissing, I feel a little more confident.
He offers me a pill, I take it with aplomb but with an ever-so-slight
panic. I don't usually take something without checking what it is.
But this is Steven, one of the good guys. 'I'm lucky,' I think to myself,
he only has eyes for me right now. I am glad we can't chat with the
loud music, because I wouldn't know what to say. I know he plays
football, and that he wants to leave school to go to trade school. I
had dreamed of me going to university and him coming with me,
maybe making us a place to live.

When Steven manages to lift me off his knees, he immediately takes my hand. I am guided out through the drunk people lining the hallway. Someone slaps him on the back, another guy catches his eye and has a grin that I don't like. Later, I will look back at that grin and wonder, but right at that moment I am leaving the party with Steven, and everyone sees. It feels like a dream.

He leads me out through the front door and over the road. As the music dims, I am aware that I am a few things: firstly, I am tongue-tied, I have no idea what to talk about. Secondly, I am drunk, but also something else is kicking in, a sort of energized thumpiness is taking hold of my body. Heart beating faster, and not in a manner I have ever experienced before. When I stumble, he drags me up, and onward.

Suddenly we are somewhere I don't recognize, a park, a green, away from everyone else. But I am here with Steven. He stops and pulls me down under a tree. It's Steven. His hair is caught in the shine of the moon, and I am thinking about tomorrow, the first day of the New Year, and how this is a great start. I might have the one boy as a boyfriend whom I have always dreamed of. I feel excited. He will be the first person I see next year. In about twenty minutes, it will be Steven who is the man kissing me when we hit midnight.

I realize I have left my phone at the party in my bag, somewhere near Diana. She's not as careful as Cheryl is, but Cheryl is not at this party, she's at another one with Albie, the stupid boy she is with—a guy she met a few weekends ago who treats her like rubbish.

Steven is kissing me with such energy that I can't catch up or take a breath. I am on the ground with him, and worried about my outfit, my dress is short and there are leaves and dirt. His hands are suddenly all over me and I realize I have to catch up, I try to do what I think is the right thing but feel self-conscious. His kissing becomes wet and slobbery. He is not a good kisser, but I don't care. I try to keep up. His hands are suddenly inside my undies and bra. He hurts my breast when he pinches it, and I try to wriggle a little. His other hand is plunging into my vagina. I am not saying no, I am not asking him to stop, but I don't feel good, it hurts. I clock it up to experience, then he pulls my head down to his trousers and opens his fly. He's insistent, but I pull away. He makes a face, asks me what is wrong with me.

He is hurting me by roughly moving a few fingers inside me, and he is trying to pull his trousers down at the same time. I don't like it. It might be Steven, but this is not what I imagined. I try to pull away, but he is insistent. Suddenly I feel repulsed by his mouth slobbering away at my face, I can't keep up. I want to go back to the party. I suggest this and he laughs in a way that I don't like. All my instincts are raised, he is not the same guy I see sober at the bus stop sometimes. The quiet, handsome guy. This is a different person. I know I need to get away.

I tell him I need a moment. He asks me if I'm frigid, and I feel like I have failed somehow. I also realize that nothing is going to plan, and while he doesn't give me a moment, I consider how to get away from him. I try to wriggle away and he pulls me closer. I tell him, 'I need to pee.' He is distracted for merely a moment, digesting this. His hand is still inside me, but it slackens. I take advantage of the moment. I stand up, and all instincts kick in, I start to run. I run as fast as I can back to the party. I don't quite know if I am running in the right direction, but I run. I turn and he is chasing me. Steven is chasing. What am I doing?

But I know danger, I have lived with violence and danger, and this is danger.

He falls, screams out all sorts of names at me. Apparently, I'm a slag, I'm a slut, and I am also a frigid bitch.

I run on, and on. I arrive at the party, heart thumping. I slip through the crowd in the dark, crawl about to find my bag and leave. I don't want to tell anyone anything.

As I leave via the back door, I hear a countdown begin. I move farther and farther away. The screams at midnight come from various sources. There are parties everywhere. Car horns toot loudly. I am heading home. I feel foolish, embarrassed. I ask myself, 'Maybe I am frigid?' but I am also wrapping my arms about myself, looking up at the stars. I am connecting with the person that is me, Tessa, the one who has bigger plans than this life. I tell myself, 'You're okay,' I tell myself, 'You're safe.' I hear myself laugh.

When I replay the night over in my head, the smart getaway: I mainly think about how I managed to escape. I am not going to be anyone's victim. I'm a fighter, I will always get away. Steven was nothing I wanted. I had a strange sense that the fear I had felt so hotly at the park was embarrassing and something I didn't want to tell anyone about. I would manufacture a story about Steven in the coming days that indicated he was not for me. But right then, as I walked backward up the hill home, in the first hour of that New Year, I was watching the stars and congratulating myself on getting away. Trying to maintain the first hour of the year as something that still held promise, that could still be lived as I wanted to live it. I blocked out any thought that I might not have had that moment of escape. I tried to convince myself that it was another sexual experience at least, so that I was catching up with everyone else who had slept with multiple boys.

And yet, right now, as I sit by the Thames on this rainy Saturday, I remember that night. In the light of what I know of the law, I see the incident with Steven for what it was. The pill, the dragging me far from the party, the determination to have what he wanted. I see the whole thing play out as it would on film. I see the rape charge papers I have read from police over and over.
This morning I did not escape, I tried, and then I gave up. 'Everyone fights,' I tell myself, I was just lucky that time in the park.
That experience was not unusual among my friends. That the boys wanted what they wanted was something we had to deal with, and managing their expectations was our responsibility. They had a sense of entitlement because we were dressed in sexy outfits and dancing. We didn't agree with this, but secretly we had subsumed so much of the rhetoric of what men felt entitled to. We took responsibility, blame for what happened to us. We didn't have a vocabulary to challenge it. We intuitively knew that if we did, we were 'the one with the problem,' seen as lacking a fun factor, that we were even 'frigid.' When you come from a housing estate, when you live in an area where survival is everything, where there are few people looking out for you, and even those who are cannot do much, when you don't have access to power, the only safety you can rely upon is the safety you create for yourself. And often, that safety doesn't work.
I think of Alice and Phoebe, even Mia. Do they understand this?

The safety net of their parents is always there, they don't even see it. Parents who know what to do, whose advice is *not* to 'keep quiet, don't make a fuss.' I feel a rising hopelessness, but then remember that perhaps it is beyond just that.

The parents of the likes of Julian are most certainly just as sure that their boys are not to be sacrificed because some woman calls rape. Didn't Alice and Mia, didn't Phoebe have to deal with those sorts of entitlements? With the possibility that the Stevens in their lives might do it differently but still had some sort of power to decide the outcome?

I saw Steven years later at a bar. I was eighteen. He was ahead of me in the drinks line. I was standing next to Jason, whom I was dating. I saw Steven's hair, his back, and I knew it was him. When he turned around laden with four beers, I saw his face. My knees were weak. I didn't tell my boyfriend, but I needed to leave. I wanted to get out of there. The look on Steven's face before he saw me was the quiet philosophical look he carried before that night at the park. The face that I had imagined a beautiful human behind. I saw him again, in that state. Then when he turned and briefly caught my eye, it changed. It wasn't fear, it wasn't anger, it was a look that indicated he remembered who I was. Momentarily I wanted to disappear, but I didn't look away. Not out of bravery or challenge, but I froze. Just as I froze this morning with Julian. Why didn't I do something? Could I have? I feel flat as I walk through to the Bakerloo line at Charing Cross station. I board the train and sit still, enjoying the ride because there is nothing I can do. A gang of boys jump on, hyped up, one of them drops a full Coke can, a woman across from me changes her seat. The spilled drink makes its way toward me. I watch it. The boys are calling out to each other, ridiculing the guy who dropped the can. Mockingly telling him to mop it up. The Coke trails along toward my feet. The can rattles around. I get off at Queen's Park and finally buy a coffee. I stand in the line at Gail's. I often love a Saturday morning here: papers, coffee, a pastry. Perhaps a browse in the indie bookshop, a walk to the park and lie in the sun. Today my coffee is in a paper cup, and I trudge back to my flat with it. The rain is over, the streets feel heavy. When I reach my flat, I convince myself to blank the feelings that wash over me. This is my flat, and he is gone. But I'm tentative.

First time through the building door, first time up the stairs, through my door. Check each room. No one there. The first time in my room since the rape. I can't stay there. I see Julian has found the sheet and duvet and piled them back on the bed neatly. Of course neatly. Julian has been brought up well. I scream out loud to no one. I pull all my clothes with their hangers off the rail in the closet, throw them on the bed in the spare room. Grab handfuls of underwear and socks, shoes, jackets, perfumes, and makeup. Put it all in the spare room on a writing desk I have in there. I'm in a frenzy of moving things. Then I shut the door of my bedroom. I don't have my phone, so I sit. Silence. I'm glad I can't call anyone. I'm glad Julian can't text me again. 'PS I hope you're ok after everything?' I am pleased I have my laptop and files home with me. I take them out and spend a long time poring over my case for Monday. I take in very little, but I am glad I am distracted. I'm not hungry at all.

In the evening I microwave a frozen Indian meal and flick through some channels on the television. I turn the television off, I sit on the sofa. I feel very, very alone. I start to tear up. I don't stop myself, I just let them fall. I feel so sad, so sad. This sadness is harder than the anger. This sadness is not something that I can fix. I hear myself gasp for breath. I wipe my eyes with my hands, bury my face in a cushion, and lie there.

Later a throw blanket on the sofa comprises the last of a makeshift bed. I switch the television on to a shopping channel, volume low but loud enough for company. Without my phone I feel terribly vulnerable. 'Not that your phone kept you safe this morning,' I think to myself. Twice I get off the sofa and check the door, even put a chair against it. I have never done anything like this before in my life. I check the windows, despite being this high up. I lock them all down properly. I have terrible images of someone pushing through the double-locked front door, past the chair, and I have no escape. The fear is exhausting.

When I wake on Sunday, I am in the spare bed. I must have gotten up and ended up here. I have a vague recollection of using the bathroom. When I first wake up, I feel sluggish, but I don't remember instantly what happened. As I lie there marveling at the spare room it all comes flooding back. I roll over and will myself back to sleep. Eventually I get up, endure a shower without looking at my body or myself in the mirror. Robotically. Trying to reclaim my flat, my home. I spend the day inside, my brief for court tomorrow is overprepared now. I realize it looks like the way Adam prepares them. So many tabs attached, even questions written out for cross-examination. All the points I need to raise. I usually prepare, but not so much of it is written—usually I hold it all in my head, intuitively laying it out so that I won't have to use notes in court unless I want to emphasize something, read it out in full, or strategically make the witness sweat a bit as I pore over what is in my folder. But I know it all, have it laid out like one of Mia's scripts in my mind, except with all sorts of branching directions to go if required, or if anything unexpected happens. I am thinking about Mia. It's past one o'clock and I type her an email. I wanted to tell her what had happened, but also that I couldn't talk about it right now. I needed her to know, so that I could not feel that only Julian and strangers know what happened. I am not wanting to tell anyone at work, the thought of anyone knowing makes me cringe. The idea of it. And yet of course if it goes to trial everyone will know. I want him to have to answer to it, to plead guilty, to take responsibility. He knows what he did. If he pleads guilty, he will be able to mitigate the sentence, to lean into his family's influence, with references and people who will stand for him. He has all that. My clients charged with sexual assault or rape do not have that. I am yo-yoing between wanting the police to take it to court and wanting something else to happen. For him to come to me and to admit he did it perhaps? An apology? The email to Mia is longer than I meant. I reread it and try to correct some of the stream of consciousness that shows my confusion about going forward. I decide it might be subpoenaed and so I delete it. This time I write a shorter email about how sure I am that I don't want him to be able to do this to other women. This time I ask her to just support me in my decision going forward; this time I say I am not confused at all. I ask her not to call me right away as I don't have my phone, that all I have is email. I ask her specifically not to FaceTime me yet. I underline that request. I'm not ready to face anyone for now. I then consider whether Mia will ignore this, I know she will, so I turn FaceTime off on my computer. Hit send.

The rest of the day I go over the brief for Monday. I am scared of going to court, of going to chambers, of seeing Julian. But I am telling myself that he will not cut me out. This is my chambers too; he will not be able to freeze me out. I will not be broken by this. I oscillate between feeling strong and outraged, and small and terrified. I don't know what to expect.

When the door buzzes from downstairs at four o'clock I bolt upright. I stay very still. Is it Julian? Has he come to tell me how sorry he is? I wonder what I shall say to him? I don't know what I should say? Or is he here because he might have left something in my bedroom? Or worse, is he thinking he can do what he did again to me? I stand against the wall and try to peep through the windows to see who is standing by the door to the building. I can't see, but across the road is a police car. I feel a little safer, then it occurs to me that the police might be here for me. Are they going to ask more questions? On their way to arrest Julian? I tentatively pick up the intercom after another series of buzzes rattle through the flat. My voice, defensive, ready for attack, scared too.

    Hello?

It's the young police officer.

    Tessa, it's Constable Kate Palmer. I have your phone.

I shake with relief, and the joy of having my phone back. I tell her I will be right down; I don't want her in my flat. As I trot down the stairwell, I can't help but think that as much as I do not want to see Julian, if he was at the door offering huge apologies about last night, at least I would know. At least I would not have to go through a trial. At least I could tell him I would speak to him only when I'm ready. I open the door to Constable Kate Palmer. She hands me my phone in a plastic bag. She shows no inclination to come up to the flat.

    I know you were worried about work tomorrow and you
       needed it.

    Thanks, I really appreciate you had to work harder to get it
       back to me.

She shrugs.

> How are you holding up?
>
> I'm fine.

I am lying but I have no energy to talk it through. She stands there for a moment.

> You've got my card if you need to call me. I'll also keep you
>> in touch with where we are with the case. I'm afraid we
>>> don't have counseling, but if you . . .

I take the plastic off my phone. It's turned off.

> When will you arrest him?
>
> Not sure, soon. I will call you tomorrow to update you.

We farewell and she moves off the curb toward her car. She is so tiny, even smaller than yesterday.

I don't sleep well that night, nor do I feel good on Monday morning. But I am not going to be the one who can't go to work—he should be the one who can't show his face. I can't eat, and I pour most of my tea down the sink before I leave.

The Hammersmith and City line is crowded, I'm on a later train than I intended. I don't absolutely have to go via chambers, I could go straight to the London inner courts, but I want to own my room, my life. I want to not be scared. My flat is feeling strange, I will not let him destroy my legal life as well.

I approach chambers, the beautiful old building that it is. I have always been so grateful to have been invited into these chambers. The old rabbit-warreny rooms have never bothered me, their lack of beauty nothing compared to the facade of this building, the long corridors without natural light; the rooms with hot desks and common areas are nothing glamorous, and yet the stairs winding their way between floors, the congeniality I felt after I recovered from my initial amazement at being offered a key and a belonging, were everything. Alice and Julian constantly complained about their mates set up in rock-star chambers with renovated rooms and luxurious fittings. But for me the tiny rooms felt good; I would never have to pay for huge floor space or some extravagantly presented desk. The long history of the building prevented any renovations that would move things about, and I relished that.

As I enter the foyer, my legs begin to shake and shudder. I breathe fast, loudly. I feel strange, clammy. I panic and run back outside. Hailey has her back to me as I exit; I take shelter to the side of the building, away from any eyes that might recognize me. My knees feel weak, and I perch on the side of a small stone wall. I can't breathe and am filled with a sense of foreboding, a terror, but more than that a desire to vomit, to retch and retch. My head spins. I am doing everything to find my phone, scratching about, through my bag, my pockets. When I find it, I call Alice. I have only one aim—that is to survive the next ten minutes and then get out of here before I humiliate myself further. Alice picks up, I remember she has just spent the weekend with friends in Sussex. I'm just relieved she is back because I know she is not in court today. Her voice is light, Sussex must have been fun. I feel a twinge. Women like Alice are not women like me. I don't understand her life really. The subtext between her and her friends. She often sighs at my unknowing, is taken aback by some of the things I say when I have no idea why she is shocked. We are so different, but right now I feel so grateful that she is on the phone and asking how I am. Speaking normally is hard. I give it my all.

Not great, Alice. I'm feeling sick.
I interrupt her considerable sympathy. She's a kind person, I remind myself soothingly.

Actually, I'm just downstairs, I had to leave chambers. Are
you free today to take my brief?
Alice is still computing that I am outside of chambers. She takes a moment, her voice a mixture of helpfulness, sympathy, and action. Underneath it I know she is thrilled to jump into court with a brief already prepared.

Which court?
She doesn't wait for an answer.

I'm coming down right now.
Before she hangs up, I tell her that I am tucked into the side. When she appears, her face is concerned for me. I have tried to stand up and have so far managed it. I am still breathing fast. My heart is racing. Alice notices.

You look like you're running a temperature. Can I get you
something?

No, no. I have an 'assault occasioning actual' case, client
        will meet you up at inner.
She is taking the file, glances at it, sees my tabs. Relief.
        Does he have a good case?
He does, but I know she needs an out if she loses.
        Look, to be honest it could go either way.
She's relieved. I see her settle; this is the sort of case she can easily
run. No pressure. We all love cases like this. She turns back to me.
        I'm hailing you a cab.
I am mid-protest, thinking I would head to the tube, but I just want
to get out of here, so I let her. She's quick, a black cab pulls up. As
she supports me to the car, she looks concerned.
        Will you be on your own at home?
        Yeah, but don't call, I'll be sleeping.
She doesn't see how I could not be with anyone.
        You should call someone to be with you.
I tell her I will, and she looks relieved. I have no intention of
doing any such thing, besides which, who would I call? Alice has
her mother and father, her brothers and their wives, her aunty and
godmother. Probably more. She is well networked in London with
family and close family friends. She feels my forehead while leaning
back.
        You're clammy.
I know she is afraid that I have something bad. Covid? A virus she
doesn't want. I reassure her.
        I think I ate something.
She's instantly relieved. Not concerned she will catch it, not concerned that I need further monitoring. She makes a sympathetic face.
        You look terrible, go to bed.
        Thanks for doing my case.
I mean it. I am suddenly aware that I just can't go to court today, I
quietly pretend even to myself that perhaps I ate something. But I
know it's something else, something that I haven't felt before, something frightening. Is this what they call a *panic attack*? No, surely
not, it's my body that's doing it. For a moment I consider it could be
a heart attack, and I know Alice must know someone who specializes

in such things, someone on Harley Street. A friend of her mother's, her father's? But I swat it away.

I am in the cab when before she closes the door, she says, heartfelt:

Thanks for the brief.

I nod. Then I am on my way home. As I finally turn into the Harrow Road, I am feeling less urgently ill, but still shaky. I check my phone. There's an email from Mia. It's a long, beautiful email filled with love and support. Filled with fury against Julian, lamenting that she is not here by my side. I read it and I lose my stamina entirely. I just want her here. She signs off, begging me to let her call, FaceTime, anything. She has abided by my request, but she needs to hear my voice. I am overcome, I need to hear hers too.

When I pay the cabbie, I sit on the corner of the street for a bit. I breathe in and dial her number, she picks up instantly, and she is there. I can barely talk; I cry but try to not let her hear. I know she knows. She says all the right things. Mostly she is angry, furious. She wants to get Julian in a room. She is in Cambodia, and this is her British phone number, I am just so happy that she can be reached. I feel less alone. I feel a bit like myself. Mia tells me that I sound shell-shocked, and that after the police interview and examination, I need to have people around me. She considers dropping out of the tour she is heading toward and coming home to be with me. I am absolute in not wanting her to do that.

I would feel pathetic. Please, please, don't.

She makes me promise I will call my mum. I tell her that Mum's at work, and she can't pick up. She insists and will not take no for an answer. She says if I don't do it, she will. Before we hang up, Mia has a little cry.

I hate that this has happened to you. How dare he? How dare he do this to my friend? Who the fuck does he think he is?

I like her outrage. I venture a question I am scared to ask.

How will I go back to work with him there?

She contemplates this, wonders if I need a break? We hang up and finally, finally, I call my mum. I wait through the first call, thinking that I would need to make two calls before she'd pick up, but to my surprise she picks up on the first try. She is not happy I have called her at work, but then quickly she asks me:

Is something wrong?

In the moment I take to frame my answer, I can hear her breathe, terrified. It's as if she knew, was waiting for the call.

I'm okay. But yes, something happened.

She's so desperate in the wait that I blurt it out.

I had a bad experience and I've been to the police to report it.

She asks me where I am and then tells me she is on her way. I am not expecting this, but she is off the phone so quickly that I don't even have a moment to protest or to ask her what will happen if she leaves work. I text her these questions, but she doesn't reply.

In the couple of hours it takes my mum to ride the train to mine, I sit on the sofa. I do nothing. This is not like me. When I see her face, I am overwhelmed with gratitude. I know what this must have taken for her. Her face is lined, worried, set. She scans my face for any hint, notes how I look.

Are you sick?

I wish I could just ask her to fill a script, make some chicken soup and I would be okay.

Mum!

It's all I can say because I choke up.

Sorry, sorry. Mum . . . I . . .

She doesn't touch me, but she leaps in.

Love, what's happened?

I have to reassure her.

No, I'm fine. I am, really . . .

Tessa?

I can't speak for a moment, but my mum looks like she is about to collapse, so I just say it.

I had a date with this guy from work on Friday night, and . . .

What? Did he hit you?

She's looking over me. Is she checking for bruises, blood? I shake my head.

No. We . . .

I can't say it. How do you say something like this to your mum?

Mum is waiting, leaning in. Tightly wound.

There's no way else to say it.

He raped me, Mum.

My eyes are hot with tears. My mother's face falls but she is silent.

I'm fine, I promise, I'll be . . .

It's out there now. My mother looks wounded, like she has taken a bullet. I start to shake. Mum notices and puts her hand on me, leading me to the sofa. She glances about the flat. I begin to blubber, saying things that are out of context, out of order. I can't talk about what happened in my bedroom. I point to the bathroom.

The bathroom, I . . . vomited, and . . . and . . .

I can't say any more. It's like my words can't find the story anymore. I feel like I have been holding it together, making my statement, moving bedrooms, holding it together and the floodgates just opened. I am still trying not to cry, but I am failing. I can't remember the last time I cried in front of my mother. She puts her arm around me awkwardly. It's too much for me. It's all too close, too intense. I tell her I haven't looked properly at the bathroom, but there was also blood in the shower.

After . . .

My mother is filled with a fury, but she asks no questions. Her knuckles are pulled tight, white.

Would you like me to clean the bathroom, love?

I nod, grateful for the intensity of the moment to shift. I hear her gather my mop and bucket. There is water, then she comes out for the scrubbing brush. When she reenters the bathroom, I peep around the corner. There is my mum in the glassed-in shower space, scrubbing the floor. I see the remnants of brown blood between the tiles and see it swirl down the drain. My blood. My mother cleaning up my blood.

When she is done, she looks up, sees me, and stands. I feel like a little girl, that I have taken a risk, done something wrong, and brought this despair into my mum's life. Despair that she doesn't need. I have done this to her.

I really had thought that I was now untouchable. That if I just did my job, didn't stand out, won my cases, I was like everyone else in chambers. But I am not. I am disposable, I am rape-able. Just like when I was a kid on the estate. Nothing has changed, just the class of man who can rape me. I feel foolish.

  Mum, I'm so sorry.
She looks up at me, shaking her head.
  No. You can't be sorry. You didn't ask for this.
She comes over to me, outraged.
Then she speaks and even if she didn't intend it, I hear the blame. I hear the fault; I hear the same disappointment I have with myself.
  I should have told you to be more careful about who you
   let in your place, Tess.
I feel defensive then, followed by the knowledge that this has happened to me, but she is blaming herself. She is in this with me. I feel a shiver. I realize it is not just Mum who will feel they have not protected me.
  Mum, you can't tell Johnny, okay?
I know I sound panicked. She nods. We both know why. My mum grabs me, she is urgent too.
  Listen to me, you must go back to work. You have worked
   so hard for what you have, and you have done so well.
   This is your job, your career. You don't get paid if you
   don't work, love. Don't let him get the better of you. Be
   strong. You go back. Just promise me that.
I'm nodding. We never get to rewind to the time before now, before Friday. I think about what I would do differently if I had known this was ahead. I have a million thoughts spiraling through my mind. I have so much guilt. My mum is still waiting.

I promise my mum I will go back tomorrow. After Mum leaves, I call Cheryl. The one person who has listened to me without judgment for most of my life. She hears me out; I wait for her fury, her usual outraged swearing, but when I stop speaking there is silence and then I realize she is quietly sobbing on the line.

CHAPTER 27

NOW

Mum is scanning my face, doesn't know what to say. I ask about the others.

> Where's everyone else?
> Your friend Mia arrived and took them to find a juice for
>   Junie.

At the mention of Junie, I anxiously remember my request.

> Cheryl knows to . . .

Mum jumps in, trying to reassure me but with a sharp tone to her voice.

> . . . take Junie out when you start . . . talking. Yes.
> No, Mum, Junie can't go into court at all.

Mum is still standing. She nods. Moving her hands around each other. It annoys me that she won't make herself at home. It's a goddamn horrible little room, but does she always need an invitation to sit down somewhere?

> You might as well sit for a bit, the jury will take a moment
>   to get sorted.

Mum takes a seat but leans in, eyes wide, shock, fear.

> There's a jury?
> Mum! Of course.

I sound exasperated. I didn't mean to. It occurs to me that my family have no idea what I am about to front up for. Still, I feel badly for my tone.

> Sorry.

Mum dismisses the apology with a flick of her hand. She buries herself in the straw bag and hands me a sandwich. My stomach can't handle the thought of eating, but the deep bags under her eyes, the worried countenance. I take it. She pushes further.

Go on, love, you'll need your energy.

Silence as I chew white bread. The taste of overly sweet strawberry jam with butter. Mum is watching my face when she suddenly rises from her chair and completely engulfs me in this gruff hug. Her voice is different.

Be your strong self, don't let the bastards get you down,
even if they get away with it—just don't let them ruin
our Tessa.

I don't open my mouth; I just sit there. I am desperately trying to not cry. I feel like young Tess all over again—I can't get away from her these days, no matter how far away she felt for so long. My mum expects very little, yet her words have pierced my heart. I feel like I might explode into a blabbering wreck. I know my mum wouldn't cope if I did. She would shatter.

I speak through a mouth of white bread.

Uh-huh. Uh-huh.

I won't cry. I won't fucking cry!

Today Julian is pleading not guilty; he will not admit what he did. The trial will run for three days at most. And it is only me giving evidence. Not Julian. I know he has that right, but it feels unfair. But I know he knows; I know he *must* know. Julian's not stupid, he's just convinced himself and all the people he has asked to write letters of support for him—people I know—he's convinced himself and all of them that I am lying, and I am doing it to, to . . . I am doing this to destroy him! He has convinced himself that he is the victim. While I, I am forced to say the words, relive it all IN FRONT OF EVERYONE. I know this is how the law works, he has a right to cross-examine his accuser. Everyone has that right, as they should. But right now, the fact that he gets to sit there through the entire thing and not be cross-examined to check whether his story has holes feels so unfair. He is the one who did this to me. But it feels like *I* am the one on trial.

My mum is back, seated. I look at her face. I think about her life. As well as the violence from my father, all she has put up with. I can't help thinking that given her life, her job, her vulnerability, she knows what it is to be sexually violated. But I'll never ask. The white bread is in lumps in my mouth. Swallowing is hard.

CHAPTER 28

THEN

I try again on Tuesday; when I arrive at chambers I put in my Air-Pods, play music that I don't recognize, but it is a welcome distraction. I manage to find my way into chambers without incident. This buoys me. I see that around me it is a regular Tuesday, and everyone is busy. When I find my way to my room, I am relieved. I close the door. A text from Alice appears on my phone. She asks how I am and tells me triumphantly that she won the case yesterday. I text back, 'Brilliant result!' She responds with a thumbs-up, she's chuffed, I'm sure. She is still typing though. I feel nervous, what does she know? When the text comes through it is just a reiteration of her concern for my health. I leave it. I gather some papers that are about my desk, open my laptop, and begin an advice that is outstanding. I feel that time is going slowly, that I am not concentrating as well as I usually do. A panic rises but I push it down. It is temporary, I'm sure. I continue, and eventually I have some semblance of calm. My work is such solace, it gives me everything I need right now. Distraction, confidence, intellectual rigor, normality, time. But then the panic comes again. I take a break and call Kate Palmer; she tells me that they are going to call Julian in to make a statement, but won't be doing it at his workplace.

I feel the shudder in my legs.

I know when they speak to him that everything is changed. She tells me she will let me know when it is about to happen to give me some warning. I am grateful.

I hang up and look through legislation I have in hard copy. I am immersed again but decide to photocopy parts of the legislation. I have the looseleaf legalization open where the pages are that I would like to copy, as I walk toward the photocopier. Most people are in court by now, so the place feels less urgent. I reassure myself that Julian will not be around, that I have some space. I wander around to the photocopier, greet another barrister who I know.

But as I turn into the photocopy bay, I almost smack right into Julian. He is dressed neatly, slim-line suit, nice purple tie with paisley swirls. I know the brand of each of them. I stare at them as I feel my body inwardly collapse. My breathing is heavy. I am standing close to him. I can smell his aftershave. I remember it, I realize that is the smell that I could smell in the Havens, and I turn all my senses off. I stand there, and he looks me in the face. I look up and he is scanning my face. He speaks.

Hey!

I think of the three letters that make up that word. H-E-Y. There's the slightest note of threat in it. Or is there? My hearing is amplified, I can smell the aftershave again. It makes me feel sick. His shirt is so white, so very starched. I wonder who does that task for him? I can't imagine he does his own shirts. He is staring at me. Emboldened by my silence. He smiles and cocks his head to one side. I know this is performative. I have seen him do it in court. Almost dismissive of me, or irritated. I am having trouble reading it, vigilantly searching over everything.

Are we good?

It is clinical, that is for sure. He knows that we are not good. How does he dare just pretend things are fine. I stand here, with legs that have forgotten how to run, and I know my face is saying no. He breathes out, irritated. As if I am some moody, indecipherable person. A disappointment. Yes, that's it, a disappointment. Then he stitches everything up, a nice, neat bundle of 'sorted.'

Tessa. I'm sorry if I have upset you in any way, let me buy
    you lunch this week?

He is gathering his stuff as he says this. I am in shock; I want to say something. He is gaslighting me right there, as he stands before me. Pretending none of it happened. I try to speak, but I'm just . . . unable. He leans in and I startle backward. He ignores this. He speaks with his smooth court voice. I know that voice. There's a note of threat in it too. Despite the singsong jokey voice. I know I am right. It's all I hear. He speaks to me directly.

I can barely remember, I drank so much.
He waits, then pointedly.
Well, we both did.
I know what he is trying to do. And God he is good, he has absolutely not missed a beat. He is claiming the narrative. I do not move a muscle, but I know what is happening. He is proposing that we could put it down to some bad drunken sex night, and if we do that then everything would go away. He offers his last phrase as if he is giving me a gesture of goodwill, a sign that he is too good for me somehow. A throwaway line that subtextually tells me that I am the problem. Not him. No apology. It is, me, Tessa, who has a problem with the other night, not him. Not Julian. The words are screaming but only inside my head. 'Upset me? Somehow? You raped me. You held me down, ignored my terror and you . . .'
Then suddenly, Alice is upon us. Julian offers her a big smile. She smiles back. Julian waves to us both.
Gotta get moving.
And Alice turns to me as I stand there. She has some papers to copy.
You look much better today. Must have been a twenty-
four-hour thing.
I nod, place my legislation on the photocopier, and I am there, photocopying. Flashing light, moving machine, Alice flicking through papers, mentioning something that I don't even compute. Over and over in my head are his words. 'Well, we both did. Well, we both did!'
He is blaming me for at least half of what happened that night. While I burn with outrage, I am also silently attacking myself. 'What, you just stand there and let him gaslight you like that?' When the photocopying is done, I try to say something to Alice, who is setting up her own copying. It feels surreal. I am aware that my legs feel shaky. I am also aware that I am not the person I was. I would never have been silent to the face of someone who did this to me, surely? I just nod to Alice as I leave. I feel so small as I return to my office. I sit at my desk for a long time, doing nothing. Trying to feel nothing. It works. For a bit.

CHAPTER 29

NOW

We have a jury.
Richard announces it like there needs to be follow-up. I ask about the composition.

How many women?
Five.
Mum pipes up.
Is that good?
Richard and I both look at each other. It's not an easy question. Is it a good thing? We both know the answer.
I turn to my mum, speaking loudly so Richard is part of the conversation.

I don't know. Women can be just as bad at believing other
women.
Richard sighs. Mum doesn't quite know what I mean, but it's enough that I am not saying it's bad. She is looking over Richard's wig and gown. He does look very regal. I reconsider the question. I have never thought deeply about why women are as bad, sometimes worse, at believing other women when they report a sexual assault. I have never had to really think it through before. But I am aware that certain cases I have run, the women have looked at me as the accused's barrister, they have looked at me and I know they have thought, 'She would never represent someone if she thought they were a rapist.' I know they have done so, and I know it has been to the benefit of my client. The fact that women—and men—are assuming that as a female acting for him, I am somehow supporting his story, that's a matter for them.
Richard talks to Mum. He is telling her about his children, Mum

is talking about Junie. Her face is trying to hold in some of the enthusiasm she usually has when Junie's name comes up; she is still afraid of what Richard thinks of her. I go over the idea of the women jury members. I have an awful thought that I have not considered before. That perhaps the reality is that sexual assault is a thing we have all had at least a brush with, a thing that mostly they don't want to acknowledge is as bad as the ones that go to court. Because what then? We weren't brave enough to call it out? We thought it was our fault! We were embarrassed it happened to us, can't bear to have to be singled out as a victim. That sitting there it is easier to say 'these things are not rape' because if they are, if the woman is telling the truth, then we must all examine our own pasts, perhaps the actions of our sons, our husbands, our brothers. Maybe it is easier to consider the woman is exaggerating, not telling the truth, not taking responsibility, re-narrativizing what happened because otherwise they must wear the blame. *Why can't women believe one another?* I think about some of my cross-examinations, how all I must do is suggest they have it wrong, and I see jury members consider that there must be more evidence they are not receiving that would show this.

I shake myself out of it. Barristers would never do, though, what they once did. Bring up the woman's unrelated sexual history. Imply she is a slut, that she wore underwear of a certain color, laciness, raciness, because she was hoping for sex. They would never necessarily call a woman an outright liar in the same way they once did. Judges would never tolerate it. I am reassured by this but then the doubt returns.

I have never had to call someone a liar to show their story has holes. I just have to imply they are lying. The juries are good at reading the subtext, especially if you speak in a certain way. You don't bully, just show them up.

I am stuck on this when Richard interrupts. He is heading back in. I feel a mild panic that we are beginning soon. That this is IT. All thoughts of juries and judges are banished; rather, I am thinking about the courtroom, and having to take the stand. Seeing Julian in there. Staring him down.

Richard speaks.

> I'm going in for the opening. I'll be sending in Constable
> Kate Palmer when they call for you.

I can't speak.

You're ready? Tessa?

I nod.

Yes.

You'll do great.

When Richard exits, Mum takes this as a sign to leave and look for a loo. She is getting prepared so she won't have to leave court, but I also know she is doing this because she is nervous.

I am waiting again. I know Mia is in there, making sure Johnny, Cheryl, and Junie know where to go, where to sit. I think about Mia. She stayed at my place last night, went down this morning and got fresh coffee and croissants. Some juice. I asked her to go ahead and meet Johnny and Cheryl's train. She was there to do anything for me. We sat up the night before talking, planning a trip for next summer. She's good talking about things. She stopped everything at one point, put her glass down. Looked me right in the eyes.

I'm proud you are doing this. I know it's not easy. But you are doing this to prove that he can't get away with it. You are doing this to show the world. I have so much admiration for you.

I roll my eyes.

No, listen to me. I can't imagine how strong you have to be to do this. I can't say I would be as strong.

I remind her that I might not even be believed by the jury, but she talks over me.

Tessa, if people can't believe you then there's so little hope for anyone. That's all I can say. You are the best witness possible; you went straight to the police and reported it. I wouldn't have even thought to do it in a timely fashion. I would have sat on it and thought about it. You're articulate, you're believable, there's no defense!

I love her belief, but I'm weary.

There's always a defense, Mia. He will just say I was consenting.

She's loud, shocked, and I love her for it.

To that! Jesus!

Mum's taking ages in the loo. I search through my texts for the message from Mia, sent as she went into court. She has come home early from an acting gig. A good gig too. She has done this just so she can be here for me, although she assures me that she was glad she could escape. I smile as I read her words. I feel stronger. She has also sent me a snap of Cheryl, Johnny, and Junie. This little group of people are my people. I know having them there doesn't change the outcome, but they are there. To bear witness. For me. I wonder how many people will be there for Julian. His family, his friends. I don't want to think about it. I know he is in there now, with his KC.

Once Richard has finished his prosecution opening address I will be called as the first witness. Julian is in there, able to listen to everything. The opening, sitting back knowing he will not have to say a word throughout the entire trial. How does he get to just sit there while I am in here waiting? How does he get to sit through the whole thing and not be cross-examined? I know he has the right to test the Crown's case. But I am the Crown's case, so I am the only one who will be tested.

I reflect on an article I had read. Something about how statistics show that any man who has sexually assaulted a woman and been found guilty has at least been disrespectful or has assaulted a woman in his past.

At the time I considered it unproven, unnecessary. Are you saying it's a pandemic or something? It's too much to think about. But now, as Richard must be opening to the jury, I think again about the possibility that Julian has done this before.

Adam had told me when he came to see me that he had heard something, nothing admissible, nothing conclusive, but something happened with a woman at university, and nothing more was ever heard about it.

I think of that now. That if she had said something, and been heard, I might not be here now. But men like Julian can find ways to cover things up, move things around, buy people off. Even if she had made a report, the law says every new case is a new case and the jury must judge him on this charge alone, not in the context of any previous convictions.

I take out my handheld mirror, fix my makeup. Tilt the mirror and check my outfit again. A perfect blend of 'I am strong, professional, I am not ashamed, and I am not a slut.' This is what Mia said about me. We both know this is what I must project.

CHAPTER 30

THEN

I know Julian's arrest is soon. Maybe this evening after work. I have a sneaking suspicion that he is somehow being given special treatment. A senior junior barrister with a father who is a silk. The police are going to have all their evidence in a line before they make a move. The big police officer, who I discover is called Dave, calls me before finalizing my statement, checks something I said. He volunteers that the Crown Prosecution Services want him to make sure he crosses all his t's and dots his i's.

He tells me:

> It's an interesting case for them over at the CPS. Two barristers, criminal ones at that!

I imagine all the jokes that are being cracked between the big officer and the CPS. Or even just around the CPS. The horrible humor in it for all of them. The CPS. They all knew me before this. I was the barrister on the other side, the one they had to watch for clever tactics, the one they had to beat. It's like the veil has been pierced, they have seen my vulnerability, they have the upper hand. This time they get to look at me and consider whether I am worthy of being believed. This time they get to look at Julian too, decide whether they will prosecute someone powerful, someone with a powerful father. I am in their hands entirely. I know that these days in chambers, where no one knows what happened, are numbered. Perhaps tomorrow it will erupt. Left leg shakes. Glance about my room, consider hiding the bottles. So many private clients hand over a bottle of scotch, something aged and single. They stack up, and every now and then we all sit around, slosh either ice or Coke in a glass and pour a generous shot.

I remember Julian wincing at Adam's scotch and Coke poured from
my bottle.

> That's a twenty-year old Lagavulin. And you put Coke in
>   there with it?

Adam just clinked Julian's glass and drank.

> The Coke takes the worst of the bite away.

I laughed. Then.

Now I count the bottles and consider whether I should remove them
in case someone considers it as evidence, a drinking problem. I check
myself.

> Stop being paranoid. My stash is no different from anyone
>   else's in this building.

Nevertheless, I take all of the opened bottles and put them in the bin.

I'm flicking through pages when outside a door slams, someone yelling. A man's voice. Bizarre. In chambers no less. Almost immediately,
the landline buzzes with an internal call and Hailey is on the line.

> Your client is back and causing a scene.
> What client?
> He's trying to get in.

I rush out and down toward reception. Bloody hell, this is all I need.

When I make my way to the front desk, I see the back of my brother.
I barge in and there is Julian standing to one side, a security guard in
front of him, and my brother being restrained by two more. Julian
looks disheveled. I don't know what is happening. Then I realize that
Johnny had asked for Julian and is now attacking him. I realize Julian
is shaken but doing a great job of hiding it. Of course, there are three
security guards there to protect him.

Then Johnny yells out:

> I'm going to rip you apart! I'll fucking kill you for what
>   you did to my sister.

My heart lurches, but I'm right in there, secretly cursing my mother,
'I told you not to tell him!'

> JOHNNY!!!

I see Hailey make her way out and join the other faces at the door.

One of the security guards has Johnny in a headlock. Johnny doesn't even acknowledge I am there. His eyes are wild, he is fighting to be free. I try to get in front of his face, but his only aim is to get to Julian. He is like a wild thing and the security guards look astonished that this is happening.

I tell them:

It's okay, he's with me.

The one in charge turns to me.

Mr. Brookes said not to call the police.

Is he asking me permission to call them or to confirm the instructions? As I respond, I consider that Julian is doing this because he knows exactly why Johnny is here. Johnny has no doubt said the words. I imagine him asking for Julian this time, Hailey calling him down, and Julian reluctantly coming to reception before Johnny launches at him. Security would have been there already, a client off the street means Hailey would have already made sure someone was there. She follows protocol, she would have sensed he was furious. Been afraid of this unruly, badly dressed 'nobody' who is 'not one of us.' She would have called for backup after calling through to Julian. I can see the fear on Hailey's face still. Fear my brother is used to at any place. He is not someone people like dealing with. My heart skips a beat. Yet he is doing this for me. My big brother is putting himself in this situation for me. But I am also furious with him, I don't want this. I have enough to deal with. Julian thinks he is safe, that he only has my brother to deal with. I know that tonight he will learn the gravity of his actions when the police come for him; it's all a lot more serious than my big brother showing up and yelling. This he can shoo away, this he can laugh over, for this he can nonchalantly declare he doesn't want the police called. He is the good guy, the one above it all. But I know he is aware that underneath Johnny's fury is *my* fury. Something is brewing. I have been quiet for days now, he must think he has gotten away with it.

Has he gotten away with it before?

I tell the security guard to walk Johnny outside.

It's okay, he's with me.

The security guard looks at me like I'm insane. Like I am asking for a wild, fully grown lion to be given over for a cuddle. I address Johnny.

Johnny, we're going outside now.

Johnny sees me, pulls the fight in a little.

Tess.

The younger security guard:

Oh, he's your client?

I nod without looking at him.

The main security guard again:

He tried to hit Jules. Yelling at him.

Julian seems to have immaterialized, and Johnny is being marched out of the building. I walk beside him. He is frog-marched all the way out to the street. People walking by with coffees, others waiting for cabs peer at us, whisper. I glare at them all. Fucking hell. Johnny is calming down, his eyes on me. Sad eyes, confused eyes, sorry but trapped eyes. I muster a professional voice.

Thanks, guys, I can take it from here.

They're not sure.

I stand my ground.

You can leave now.

I hear my own voice; it is pissed off. I don't intend it, but this whole scene in the street is upsetting me, I want them to go. I don't want strangers gawking at my brother like a criminal when the real criminal is hiding inside, is the one being protected! The guards let go. My voice softens, I thank them for their troubles. They leave, glance back, and see that Johnny is standing beside me, chastened, without any trouble. I take him by the arm and walk him around the corner, the same place I hid on my first day back to chambers after, after the rape. He's fuming, spits on the ground. I look at the spit. I don't know why.

Johnny!

He looks despairing. I know this is compassion for me. He speaks with force because he can't tell me he is worried about me.

I'll fucking kill him, Tess! I'll cut his fucking dick off.

I know he wants to hit something, anything, but he doesn't. He stands there waiting for me to speak.

I can't believe Mum told you.

Instinctively he protects Mum. He knows he's blown it.

I saw Cheryl crying.

She wouldn't tell you!

Yeah. I hassled mum.

But then Cheryl let you come here?

Not exactly.

Everything feels overwhelming. Johnny is unpredictable, or rather too predictable. I need to get him home before he barges back in there. I need to stop this. He speaks again.

Tell me where he lives.

Fuck, Johnny!

My heart is still racing. Johnny fires up again.

I'm going to pound his fucking head until it's nothing but
    pulp.

It sets me off.

Stop it! Stop it, stop it.

He looks confused as I start to pummel his upper arm.

What are you doing?

He's alarmed, sees my face start to tremble. He thinks he must explain himself.

I can't just let him get away with this. You're my little sister.

I start pounding his chest, I am screaming at him.

I don't need you being arrested for assault or . . . worse.

I go to pound him again; he grabs hold of my hands. I panic.

Let go of me!

He does. Gently. More confused than ever. A man puts his head into the small area we are in, asks if I am being bothered by 'this man.'

No. no. All good.

The man looks at me directly, questioningly. I answer the look, careful voice, almost jolly.

He's my brother, it's fine.

When the man takes his leave, we stand in silence. I tell Johnny.

Julian is about to be charged. The police are dealing with it.

This doesn't placate Johnny.

They won't do nothin'!

I feel exhausted and say:

I just want justice.

I'm jolted as Johnny laughs maniacally.

I'll give him fucking justice.

I'm angry at his laugh, at his menacing voice. But I don't want things getting out of hand. I stand tall, breathe in deeply. Muster my strong voice.

Listen to me, you do nothing because this happened to
    ME. It didn't happen to you, and I am NOT your
    property to fight for.
He looks slightly hurt; I feel bad, but he has to listen.
He can't help himself.
    What the fuck?
    I'm fighting this *my* way.
He waits. Still confused, but I need him to see sense now. I try to
modulate my words.
    You're going to have a family. You think your kid wants you
        in prison? You going to be an absent father like ours? I
        don't need this shit.
His offense dissolves when he sees I am upset. My voice wobbles on
the last line.
    I need you to care about what I want. Or else you're all the
        fucking same.
I'm crying softly now, and he tentatively reaches out to me. I am clear.
    Please. Don't make me worry about you on top of
        everything else.
His shoulders drop, he puts his arm on my back like I'm fourteen
again. But it makes me sadder somehow. I gulp loudly. Johnny is
whispering, rubbing my back.
    Hey. Shh. Yeah, I hear you.
I try to sniff away mucus.
    Hey. Shh. It's okay. I'm not doing nothing but what you
        want. Shh, your brother's right here, trying not to be a
        dickhead. Okay?
I nod, grateful. Pull away.
    Thank you.
He makes a comically shocked face.
    Eee. That posh accent!
    Fuck off!
I say this roughly, laughing, but in my toughest voice. Johnny beams.
    There she is!
And I squeeze his hand.

CHAPTER 31

NOW

Mum walks back in from the loo, just as Constable Palmer does. Kate, still so tiny in her uniform. A baton in her holster. She wants this trial to come out in my favor. She believes in me. Her face etched with hope.

They're calling for you now, Tessa.

I look at my mum. A shadow of terror flickers across her face.

Look back at Kate.

Can you take my mum with you?

She nods. Mum collects her things. Straw bag under her arm. Kate takes Mum by the arm but before she does, she turns back. Then . . . she squeezes my upper arm like a friend, a sister. It's a perfect gesture. I smile at her before following them both through the door. As we leave the small room, I see a woman with a small boy. The boy is playing with the abacus, no idea what it actually is, just spinning beads about. There are a few more people in the common area, some look up, then quickly away as we pass through. I hear my heels on the marble floor as we make our way forward.

I am doing this, but I can't feel myself doing it. Click, click. Heels, one large marble tile after another. In my head I count my steps. It feels surreal. I am calm but each step takes me closer and closer. We make our way down some stairs. Mum clinging to Kate, me in a bubble all my own. Evidence being carefully held in my mind. I know I can do this, but it still feels otherworldly. I think of everyone in the gallery.

Once we are near court one, Mum and Kate peel off. Wishing me luck. I hear my name and I am heading into court.

This is me walking into courtroom one at the Old Bailey in London. This is me following the court officer, standing in the witness box. This is me looking at the judge.

My Lord.

Looking right at him as I declare that the evidence I shall give shall be the truth, the whole truth, and nothing but the truth. The air is still. I turn from the judge slowly. Look straight out and there is Julian's father, his mother and brother, seated up front in the gallery. How they hate me.

I turn deliberately to see Julian. There he is, seated in the dock, suited up. Knowing his KC is there, waiting at the starting gate. Julian looks back at me. Eye to eye. I know that face, it feels like he is going to mouth 'I'm sorry,' but, of course, he doesn't. Instead, almost imperceptible, a shake of his head, seemingly saying, 'What have you done?' I look at the jury. I have never looked at a jury from this vantage point before. Never felt this vulnerability of what they might decide. These will be the ones, these strangers. I look up at the judge again, he is looking at his laptop. Scan the members of the bar, those assisting the judge at the bench. Panic. All the barristers are men! The judge; the judge's clerk; Richard, the prosecuting counsel; Julian's KC; the police informant; and the instructing solicitor. I am the only woman. Even the court usher is a man! I am the only woman. Heart thumping. I can feel the blood rushing through me. After 782 days, I am here. After being asked over and over, 'Are you sure you want to go through with this?' After all the snide remarks or embarrassed looks at work. The doubts people have expressed about me, the statements, the rape kit, the ongoing souring of my own body every day. After the ongoing nightmares, the vomiting, the constant digging into my own flesh. The system I've dedicated my life to is called upon by me, to find the truth. To provide justice. As if on cue, Richard, the Crown prosecutor, moves some papers. He looks different over there in the wash of gowns and suits, but he is here to help me. I look at him, he nods in my direction calmly. I fidget a little. A sudden need to see my family comes from nowhere. I scan the gallery. There is Mum, seated beside Constable Palmer, the young woman holding her arm. My mother's face grim, set. I zigzag about and see Mia and Johnny. Cheryl has tiny Junie outside, thank God. Mia reads my mind, she nods at me— everyone is where they should be. I breathe again. In, out. And then the Crown prosecutor, Richard Lawson KC, stands to start the pros- ecution case.

CHAPTER 32

THEN

The day after I know they have arrested Julian, I am waiting for what happens next. But there is silence. Alice has been off circuit doing a case in the Midlands; she has texted me a few times. I can tell from her breezy texts she knows nothing, which is partly a relief and partly a loaded gun. When she finds out, I have no idea what her response will be. I cannot read Alice; we are so different. I want to give Adam a heads-up about what has happened, but I don't seek him out, and he is obviously busy in court. Every time I imagine Adam knowing I feel a sense of shame. I don't know why? I suppose I fear that Adam, as a defense barrister, will consider Julian someone in need. His default will be innocent until proven guilty, which is right; of course, in any other situation I would agree with him, but I was there, he is not innocent.

I have an awful feeling that Adam will distance himself from me. I feel distraught over this, then think onward about how Julian might ask Adam to defend him. This new thought has me shaking. Brilliant Adam, standing up in court and cross-examining me. Brilliant Adam, who barely loses a case. No, no, surely, he wouldn't take the case. I hear 'cab rank rule' roll around in my subconscious. I argue the point, surely there's a conflict? I think about Diana at school all those years ago. We were all at her older sister's hen do, at the pre-drinks before we all tried to sneak into the pub to celebrate her sister's last night out as a single woman. Her sister was fretting about the bachelor night and the plans they had made. She talked about how there were going to be strippers and a pub crawl. Diana shrugged it off. Her sister wasn't sure. The best man had told someone his aim was to make sure the groom got laid. Diana's sister sighed. Not happy.

Diana exaggeratedly loudly:

    Boys will be boys.

Everyone laughed. Another voice added to it.

    And men will be boys too.

I caught Cheryl with a side eye. We were both not laughing. She leaned into me and whispered in my ear.

    And girls will be women!

I'm thinking of this now as I wait. Wait for what? Wait for the word to be out, for the talk to begin. I am afraid. Not just of what lies ahead, but of what the men about me will do. The barristers who nod at me with a smile as I walk through the corridors. The ones in court who have congratulated me on my wins or successes. I consider how tainted I will be. 'She's the one, she accused poor Julian of rape.' *I* know how it goes. Julian is one of these men, they know his father. Julian has a fucking pedigree! I am the mongrel from Luton. I can hear them: 'She grew up on an estate; a scholarship girl.' They are thinking, 'We let her in and now this? To one of our own.' They will find ways to prove that I trapped him, to convince themselves that I did this to undermine him. That I am jealous of who he is, that I am chasing a compensation claim from his rich family. I feel anxious about being here, imagining Adam being nervous to be alone with me. What if he is afraid I am a loose cannon, afraid that I would accuse him. Adam has no background, no context. He doesn't know we were having a, a . . . 'thing.' He didn't see us dancing at Inflation, didn't know Julian was taking me out. I know Julian didn't tell him because Adam would have said something, surely. To me? Is his friendship with Julian close? They play touch football together sometimes, less so now that Adam has his daughter. There's a knock at my door. I freeze. Julian? A voice rings through it. Female.

    Tessa. Knock-knock. It's me, Hailey.

Hailey has never come to my room before; I am on edge.

    Come in.

She lets herself in. Something is different, of course I am waiting for her to say she has heard. Why else would Hailey be in my room?

    Just checking you're okay?

I nod. She explains.

After that guy the other day . . .

She is asking for information. This is how it starts. Possibly picked up on Johnny's screams, perhaps Julian has sent her to ask questions. I don't trust her. I nod. Shrug.

All fine.

I look at the screen on my computer. I know she is considering her next line, but she is too slow, and I manage to speak just as she opens her mouth.

I have a case conference starting online.

Hailey backs away, I glance at my screen, then back at her as she lets herself out. Professional voice, with a touch of friendliness:

Can you shut the door for me? Thanks.

I hear the latch. I fumble through my drawers, find Hugh Dalton's card, the KC who had invited me to talk about taking the room in his chambers. I call Mia in Australia, it's late there but she picks up immediately. I tell her that Julian has been arrested. Wherever she is, she moves about a bit and finds a private space. She is reassuring. We had spoken a few days ago, I had told her how hard it is for me to be in my flat. I asked her if I should sell it, move away. She was firm.

This is your flat, we will find a way for you to reclaim
     it. He doesn't get to disrupt your life so that you lose
     money as well as your home. Stay there, this is your
     place, you loved that place, and you will love it again.

I wasn't convinced but I wanted to stay, wanted to be safe there again. I still do. It was the right decision. I have thrown out all my sheets and duvet, the guy downstairs helped me move my bed so it is against the opposite wall. I still don't sleep there, but I bought new sheets.

Today, though, I tell Mia I'm afraid in chambers, I don't like being this close to Julian. I feel he is around every corner. It's going to be awful to work with him here. I am already feeling panicky whenever I walk into the building. Mia considers this, asks if I can get him removed.

It's not just him, though, it's everything. Even the
     receptionist is friends with him. Everyone loves Julian
     here. He is a big hitter; his father's clients brief barristers

here when they can't get onto him. Julian is on the board
here as the senior junior representative.
As Mia considers this, I finger the card in my hand.

Mia, I have another option. I was flattered to be
considered, but I can't really afford it, so I shelved the idea.
What? Another chambers?
I mean I could sell my flat, rent somewhere, and then I
could afford it.
Is it more expensive?
I tell her about Dalton's offer. A plush, beautifully fitted-out cham-
bers. Prestigious, human rights and test cases.
Her voice is excited.

Sounds perfect.
But I was always happy here.
I expect Mia to say something like, 'Stay where you are, he doesn't
get to drive you out of your chambers.' I wait for her to say that. But
she doesn't.

I think you should take it.
I'm gobsmacked. She continues.

There will be talk, and it will be so hard for you where you
are now. People will get his story, will feel for him. They
won't know what to say to you; you're on the same clerk's
list as Julian, it's just too hard. Besides. Dalton is huge.
Of course, Mia, who isn't even a lawyer, knows who Dalton is, knows
the inner workings of chambers. She has grown up knowing this
stuff. I'm grateful for her advice.
Then she says:

Tess, don't sell the flat. You know I hate talking about it,
but I have my fund. I can lend you the money. Fuck, I
could give it to you.
She's laughing. I know she is trying to make light of it. I'm briefly
speechless. No one in my life has ever offered to do something like
this for me. I tell her no. I tell her I will just work harder to make it
work, I will just take on more briefs. She attempts to delicately press
it, but I am firm. No way would I accept money from Mia. Or anyone. I reassure her I will try to keep the flat. I tell her that I love her. I
tell her that no one has ever said something like this to me before, no

one has ever offered me something like this. She tells me it's there if I need it, and she is embarrassed that she has the trust fund anyway. I am a little surprised she has told me; I cringe when I reflect on all the jokes I had made in the past about the 'Trustafarians' around Notting Hill, the bohemian sorts who are all 'event managers' who seem to spend all day drinking coffee, eating lunch, and going for drinks. Mia tries to never talk money with me, she is careful and, I realize now, completely aware of my lack of safety net. I think of her as a rare sort. I think of how impossible it would have been to even meet Mia if I hadn't won my place and scholarship to Cambridge.

When I'm off the phone with her, I feel stronger. I have a way out of here. I recognize that I must act today. Before the gossip is everywhere. Mia had made it super clear: 'Do it right now and text me when it's done.' I call Dalton on the landline. Reach his administrative assistant. I tell her that I am calling for him, she asks my name and, remarkably, puts me through. A small sense of being significant. He is delighted to hear from me and organizes coffee that day.

When we meet, he explains all the attributes of his chambers, the amazing legal minds I would be working with. I tell him I would be delighted to accept tenancy at his chambers. He is delighted. We shake hands. I text Mia afterward, she is well asleep by now, but I know she will smile when she reads it.

CHAPTER 33

NOW

Richard clears his throat, gives me a sympathetic smile, then it's all professional.

Can you tell the court your full name and occupation?

I answer. I will not take my eyes off Richard. He continues. Asks me various questions about where I work, how long Julian and I have known each other, what the working relationship is like. As he zones in on what the matter is about, I start to feel panicky, my throat is a bit closed. He keeps going.

In your own words, can you tell the court about the first night you spent with Julian Brookes?

When I speak about that first night in chambers, I hear a snicker. My eyes involuntarily dart about, seeking where it came from. There are extra people who have arrived in the gallery. Perhaps a group of Julian's friends? Old school buddies? They all look the same. It dawns on me that this is a show of support for one of their own. There are about twelve of them. I lamely finish answering. Richard continues.

And then after the vodka in Mr. Brookes's room?

My mum must hear how her daughter had sex with this man here in court, in his office on his corner sofa. I cringe when I am asked for a detail, catch her face. She looks straight ahead, she is not looking down or away. I want to hug her right in that moment. She is not ashamed of me. I return to Richard. He asks whether I was consenting to sex that night.

Yes, yes, I was consenting.

I feel my energy sway. I remember my feelings that night, I was a completely different person, so confident, so . . . Richard is asking me: What did you do while Julian slept?

I explain that he snored a little, and I was looking about the room. I don't mention that I went through his things.

> I read a case. A few cases actually.

Another snicker. I feel my heart start to race, but Richard is asking me what time we left.

> About three a.m. or four, I think. I needed to get home,
>> some sleep and . . . I don't know. I didn't want to stay in
>> the room and wake up when barristers were arriving.

When I describe waking Julian, Richard asks me what I said.

> I told him I had to go home. He didn't at first seem to
>> understand, but I said I had to. I told him I had to feed
>> my cat.

I've been over this with Richard, the fact that I have no cat. Not that I would be caught out on it. The fact is that Julian never asked where my cat was once he did come over. But I have to tell the court I was lying about having a pet to feed. I want to do everything by the book.

> It was an excuse. I don't really have a cat.

Richard and I had discussed and agreed that by raising and admitting this in court, I would be indicating to the judge and jury that it proved I was prepared to admit when something wasn't true. A strategy to show I can admit to lies when I have said them. I have said it now. I watch Julian's KC, Daniel Stenham, he is a top top silk. I watch Stenham make a mark in his notes. A solicitor behind him sits and seems to write a long sentence about this. I look over at the jury. There's a man sitting in the middle, a woman juror is looking right at me. Her eyes boring into me as if I am a figure on a screen, not live here in person in court. I look away, avoid her eye. I think I do it because I don't want anyone accusing me of trying to influence the jury, of attempting to manipulate them, but if I'm honest she makes me nervous.

There are journalists in the court, three of them now. I realize this is a case that would be interesting to read about on the tube. Rachel Myers is there from the *Times*. I imagine all of Julian's father's friends opening it the next day and tut-tutting the woman who dragged poor Brookes's son through such a scheming story. 'Poor man,' they would think to themselves. 'Even the best of us is not safe from lying opportunists.' But perhaps I am being unfair. I hope I'm being unfair.

I see a court artist sitting near the journalists. I am being sketched in court. I feel self-conscious. Block it out. I talk about dialing the Uber, about Julian attempting to get into the car with me, and me questioning him. I am asked why I did not want to bring him home after we had just had sex.

I wanted to sleep.

Julian's instructing solicitor takes off writing again. I wonder if I have said something else in a statement somewhere. I am speaking the truth here. I guess the solicitor thinks he can use this to compare with me letting him stay with me on the night.

The night. We are getting closer to the night. Richard asks if anything else was said.

Julian invited me to have dinner with him the following
week. He seemed nervous. I remember that I was
surprised at that.

I find myself glancing at Julian. He is holding himself well, looks very out of place in the dock. He does not look nervous now. I mentally compute that Julian looked more nervous that night asking me out than he does in here, being tried for a serious crime. He must be confident now, then. Or perhaps he wasn't nervous at all, all those days ago, maybe his voice was sleepy, and I just thought he was nervous. Maybe he was planning all along how he would get what he wanted. I had assumed there was something tender about it. I think about how I told Julian that night in chambers about my dad. I wish with all my heart I hadn't told him anything personal like that. He had seemed so understanding in the light of all that vodka, vulnerable even, but was I just a curiosity of sorts? Slumming it. Fucking a woman in his office, whose father might have been to prison. I don't know. I can't know anymore. I feel foolish for ever trusting him. I realize these days I can no longer trust what is real anymore.

CHAPTER 34

THEN

By the time the moving van arrives I am so glad to leave chambers it's a relief to go.

When the news got out that Julian Brookes was charged and going to trial for sexual assault, everyone must have known right away. I had turned my phone off for the night, but when I turned it back on in the morning, with a sense of impending doom, it was ominously silent. I thought there would be something, anything. Julian even. Possibly yelling at me down the phone in a voice message before he caught his senses that he probably shouldn't threaten me. But nothing.

I called Kate and she confirmed he had been charged. She posited that perhaps he was seeking advice about pleading guilty. In my heart I didn't think this was going to happen, but I hung on to it and even convinced myself that he might be too ashamed to tell anyone, and that perhaps it would all be okay at chambers.

The minute I arrived, the look on Hailey's face said it all. She couldn't help but stare at me. And from then on the atmosphere was stark. Alice was still off circuit, working outside of London, it seemed, but was calling me and calling me. I didn't pick up. Eventually she sent me a text, saying, 'What the hell is going on?' Everyone in chambers seemed to talk to me differently: my clerk, the man in the next office, even the women that I usually chat to downstairs.

Phoebe burst into my room, hair streaming.

>	Have you heard what Julian is saying about you? It's a joke, right?

When I somehow spat out that it was no joke, she was confused. So used to being surrounded by defense lawyers, she didn't know what to say.

Fuck, are you sure you want to do this?

I didn't say anything. At least Phoebe was honest. I liked that more than the formal greetings I was now receiving in the hallways, as men almost clutched the wall to be away from me. Julian wasn't about, he was avoiding me completely, as he had been for all the time since. I lived in fear of running into him every time I left my room. I felt myself look to the ground, my breathing hot and loud, my legs shaking and heart pounding. One day I sat in my room and put my head on the desk, rested my cheek against the cool surface. I jumped when the cleaner came in. It was Magda.

You feeling sick, miss?

She looked concerned. I wanted her to stay, to sit, to tell me about her day. Anything that wasn't about me, about what was happening. I reassured her I was just tired, and she told me some theory about how it was the weather. I wished so hard it could be the weather, but the truth was I couldn't sleep through the nights anymore. I was still in the spare room, I always fell asleep fully dressed, and any noise outside had me wake in fright.

The moving to new chambers took a week or so; the new room was available before I moved, but I had to wait until the month was up where I was or pay for two rooms. At least once Julian had been arrested the notice period was waived by the heads of chambers, and I was out fast. I had the feeling they couldn't wait to get rid of me. Each day after the arrest I wondered why Adam hadn't contacted me. It was like a knife to my heart, I tried not to think about it, considered that Julian and Adam must have talked it over, possibly Adam was already briefed to advise him and therefore wouldn't be able to talk to me about it. Still. It hurt.

So, it was a surprise when Adam appeared at my door one afternoon, two days before I moved out.

Tessa, can I come in?

He looks alarmed, and I feel teary at seeing him. I realize I don't trust Adam anymore. He gingerly takes my non-answer as a yes and slides into my room, considers closing the door but doesn't. He asks me:

Is it true?

I answer flatly:

I wouldn't make it up, Adam.

Silence.

Then he tells me:

> I wasn't sure if Julian was making something up, the whole
> arrest. And then . . .

I shrug; however, I'm slightly touched by his doubting what Julian
might say.

He continues.

> How are you?

Then I tell Adam that I'm leaving chambers, but that I assume he
already knows. It dawns on me that all of this is news to Adam.
He wants me to know why he hasn't been in touch. He's been at
home with Covid, the baby also had Covid. He was wondering why
I hadn't checked in with him after ten days of no-show. He said he
had a few missed calls from Alice and Julian but nothing more, no
messages. And now today, he has just heard everything. A tiny spark
flickers—Adam didn't avoid me. I have avoided him!

I ask him about his illness, but he brushes it aside. He asks questions,
not prying, but he comments on not knowing I had a connection with
Julian. I feel like I have betrayed him by not sharing any information. I
don't want to be dishonest, but I also can't help but wonder if my sleeping with Julian in chambers would make him think of me differently.

> It was consensual at first.

I suddenly feel nauseous. I excuse myself and rush to the loo, but
when I get there, I am unable to vomit. I make my way back to my
room and Adam is still there. He has been thinking. Tells me to come
over for supper with him and his wife this week. It occurs to me he
will tell his wife. That I was raped. I have to get used to this, but it's
awful each time I realize that I am public fodder. I feel ripped apart
for all to see. I imagine the horrible things being said, the jokes. I
know how people are. I've probably made jokes myself about people
in despair. I feel like an awful person right now. So much shame, so
much damage. I think of my mum, 'don't get ahead of yourself.' As if
Adam can read my mind he speaks.

> It's not your fault this happened to you, Tessa.

I tell him I have two days before I leave, and he asks which chambers.
He's impressed when I tell him. A tiny win at least. He says he will

be here that day and help me pack. The offer makes me want to cry.
I tell him I need a moment. Adam hesitates, then leaves. Telling me
he'll be back to check on me. When I'm alone I hug myself tightly,
arms on the opposite shoulders. It doesn't feel real.

When the movers start to take my boxes out to the truck, I notice Hailey has taken a lunch break. Relief. I imagine she is Team Julian and
would not want to have to face me there in reception for the move. I
don't have much, mostly just books and papers to go. The boxes were
packed well into the night last night, Adam stayed and helped me. We
didn't talk anything other than logistics. I was aware that it was the
first time I had ever seen Adam in chambers after hours. The movers
have already packed my desk and shelving. It looked so meager being
carried out, it will be dwarfed in my new, much larger room. As the
younger furniture mover bounds past me, he calls out:
      Last trip, then we're off.
As if from nowhere Alice appears. She is upset, frazzled.
      Tessa, you can't leave!
It's not the time for this. Her texts have become difficult to read.
Checking how I am and saying she's worried about 'you, and Julian
too.' Sitting on the fence. I really do not understand Alice. She comes
right up to me.
      Tessa. Don't leave like this.
She looks desperate, but I can't.
      I don't want to talk about it, Alice.
But Alice feels she has this one last moment to fix it. She would not
normally speak so directly but I can feel her agitation. It's contagious.
      Jules has been charged, Tessa. With a serious crime!
I look at her, what does she want from me? She's incredulous.
      You'll have to stand up in court and give evidence.
I look at her, thinking to myself, 'Do I even know you?'
      I know how court works, Alice.
She puts her hand on my arm; it's a gesture that feels cloying, but she
is trying to reach me, she has something to say.
      You know I support you.
I do a double take. I didn't know that. I meet her eyes. But she
continues.

And I also want to support Jules.
Slap.
Tessa, it's all a huge misunderstanding, let's all get to the
bottom of it. Together.
I must have looked at her like she was deluded. She tries to make me
understand.
Jules is beside himself! This is a disaster for him. And
probably for you.
I just stare at her.
I mean, surely there's another way to fix this?
I am looking at a face I have looked upon so many times, but this
time it takes on a surreal quality. I do not recognize Alice. How could
I have spent so much time with her? Sure, it was because we were
in the same space, but how could I ever have considered this to be
friendship. I think to myself how much I wish I had never taken
Julian back to my place. I think back to Alice telling me, 'He's a really
great guy.' Telling me to 'enjoy it.' I want to strike out at her, a verbal
torrent, but I don't. Adam arrives with a box, he stops.
There's nothing else up there now.
The younger furniture mover walks past with two boxes. I see in one
of them the photo of Johnny, my mum, and me on the day I was
called to the bar. Everything feels lost. I have no words for Alice, who
follows me nevertheless. Adam walks beside me, places the box he
has in the back of the van. The guys have to push off, and I am hail-
ing a cab. Adam looks at me, reminds me that he will see me soon.
Then squarely he makes it very clear.
I am here for you. Anything. ANYTHING.
I nod, I know I am going to cry soon.
Then in front of Alice, he says:
You did the right thing.
Alice looks at Adam. Surprised. Adam hugs me, but I pull away and
take off.
I don't look back, not just because I am leaving chambers, where I
have been so comfortable.
But because I don't even know who I am anymore.

CHAPTER 35

THEN

Numb. I realize weeks have passed. Ensconced in new chambers, not too far from my old ones but somehow a life away. My room is big, and empty mostly. The members of the new chambers polite, warm, and respectful. I am not engaging directly with any of them. Not sure how to; I keep wondering what they have heard. I've mentioned nothing to any of them.

My mum was shocked when she saw me the other day; I had dropped in mainly to stop her from coming up to London—she said if I didn't come to see her, she would come to me. I didn't stay long, and I know she didn't like my new, *much* shorter hair. Cheryl came by, we had all seen one another a few times since . . . since. Cheryl was starting to bulge. It occurred to me that there was not much time left before she had the baby. My niece. It was like I was watching life unfold on a screen and I was not part of the story. Everywhere I went I was not part of the story. I felt flat, but it didn't affect my work.

I have tried unsuccessfully to stop the panic attacks, but they are still as bad as ever. I spoke briefly to a therapist but I couldn't talk about what had happened, and the therapist wanted to talk about my father. I hadn't the time for that.

I didn't stay at Mum's place for dinner in the end. I felt different, I couldn't smile the way I used to, couldn't laugh. At one moment I was looking over at Mum, Cheryl, and Johnny, all grinning at a joke Johnny had made, and it was like I wasn't there. I was studying their faces as if I were invisible, looking at them, and wondering how they made their mouths do that thing, that smile thing.

Cheryl looked over at me.

    Hey?

She was gentle, asking me outright. But I just apologized, took my glass to the kitchen, and when Mum followed me in, I told her I had to get home.

I waited a long while before I started 'Operation Get Back to It.' Mia had offered the terminology as a fun thing, and I tried to think it over. I kept calling Kate Palmer, who told me that she was still awaiting some elements of the brief for the trial. She seemed frustrated that she couldn't make more happen for me.

I didn't go to the first court mention. It was just administrative; instead, I waited to hear when it would be set down.

Eventually I did it, I went on a date. Operation Get Back to It. I have always loved sex, enjoyed the exploration of another's body, the joy of engaging with a man. It never seemed foreign, or anxiety producing; at times a little embarrassing but that usually lifted, and such fun could be had. So much of my own body had been a source of joy. I relished the feeling of arousal, of seeing someone else aroused. But since the rape I have had no feelings, nothing. I couldn't even look at my body. Mostly I made myself feel something by digging in my nails. Scrubbing my skin harshly in the shower.

I knew it was strange, different. Unfamiliar to me, this new numbness. Yet the thought of fucking someone, letting them in my house, the thought of even touching myself, allowing myself pleasure, was warped into a guilty anger. A betrayal of vigilance. A warning to remember. Somewhere in my body there was a despicable self-hatred. I couldn't mark it, but I knew it was there.

I knew being the first person after the rape would be a hard role, so I didn't tell him. I agree to dinner, then another dinner, and then I ask him up to mine on a Tuesday night. I'm still sleeping in the spare room, so I figure it won't trigger anything. I have a knife I bought on the Harrow Road underneath my bed. It doesn't make me feel much better though. Sam is smaller than I am, which makes me feel physically safer. The dinner talk is almost congenial, a nice guy, it seems. But then so was Julian once.

When Sam comes up to mine, he is sweet, but my heart is wildly beating. He follows me into the kitchen, and I take the promised bottle of sauvignon blanc from the fridge. Pour two glasses. I finish mine quickly and sneak in a refill as he makes his way through to the living room. Sam works at the gallery near where I work. He's not artistic, he tells me, rather he enjoys just having a job where the days are easy. He sells the work and sits there all day with the opportunity to read books. He's an avid walker, he tells me. Scotland mainly, but occasionally on the continent. I sip my wine and ask questions. Eventually he puts his drink on the table and gazes into my eyes. I try to look back, this is the ritual, but I am aware that the main thing Sam and I have in common is a cigarette or a vape on the street on an afternoon. Usually when I am walking back from court, he is there, standing outside, and I join him. It's this commonality that has brought us here. I want to like him, I want to feel my blood rush, the gorgeous moment when you realize you are going to fuck someone, and they start to reveal previously hidden parts of themselves to you.

I'm ready, I tell myself. He is trustworthy, and if he isn't, he is short and thin enough to kick to the ground. Or is he? Stop.

I put my glass on the table, he leans in slowly, too slowly, and I don't want this. Romance. This tenderness. No. I just want to get it over with.

I kiss him hard on the mouth, and he is surprised. Tries to keep up. Eventually he is pulling me toward him, kissing me deeply. I go through the motions, he is aroused, excited, intensely involved. I kiss him more actively. This triggers him. He tugs at my top, my trousers. And his hands are on my breasts. His hand slides down my underwear and I stop kissing him. I pull away. I'm scared, and feel my heart start the panic. I stand up, look down and he is there, panting, looking up at me. Bewildered. I grab my phone.

He starts to straighten up.

Is something wrong?

I hold on to my phone. It feels like protection.

I'm sorry. I'm just not . . .

He is silent.

Actually, do you think you could leave?

He tries to speak but I talk over him.

It's just not a good time.

He rearranges his clothing, resurrecting some of his standing. He stands up and runs his fingers through his hair. He goes to say something. But I walk toward the door. I give him a look, sheepish, 'I don't want to talk about it.' I open the door and he approaches. He goes to kiss me on the cheek, but I am too shaky. I move my face. I don't want to be touched. He must be searching my face for a message, a hint, a vulnerability. But all he is getting is numbness. Inside though, my heart is racing, my body is screaming. Everything feels wrong. When he walks out the door he says:

See you around?

Bye.

Unexpectedly upbeat, I'm sure. But I close the door and stand as I hear his footsteps descend the stairs. The door to the street slams, and I lean against the door. Feel myself slide down the wall until I land on the floor in a heap. I stay there for a long time.

CHAPTER 36

NOW

After a few more questions, where Richard establishes that Julian asked me to consider a date in the week to follow, I hear Richard's voice slightly change. I hear the change, it triggers something in me, a fear. A sense of being outside my body. Here it comes, I tell myself. This is the part. I dig my fingernails into the palms of my hands. The pain focusing my attention.

> Turning to the night in question, can you please tell the court, in your own words, what happened?

I am not even aware that I am speaking. I am only aware that words are in the air about me. I feel the need to make sure I am accurate, that I don't sound hysterical. I pause for a moment and continue. I hear myself talk about meeting Jules on the corner before we had dinner at the Japanese place.

> We walked in together and were sat at a table near the back.
> We ordered sake and then looked through the menu.

Richard asks about the conversation at the restaurant. I reply:

> We talked about many things, work, books, people at
> work. We chatted about clients, he told me a story about
> a case he had run. I told him about a conference I had
> been to where they talked of ID evidence. We laughed,
> then ordered food.

I go back to that night; I feel myself shudder. I train my attention so that I am not stuck in the memory. I think about who the men were having dinner at the same restaurant. The ones we didn't want to see us. I can't remember. This bothers me. I know I was concerned they would see me a bit drunk, dressed all sexy, and make assumptions about me. All women fear the assumptions that can be made about

them at the bar. The senior men are the ones who choose junior barristers to assist them, whom they decide to refer to when overbooked.
They will not take a risk with someone they think is unreliable, or
who stands out too much! I consider why Julian didn't want them to
see us. For the first time ever it occurs to me that he might not have
wanted there to be a witness. A witness to my stumbling drunk out
of the restaurant, with him leading me. I move on.

I have to talk about the gelato, the off-license, the Uber drive home
to mine.

 Yes, it was my idea to go to my place.

Actually, I think it might have been his. He suggested it first, but
they are already asking me why, if he wanted to go to his own place.

 No, he didn't suggest his own place.

I'm thinking, thinking. Why? Why didn't he take me to his place? I
feel uneasy that maybe I was a secret, something shameful.

Richard asks:

 Can you describe the first occasion of sexual intercourse
  that night?

I talk about us having sex, laughing. How we were in my bed, it was
expected.

Richard asks me specifically:

 Taking you to that first occasion, was the sexual intercourse
  consensual?

 Yes. I consented that time.

Then he asks me what happened next. I talk of waking up to Julian
touching me, and how we were probably about to have sex. I feel
embarrassed; Johnny is hearing this, it feels wrong that everyone learns
about this, that I have to say it out loud. In front of everyone. I must
tell it straight, tell the truth—which means I have to say things I liked
about Julian. It's hard. He's just there. I feel like a foolish teenager.
'Why did you let him give you that pill and drag you out to the park?'
I hear myself.

 I liked him then.

Now I have to talk about the vomiting in the bathroom.

Richard asks me:

 Were you naked? How long were you there for?

I try to answer the second one. I know everyone in the gallery is hearing me talk about my naked body vomiting. They are all looking at me, imagining, imagining . . .

Then Richard asks me how I got back into the bedroom. I explain that Julian came in some time later. Quite some time, as I had fallen asleep on the tiles.

I couldn't say how long exactly. Then he lifted me up and carried me. He carried me carefully back to bed. It occurs to me, in this moment, here in court, while I'm answering this question, that Julian said that day at the photocopier, 'I barely remember, I was so drunk . . .' but he wasn't too drunk that he couldn't remember at all. He lied to me when he said he was drunk, he was able to lift me and walk steadily back to the bed. He didn't fall or stumble. He KNEW what he was doing. I feel a fury rise to my throat. But my legal training kicks in, I know that this will be used against me. They'll say that I was the only one drunk in this story, so I am therefore the less reliable one. I answer the questions, clearly, out loud. Richard asks them one by one, steadily, moving toward the rape. I answer out loud, but in my head, I'm cross-examining myself. Using my own defense skills to doubt my very own narrative. I realize with a jolt that I have been doing this almost every waking moment for two years and fifty-two days. Finding fault in my version of events. Blaming myself. Trapped again and again and again. I dig my nails more deeply into my palms. Richard is making his way to the part that is in contention. The voice inside my head is demanding, it is reminding me loudly.

I will not freeze up this time.

I will not question my memory.

I will not minimize what happened.

I will not embellish.

The truth will be revealed by me saying exactly what happened. I know what happened that night. I know. And then Richard. The rape.

What happened next, Ms. Ensler?

He is speaking gently. I pause and courtroom one is utterly silent. Some shuffles, each sound amplified. I try to keep calm. It's hard, but I don't want my voice to falter. I am going to be the best possible witness. I talk about Julian's attempts to kiss me and then I step through the worst of it. About how I was trying to politely refuse, and how he was insistent.

How he stopped saying anything and started pinning me down. How he was holding my wrists, and, and . . . My heart is beating so fast, so loudly. My foot feels numb, I realize I have it shoved up against something.

Richard asks for clarification.

>Please explain to the court where each of your limbs were.

I tell Richard. Eyes on his face alone. But I'm not as clear as I want to be. I see the solicitor instructing Julian's KC, writing madly. This is a huge issue of cross-examination. I pull myself back to focus.

Richard continues.

>Ms. Ensler, can you tell me what happened next?

Sharp intake of breath, my throat feels tight. I can only hear my heartbeat. I'm trying, but nothing is coming out. I focus my memory. Limbs, hands, skin.

Trying to explain it.

>So, he was holding my arms and I was pinned to the bed.

I feel like I am underwater, Richard's questions keep coming. I have gone over and over it with him.

But I am not doing it right.

>Sorry, it's a little confusing.

Never say 'confusing.' I am furious with myself. Glance at Julian's instructing solicitor; yep, madly scribbling. Richard snaps me back with more questions. His voice still underwater, but I hear them all. I answer Richard's questions. I am talking about the rape, and it starts coming back, what I felt, it's happening all over again. I stop. Drink some water from a plastic cup. My hand is shaking. I see some marks on my palms made by my own nails. Cup down.

Richard asks:

>Are you all right?

>Yes.

He continues:

>Can you tell the court what you were thinking at the time?

>How I didn't want this. How I felt trapped. I couldn't move
>>properly. I felt fear.

Richard keeps it going.

>Did you make it clear to Mr. Brookes that you were not
>>consenting to sexual intercourse?

I hear my voice. Sure. Eyes closed.

    I did. I told him, 'No.' 'Stop.' I, I tried to push him away.

I stop answering.

Richard is forthright.

    Did you say anything else? Scream?

Oh yes, of course, this part.

    Yes, I tried, but his hand was over my mouth.

    What happened then?

    I could hardly breathe . . . was terrified. I froze and
        then . . .

I gulp.

    There was pain. Searing through my body.

I think of the pain, and how long it went on for. I can see myself lying there, scared.

    Then shock. I felt a sort of dissociation.

I want to say, 'I'm feeling the dissociation right now,' because I am, I am here but I am not here. Suddenly Julian's KC is on his feet.

    My Lord . . .

He continues but I don't hear what he says. I am outside my body, looking at myself giving evidence. Julian's KC is down, Richard rises again. More questions. More details. More humiliations. This is me. Tessa Ensler. Giving my testimony. In court.

Final questions from Richard and then he takes his seat. He looks up at me, smiles at me. Pleased with the examination in chief. It has gone well.

I'm alone again. Waiting. I look up to where Mia will be. She's smiling, I can just make out her face. Behind her I see Adam, and Alice. They must have come in after finishing something this morning. Adam has a beard now. I've been out of touch with them both for so long. The last two years in my new chambers has made it easy to avoid them both. Alice tried to make amends but we're not close anymore, if we ever were. But Adam. Adam kept leaving me messages. Checked in on me. Adam was my friend.

Why didn't I keep in touch with Adam?

CHAPTER 37

THEN

Waiting for Adam to show and I feel awkward. It's Saturday morning; I know how important his weekends are with his family, and I don't have much to talk about. He arrives pushing a stroller, his daughter, Lila, is sleeping inside. I peek in at her. She's long and dark, beautiful. Adam had suggested we meet, but I only had weekends. I tell him about Junie, she is a few months old now. Lila is about ten months or maybe a year now, and Adam is a willing listener to Junie stories. I relate the birth, the homecoming, how my mother is super nan. I talk about how much more work it is than I ever expected, but how she is the light of my life right now.

I feel that for the first time since forever, I am having a conversation that has me animated. I take a mental note that it is still possible.

Adam is here because he reached out about who I was dealing with at the CPS. I had been frustrated because I had a series of junior lawyers on the case for so long, and I wanted to make sure that when they chose counsel it would be one of the barristers I admire. I don't know that many Crown prosecutors, except the ones I have pissed off because I have beaten them in court. I knew Adam would know what to do.

Our coffees arrive after he has told me that I look really well, he has read up on some of the cases I have run. He is excited for my new chambers. A very welcome boost. I am nervous though, why isn't he telling me what he knows.

I jump in.

Adam, you're killing me here, what do you know?

When his face lights up, I realize I am behaving like my old self. Yet I am behaving like my old self while I am here on a Saturday to ask about how I should strategically manage the CPS about a rape case where I am the victim.

He sips his latte.

> So good news. I spoke with my friend Mark; he's going to
> make sure you get Richard Lawson prosecuting.

I'm thrilled.

> How?

> Mark spoke to someone at the CPS, said it is a high-profile
> case, that they need a KC and he had already checked
> and saved the date with Lawson. And as we know
> Richard Lawson is . . .

Huge relief.

> He's really good.

> The best.

I breathe.

> Adam. Does Mark think I'm crazy to go forward with it?

Adam fixes his eyes on me. I go further.

> Do you think I'm crazy?

He puts down his latte. Holds both my hands across the table.

> No. It's courageous. This is what the justice system is there
> for.

He takes his hands away. I push further.

> I'll bet the entire criminal bar is gossiping?

> What do we care?

I love that he didn't lie to me, of course they are gossiping. But Adam said 'we' and it makes me feel less alone. He hesitates before he speaks.

> Someone else has spoken about being sexually assaulted by
> Julian.

> What? Who?

I'm more excited than I should be. Adam sighs. He regrets telling me.

> She won't go to the police, she's not ready.

> But if she did?

> She won't.

A pause then.

> I don't even know the details, but I thought you should
> know.

I slump back in my chair.
        So, it's my word against his.
Adam leans in, speaks with authority.
        But you're telling the truth.
I appreciate him, but I feel very small suddenly.
Very small.

CHAPTER 38

NOW

Waiting.

Fingers jittery. Hands, armpits, shins sweating.

Look up and check Mum. She hasn't moved a muscle. Beach bag clutched on her lap, the young woman Kate by her side. I look back at the bench, barristers all with their eyes on me. I wait. I know more than anyone, this is where the real work is done. Julian's KC stands slowly for effect. I go to take a sip of the water, but my hand is shaking.

This is it. The cross-examination. By the best King's Counsel money can buy. Thoroughbred. He nods benevolently toward Julian in the dock, then his eyes fix hard on my face. And. Bang. His voice is sharp, velvety, with that magical, practiced edge to it. That edge that we all hope we have. A silent communication to the jury that this is a waste of everyone's time, this should never be in court. It says it all without a word, just a tone. An arrogance. It's not a shock to me, I was expecting it. What I wasn't expecting was that when it is aimed at me, I feel it pulling me apart. I pull myself upright, answer the questions that are fired at me with a carefully modulated, unintimidating, helpful voice. I hear it and I am proud of myself. Each answer without hesitation.

Yes.

Yes.

Yes.

My voice inside tells me in a much sterner version, 'Hold it together.'

I'm briefly confused.

Then:

No.

I think so.

Inner voice telling me, 'Don't say you think so, be SURE.' My heart starts really thumping.

I'm quick with my next answer.

No, it was the second time.

I keep my eyes on the KC. I will not be accused of trying to shirk a question. I'm doing well, sharp, thoughtful, clear answers.

Then:

Yes, I think so . . .

Fuck. Sound sure, none of this 'I think so.' Julian's KC asks around the question. He is trying to rattle me; I keep my face still.

Sorry?

Oh. My answer is yes. Yes, I'm sure.

Temples pounding, heart pumping blood faster and faster. Wrists. Temples.

Then a stumble.

I don't know.

I look at Richard. He sits without emotion. I think, think. Asking myself, 'Whose idea *was* it to go to my place?' I do a mental calculation on the spot and answer the same way I did in examination in chief, even though I'm thinking he might have suggested it. I can feel they are trying to catch me out.

I want to be consistent.

Maybe my idea.

He's asking about gelato, red wine. My hand goes up to the side of my head. I pull it back down. I know what he is doing, establishing how drunk I was.

I answer a question.

I think so.

Thoughts ricochet within my mind. I'm furious with myself. Stop it. Not 'I think'—be sure. I am breathing heavily. I can hear it. In, out.

He asks me:

Do you agree with me that you were drunk?

I answer honestly.

Do I agree? Yes.

He lists various drinks. I will not fall for this; I use this trick myself.

Yes.

Yes.

I have agreed to all the drinks I had, sake, red wine, whatever else. I sneak a quick look at Mum. She is rigid. He is asking for amounts. He asks question after question. I barely hear them before I snap back the answers. I will not be made to feel that I was 'asking for it' by drinking.

A few. Six.

Breathe, don't look guilty. He corrects me, I don't take the bait.

Yes, maybe seven.

Richard is on his feet.

My Lord, Ms. Ensler has already given evidence about . . .

It's hot and I can't concentrate. I just hear blah-blah-blah.

The judge refuses Richard's application.

Defense counsel can continue. Mr. Stenham.

Julian's KC rises.

Thank you, My Lord.

His voice like honey when speaking to the judge, then back to stern with me. I know this tactic, message to jury: 'I show respect to those who deserve it'—she doesn't deserve it. Yet, he has distilled his technique so perfectly that it is all subtext. He is not rude to me, just undermining, which is exactly what his client expects. I answer him over and over, then he digs in deep about how drunk I was. Questions. Questions.

I start to falter.

Yes.

Yes.

Um, I don't remember.

I'm still cross that I don't remember when he starts up again.

I can't keep up.

I, I . . . I don't know.

Then:

Yes. I vomited.

He lets it hang in the air, recoils as if I have just projectile vomited at him right there in court. I feel dizzy, I'm panting. I look at Richard but there's nothing he can do. I do a quick glance about the courtroom, but there is nothing to hang on to. I feel like my words are out of sync with my mouth as I answer the next questions. I feel the words, but I don't hear them for a few seconds after I think I've said them.

No. I don't know for sure.

Fuck! Then:

Uh, I don't understand.

He calmly restates the question.

I don't know.

I'm breathing heavily, asking myself, 'What the fuck is wrong with you?'

Yes . . . I think so.

I flash Richard a beseeching look. Inside I'm screaming, 'Richard, help me. I'm not being clear.'

CHAPTER 39

THEN

Nearly two years before I go to court I meet Richard. After two hours of legal strategy, Richard sums it up:

> As long as you're clear on all your evidence you should be fine.

I'm at his chambers, it's neat and warm. There's lots of folders lining the walls. Methodical but not clinical. We have really bonded, and I know I am going to be in great hands going forward. We have talked through all the different ways that a rape case can go in court and have laughingly shared some of our own secrets from court cases past. He has read the brief and my statements. He has studied the pathology and the photographs of my vagina. I wince when I imagine what he had seen. He has told me that the forensics didn't come up with any internal bleeding or bruising. Nor did they come up with any specific DNA from my mouth swab indicating I bit him. He pointed out that there was a small cut on my leg; I know that this was made by me in the shower. I told him it wasn't related. He said he thought as much. He realizes the forensic report is not helpful, and that I might have been unduly disappointed. The case is basically my word against Julian's. But Richard adds:

> You're a terrific witness though.
> Thanks.

It feels odd to be thanking someone for flattering me by telling me I'm a terrific rape witness.

I add, jokingly:

> I think!

He shakes his head.

Terrible thing to say, so sorry. I mean I have had cases
       where I know we need to take it to court, but the
       witness's testimony just won't stand up.
We both think on this. A pause.
Then I ask him:
       Have you ever had any other barristers in my situation
       before?
He nods.
       Yes, a few. Most of them didn't take it any further, they
       withdrew. I think they felt there was too much to lose.
He jumps in again.
       You know if you want to pull out, change your mind about
       giving evidence, that you have that right. Don't you?
       I know.
       You're a terrific criminal barrister, no doubt you know more
       than me about all the rules.
       No. I just . . .
I think a moment.
       I often wonder if I should have pulled out. But I couldn't.
       And now everyone knows, so if I didn't show up in
       court, then Julian would just spin the story. Say that I
       made it up and was afraid of taking it to court in case I
       perjured myself.
We both sit in this reality.
       I also think, if I didn't report it and found out he did it to
       someone else . . .
       I think that's very noble.
But I don't want to hide anything from him.
       To be honest it was as much about me not wanting to
       disappear. And I could feel that happening to me when I
       was silent.
The air is still. He tells me the statistics for reporting sexual assault
are low, that while it is suspected that one-third of women have had
a sexual assault or harassment, only one in ten of them report it. That
only one in ten rapes are reported to the police. I look at the photos
on Richard's desk. Two boys climbing a climbing wall. Another of
him and an attractive woman. He sees me looking.

Those photos are old now, the little monsters are now
     monstrous teens.
I smile. I'm still thinking that out of all those women only one in ten
report it. I say something out loud.
     It is hard to report something like this. I mean . . .
I shake my head as I point to the pathology file. Then I continue.
     But then I think, here I am, I work in the law. I know
          how it operates. If I'm scared to report it, then what
          chance . . . ?
He nods.
     And yet, they do, you know. They still know that justice
          should be done.
I think of those women, that report. He must be thinking about
them too. I want to know conviction rates.
     What percentage of rape trials end in conviction?
     Low.
     How low?
     One point three percent conviction rate.
I reel. I feel anxious. Then I run that figure through a different filter.
My voice is wry, I can hear it.
     You know, whenever I did a rape case, I always thought I
          won because I was great at defending!
Richard is gracious.
     Ahh, well, that's the prerogative of a smart defense barrister,
          I imagine.
I take another look at those boys on their climbing frame; I wonder
what it would be like to have had a dad like Richard.

CHAPTER 40

THEN

I'm out of court and back in chambers, working through tomorrow's case. I still haven't added any furniture to my new room. I have to work harder to make the extra cost of this room each month, but so far, I have managed it. I consider Cheryl and Johnny's place together, tiny, with a little alcove for Junie. I know I would garner way more joy by helping them set up than by putting extra stuff in this room. I also know it would be hard to rock up to their place with anything too sizable. We all have our pride. Johnny is still scaffolding, and so far (fingers crossed) he hasn't had any accidents. When I speak with Cheryl she is quite sanguine about it, thinks Mum and I worry too much. She wasn't there when Johnny had all his accidents as a kid. The bike one that left him with no teeth for a few months, then there was the one over the fence. The 'accidents' at the pub with a beer jug or glass. I've pulled so much glass out of my brother's face with my mum's eyebrow tweezers.

The door of my room moves. I look up, a knock.

Come in.

I have no idea who it could be, but most certainly I didn't expect Alice. She has tried to text me for breezy lunch get-togethers from time to time, but I am still hurting from her words when I moved over here. She looks slightly different; I can't put my finger on it. Maybe new clothes, differently styled suit? She is carrying a bunch of daffodils, and of course, being Alice, she also has a vase with her to put them in. I'm not pleased to see her; she can tell that.

These are for you.

I'm cool with her. Formal.

Thanks, Alice.

I don't rush up to collect them, she lays them down. Looks around, taking in my space.

> Nice room.

I know she would have a million critiques about how to make it 'feel homey,' but I'm not interested in encouraging chat. I wait. Suddenly wary that she will report anything I say, right back to Julian.

> Are you here for a reason?

I'm so direct she hesitates.

> I'm not staying.

She goes to take a chair, then rethinks it and stands behind it.

> I just wanted to come and apologize to your face . . . I
> made a mistake.

Silence. I'm not sure how to respond. She fills the silence.

> When you moved out that day, I had only heard about . . .
> everything. And I didn't even know you two were having
> an . . . whatever.

She's making a mess of it, and she knows.

> And we were all such good friends, and . . .

I don't move.

> I think I always felt that given you've always defended so
> many sexual assault matters that . . .

I jump in. Livid.

> What? That I would find an excuse for what happened to
> me?

> No. No. Of course not. Tessa. Please. It was just that we all
> knew Julian, and . . .

She looks again around the room, searching for something. Lands on a thought.

> I was wrong, and I'm really, really sorry.

I don't know if I feel indifferent, or it's all too late.

She speaks again.

> Tessa, please. I feel awful.

I look over at Alice, whom I have had so many drinks with, so many ghastly green teas, so many legal conversations; Alice, who chattered away and ate lunch with me for years. She must be thinking the same thing.

> Tessa, I miss you.

I know Alice and I will never really be close again; we were always an unlikely match and mostly connected by proximity. It's hard to be a woman at the bar.

I nod my head with a small smile. It's all I have for now. Alice's face shows pure relief. She tells me she will put water in the vase before she leaves. I look over at the daffodils, so perfect in their pure yellow, the exquisite form repeated over and over, green stems lined up. She gathers up what she brought in, and I ask her about Phoebe.

Oh yes, she says hi. She decided to take up an offer from
    Dean's Court Chambers.
Manchester?
Yeah. Manchester. She met a man up there too. She's doing
    a bunch of white-collar matters. Says hi by the way; if
    ever you're off circuit up there, she has a spare room.

She leaves my room, obviously knows she can poke around and find the kitchen or loo. I know I won't be seeing much of Alice, but it's nice to think I won't have to cringe if I see her in a court foyer or barristers' drinks thing. I'm glad she hasn't mentioned Jules, I don't want to know what he's doing. I think about the daffodils, the photos most people have in their office. I still haven't unpacked the photos from my old room. I go over and look for them, they are still there, right on top of a box of files. I take out the one of Johnny, Mum, and me and put it on my desk. I make a mental note to have Johnny and Cheryl take a great one of Junie for me.

CHAPTER 41

NOW

I gather my thoughts as Julian's KC asks me a question; again I hear his underwater voice, coming at me in ripples like waves of words. I am trying to compose myself.
My temples pulsing.

Yes, I liked him THEN, but . . .

My heartbeat feels so loud that I think everyone can hear it. The room feels larger, more spread out. I want to add to what I said. The question was, 'When you slept with Julian in chambers, did you like him?' Julian's KC awaits the rest of my answer.
I lamely respond.

I don't know.

He presses on.

What did you like about him?

I hate the question. He is telling me to tell the court what I liked about Julian, what was good about him. It's a trick question, deliberately used to provoke me. I feel the rise of anger in me. You want to know what I liked about my rapist? Fucker, is that what you want to know, well, guess what, I am not going to rise to it, I am going to tell you.

He seemed smart and fun to be around.

I say it blandly. I want to add, 'Obviously I was being fooled, I am a bad judge of male character.' But I don't. I'm fuming, which briefly takes away my anxiety. It's killing me to have to say what was good about Julian. But I stare Julian's KC down. 'Take that, sir, I am not going to say, "I don't remember"; rather, I am going to kill you with honesty.'

Richard rises slowly and addresses the judge. Julian's KC listens, then rises to respond. I don't hear any of it. I am trying to drink the water without spilling it. White-hot rage flows through me. I see their mouths moving, the judge's mouth moving, but I am not hearing any of it. I replace the water cup.

Julian's KC is waiting for me.

> You wanted a relationship with Mr. Brookes though, didn't
> you?

He is on slippery ground here, I told no one that. Maybe Cheryl or Mia, but no one he has spoken to.

> I was merely considering it as a possibility, but that was
> before he was violent with me.

He doesn't like the sting at the end of my sentence. 'I have you figured,' I think to myself, then remind myself that that's exactly what he wants me to think, and I back down.

> People describe you as ambitious, Ms. Ensler, would you
> agree with that?

Richard is on his feet.

> No evidence has been tendered or given from the
> witness stand to prove that 'people think Ms. Ensler is
> ambitious.'

I see his point, but I want to answer the question. I see the double edge it is, and I can't help it. Richard sits down and I volunteer the answer.

> I do consider myself to be ambitious, Mr. Palmer, and I
> would hope that most women are free to be ambitious
> without it leading people to cast aspersions.

He deliberately ignores me, cocks his head to one side and changes tack.

> Are you often drunk, Ms. Ensler?

Richard is up again, I am computing that Julian's KC has heard about drinking at Inflation, drinking in Julian's room, and then on the night of the rape. It feels unfair, Julian was also drinking on each of those occasions, and he was the one who supplied the vodka in his room. In fact, he also bought most of the tequila shots whenever we were out, and . . . the two bottles of red on the night. The judge decides that Mr. Palmer KC can continue this line of questioning. He turns to me and in a sugary voice repeats his question.

> Are you often drunk, Ms. Ensler?

The outrage is still firing, I like it, it makes me less afraid. I go over
the possible answers in my head. 'Yes, I happen to be drunk every
day. Is that what you want me to say, you fucker? Is that it? That I go
to court drunk? That I'm drunk right now?'
But of course, I just say:

    No.

He goes at me again.

    How often would you say you vomit?

I know I am being provoked, but it comes out fast.

    Do you mean in the time before I was raped, or in the time
        after I was raped?

Julian's KC looks at me sharply. I look up at the judge innocently,
as if I am not sure which period he is talking about. I turn back
to Julian's KC. I feel like I finally won a point. In my mind I am
reminding him that I am also a defense barrister, and sure, he might
have taken silk, but I will not be fucked with. Richard is looking
down at his papers, but I feel that he liked my answer.

CHAPTER 42

THEN

Robing room, Southwark Court. Going over evidence from the brief in my mind. Terrorism charge, my client arrested along with the others but had no idea what they were involved in. Concocting some homemade fertilizer bomb of sorts; police were onto them from day one. My client's just turned eighteen, cried in our initial conference, has significant cognitive dysfunction but is charged anyway. Robe adjusted, straightening my collar carefully in my handheld mirror. These days I don't socialize with the other women in the robing room; I have gotten into the habit of keeping to myself.

A month or so ago, a barrister robing beside me said to her friend:

> You know my friend, Julian Brookes, great guy. He's having
> a dinner next week; would you like to come along?
> Saturday night. Great company, great food as always.

I froze, knowing by her volume and tone that this was meant for me to hear.

I felt the usual anxiety rise, kept my head down, pretended to open a file and read through it. As the woman left the robing room, she flashed me a look. Caught me as I looked up inadvertently. I feigned ignorance, though I was fragile, unsteady. The woman's face, a flash of righteousness across a horsey mouth. She was gone. I sat there, trying to breathe like the counselor taught me. Counting down the minutes before I leave the robing room and make my way to court. I think to myself, 'So Julian is still out there being admired, even adored.'

I wonder to myself if he has any difficult encounters with other women or men. I know if he does, they are few. Only Adam has completely broken ties with him. Everyone else is afraid to rock the boat. Everyone else is sticking to neutral. Or else they are, like the horsey woman, standing up strong for him. No doubt there is some reward for those who speak out for him, more than just a well-catered dinner party; the reward of being tight with his family, the reward of being part of the powerful. Can't offer them that. Clearly. I know that keeping to myself makes me feel a little safer. Don't try to be part of the circle, don't plead my case. Wait for court. It's lonely though, and the days are long.

This terrorism case has taken hours of preparation. I am not in the same robing room as the encounter with horse face, and it is sparse here. I imagine there aren't many women barristers running long terrorism cases. This is my first, and in any event, even if my client goes down, I know there are mitigating circumstances that I can use in sentencing.

I also, not that it matters, believe him. Sure, it makes no difference to how I run the case, but all I see is a kid desperate to be part of the gang—and now look where it's got him, staring down the barrel at a lifetime of horror over something he doesn't even understand. Comb my hair flat and put on my wig, tuck in flyaway hairs, and head toward the courtroom. Bag of books, terrorism legislation, cases, updates, and various notes taken over weeks of preparation. All those eyes on me in the courtroom means if I do well, the King's Counsel acting for the others will see me in action, consider me as a good referral when someone can't afford silk prices in a private case. That is, assuming they are not just watching me out of curiosity as the woman who accused Brookes KC's son. I just hope that some people don't hear the gossip, or don't listen to it, are too senior for blabbing junior mouths to address. Surely, I think to myself, surely Julian does not want everyone knowing he has been accused of rape?

It appears he has jumped ahead of it, like he has some sort of understanding that if he claims the narrative as bullshit, then he is ahead of it, he is more believable. He could be right. It's all too late for me on that front now. I have no idea when the trial will be set for, it seems that there is a massive delay. Richard says it's normal, but no one is thinking about how stuck I am as I wait. The waiting wears me out. I just want it to be over. Move forward; I can see why so many people give up.

The courtroom is filled with onlookers, interested parties, family members of all the accused. There are five in all; all of them bar my guy are angry, confident, sitting tall. My guy sits apart. Lost. 'Fuck the world,' I think. At least be nice to him, he's in this with you, you tricked him into it. At least don't make him feel like an outsider. But perhaps it is good for my little guy; the judge can see he is not 'one of them,' that he is a lost soul.

By four o'clock the case is adjourned until the next day. As I walk through the court foyer, I am going over the question I asked, the one that made the others sit up and take note. I smile to myself; it feels good.

I am heading back to the robing room to de-robe so I can leave when I come face-to-face with Julian.
He is just there, in front of me. Not in legal dress, clearly on his way out. 'What is he doing at Southwark?' is my first thought, followed by the bottom falling out of my stomach.
I just stand, he is a few meters away. I can't turn because then I am going in his direction, I can't walk forward or I will be closer to him. I know I should walk right past him, as he should walk right past me; we're not supposed to talk. But stupidly my eyes just stare right at him. I have no idea what expression is on my face. My blood is racing. I literally can't move. Julian looks around quickly, then speaks directly at me.
A voice laced with outrage, confusion, mock vulnerability.
        How could you do this to me?
He's convincing. I recoil but stand still. Then, his head leaning in toward me, he takes a small step forward, and in a loud whisper:
        I really liked you, Tessa. I was hoping we'd find something
            special.
I'm mute. I start to feel dizzy. He adds:
        I held your hair while you vomited for chrissakes!
I reel, confused, mixed-up.

I also remember, he never held my hair! He never saw me vomiting.
He waits for me to say something. I don't.
Then with force, he almost spits at me:

>   But this. What you have said.

His eyes narrow. I feel scared, yet I'm glued to the spot. With real
vitriol he shows what he is capable of. He continues.

>   Are you out of your fucking mind?

I am still stuck but despite myself I respond.

>   You know what happened.

This is not what he expected. It rocks him a little. He digs himself in.

>   Whatever it was, I'm not a criminal, Tessa. That's not who
>   I am.

He speaks in a growl. What I hear is a man who believes that whatever happened it wasn't a big deal. It doesn't shock me, but it reminds
me of how much he feels entitled to what he wants. The facade is
down. I see him for the man who isn't going to be held to account by
the likes of me. As he looks me over, he radiates disgust. I know this
look. I've had this before; it fills me with fury.
He bursts out:

>   And God, you're not a victim!

He says it like I'm a schemer, a criminal, not a victim. That I have
done this to him, to hurt him. That I don't have the right to complain
about the likes of him. Basically, he is saying 'How dare you?' I stand
there, wishing someone else would come by. I wish also that I could
make my legs move, that I would say something back. But I am computing what he is saying, this is his version of the story. It shocks me
that he said, 'Whatever it was, I'm not a criminal.'
What does he think it was? I mean he's a criminal lawyer, he knows
the law, or does it just not apply to him! That he can hold me down
and ignore my resistance, my loud 'no,' my desperate 'stop,' that he
had the right to override that. That he could cover my mouth, push
himself inside of me while I was fighting, writhing, trapped.
I'm not sure what my face is revealing to him, I hope anger, but I fear
it is just blank.
He tries one more time.

>   You know if you continue to go through with this, you'll
>   destroy my career. You do realize that, don't you?

I feel a wave of guilt. I never wanted to destroy anyone. But I am the one who has been damaged, not him. This is not an apology; this is a guilt trip. He is casting himself as the wronged party! I feel all muddled up; want to be the one who takes leave. But he flashes me a look of disgust and walks away. I stand a little longer, not turning to look where he walks. I consider telling the police. He spoke to me, breached his bail conditions. But . . . I'm not supposed to speak to him either.

I walk straight to the toilet. Enter a cubicle. Take off my wig. I open the toilet seat and I vomit. I leave the cubicle, and I wash my face.

In the mirror I don't see me, I see a diminished version of myself looking back at me. A haunted look. A stressed face. I see some-one I don't know how to look after anymore. I stare at her. And in that deserted women's room, I make eye contact with myself, I feel despair at all I have lost, both the things that I know about and the ones I feel inside my body. And I cry and I cry, and I cry.

CHAPTER 43

NOW

The KC asks me so many questions about vomiting in my bathroom, how I was clearly so drunk I had made myself sick. It goes on forever. What time was it? How long had I vomited for? How long had I slept on the floor for? How I must have felt better after vomiting for so long, and 'getting everything out of your system, so to speak.' I know there is some point for the defense in all this and I feel myself not wanting to give up anything. I realize as a witness, I am doing what all witnesses try to do, the very thing that undoes them. I am trying to control the narrative, when I should just answer the questions and not try to consider what he is going to ask me next. I remind myself that Julian's counsel, Mr. Stenham, is smart, he is a good KC, he won't even let on when he has got what he needs; God knows what I have already given him. Most witnesses up here wouldn't even know they were being played with, would start to offer up elements to make themselves more believable. I remind myself that that is when a witness starts to embellish; they feel afraid that they are letting themselves down, letting down all the people trying to help them, the prosecution, the police. Their story should be better. But none of them realize there is no perfect story, and that people are messy and sometimes drunk, and sometimes vomit.

I remind myself that my truth must be enough, because it's what happened to me. I will not give him something to accuse me of by losing my way forward. I try to calm down; I see how hard it is to be cool with someone suggesting such things to you. Finding the thing you are ashamed of and making sure that it is visible for all to see. Yes, I was drunk, yes, I was on the tiles in the bathroom vomiting my guts out, yes, I put my face on the bathroom floor. That does not mean that what happened next didn't happen.

I realize I am agitated because I know what he is going to ask me next. If I am this hot under the collar with the vomiting, I hate to think what I will be like in the next series of questions. I sense the solicitor pass notes to Julian's KC; I know they are what he wrote down during my examination in chief. I know it is about the next part. The rape. I feel it getting closer.

Then the KC sideswipes me.

> How many people did you brag to that you were sleeping with Julian Brookes?

I just look at him. Breathe.

> I did not brag about it. I told two of my closest friends that I was going on a date with him.

> Were you excited to tell them you were going on a date with him?

I feel humiliated, but I remind myself not to let him catch me out. I answer with confidence, but it comes out with vulnerability.

> Yes.

> And did you consider you would be sleeping with him again that night?

Richard is on his feet; he seeks to have this line of questioning stopped. Julian's KC returns to me on the bathroom floor, face to the tiles.

> You did return to your bed though, didn't you?

> Yes.

> And how did that happen?

> Mr. Brookes came and got me.

> And did you walk with him back to your bed?

> No.

> How did you manage to get back?

> He carried me.

The KC looks impressed, flashes a look at his client, at Julian, as if to say, 'That's nice.'

> He cared and he carried you back to your bed.

I didn't hear a question, so I stay silent.

> Is that right?

I don't know if he cared, but yes, he carried me back to
    bed.

He puts his head to one side.

    Did you brush your teeth before you were carried back?
    No.
    And did Julian carry you back because you weren't *able* to
    walk?
    No. I could have walked, I could have easily walked back to
      my bed.

My throat feels dry, I realize I could have said I was so out of it that
there was no way I could have managed it. I could have led the jury
to believe I was too sick for sex. But I have no time for regrets. It
is the truth, I could have made my way back, I wasn't so drunk I
couldn't walk. I'm waiting for it. The defense pauses. He looks at his
notes, turns and asks for the solicitor to pass him something. I wait.
Waiting. I feel afraid, I want this done. Then the defense turns back,
still; he changes his stance. I dig my nails into my thighs.

Another long pause. He hasn't made the major defense arguments
yet, but I can feel them coming. Richard is in the dark as much as
I am, he looks alert. My eyes are searching, I go from Richard's face
to the KC's face, back to Richard's face to the KC's face again. And
then. When the first of their points arrive, I am dumbstruck.

    I'm sorry, what are you saying?

He repeats his question.

    Julian didn't have his hand over your mouth at all, did he?
    No. No.

The KC digs in.

    It was your own hand over your own mouth, wasn't it?

I panic, then add:

    I don't understand.

He seems to relax into this unease. He has found one of the areas
where he could win this trial. He rephrases it. The truth is I do
understand the question, but I can't compute that he is leading with
this. I can't follow except I can, and I don't like it.

    What? It was not my hand over my own mouth!

He says something else.

    My own hand? No. It was Julian's hand.

He asks me about how bad my breath was. Suggests I was concerned that I had sour breath after vomiting.

> My breath?

I think through, but I'm muddled.

> Yes. I didn't have great-tasting breath. I remember that.

He tells me again, 'suggests,' that I had my own hand over my own mouth.

> What? No.

I think back.

> I might have touched my own mouth but—

Again with my hand on my mouth.

> Yes, but I touched it before, when he was only trying to
> kiss me. Not when he . . .

He has said something else. I jump back in.

> That's not what happened. I didn't want to have sex. I felt
> sick.

He suggests again that my only concern was not upsetting Julian with sour breath.

> No, you're wrong. I didn't want to have sex, because I
> felt *awful*, not just because my breath was sour from
> vomiting.

He suggests I am not remembering it clearly. He starts to give a different version of what happened, but I can't let him do this.

I interrupt him.

> No, I remember it very well.

He finishes his line of questioning, completely unruffled. I know I am rising to it, which is what he wants, but I must rise to it. This is completely untrue.

> What?

I take a breath and try to spell it out. Speak in a certain, very clear voice. I look over at the jury.

> No. I did not put my hand over my mouth to protect
> Julian from my sour breath. He put HIS hand over my
> mouth.

I am firm. Digging in. Then Julian's KC flips entirely and starts another line of questioning. At first, I can't follow. I am still catching up after the fury. He speaks almost patronizingly to me. A tactic. A reminder to me that he is in charge here.

> I imagine, Ms. Ensler, that you would be clearer about
> what happened if there was CCTV footage of the
> incident?

I inwardly groan. I know this line of questioning. I have used it myself. Later he will tell the jury that if they knew there was CCTV footage and they watched it, then they wouldn't be really sure that they could believe my version of events. This plants a doubt for them. They are not as sure as they should be to convict his client. I try to manage the question and the outcome with as much precision as possible.

> Even if there was CCTV footage, Mr. Stenham, I would not
> have to watch it because I am very clear about what hap-
> pened. I remember it very clearly.

He makes a leap now.

> And of course, there is no other evidence, is there, Ms.
> Ensler?

> I'm sorry?

He tilts his head.

> I mean you have no photographs of that night, do you?

I feel angry now. This is an old trick. He should know better. I lean into my own legal skills.

> Take photos of myself being raped?

> Any photos at all? Or video footage?

Richard is on his feet. Somehow, I miss hearing what the judge says. I'm still fuming. Thinking to myself, 'Yeah, I spent all my time while I was trapped under him snapping photos, taking selfies, making videos.' He is back at me.

> But they did take photographs when you undertook a
> forensic medical examination, didn't they?

> Yes.

> And yet there were no bruises in those photos, no bleeding,
> was there, Ms. Ensler?

I hate him. I know he is doing his job, pointing out that there is no objective evidence, so I try to collect myself. Calmly I say:

I haven't studied the photos, Mr. Stenham, because I am
    not a pathologist.
He nods gently. Then says in a sad voice, as if it is just all too
hard:
    So, really, we only have your own word against Mr.
    Brookes's word, don't we?
I start to feel like I am falling. I look around the room and swallow.
Julian's KC has already moved on, but the punch is clear. It has made
me feel that I can't be believed. I was drunk. I was vomiting. I was not
the reliable one in this story; it was Julian carefully carrying me back to
bed who was the 'reliable' one. Mr. Stenham KC is asking more questions; his voice has reverted to the underwater quality. What is this?
Why does it keep happening? His mouth is moving, and I am watching it. I know the jury are glued to his every word; he is leading them
through the mess of the night. He is talking about me giggling when
Julian tried to kiss me, talking about my sour breath. He suggests that
out of embarrassment, or camaraderie, I was attempting to shield Julian
from my sour breath. He thinks I was being considerate and placed
perhaps a few fingers by my mouth while we were getting intimate.
He goes on:
    While you were, once again, that night, getting intimate
        with the man you had liked, that you had consented
        to have sex with, who you were considering 'boyfriend
        material'?
    No. No.
Richard rises and suggests that there were too many questions in the
one line. He is really just trying to buy me time to compose myself. I
know this tactic by barristers. I try to compose myself. But the questioning continues to upset me.
    I didn't want to have sex.
In my mind my voice is screaming. I did NOT want to have sex. I
add to it, even though I might not be answering the question he just
put to me.
    I didn't want to have sex because I felt sick.
I am feeling sick right now. I feel flustered, remembering how I felt.
Remembering how I was trapped, terrified. Shocked. Then a series of
questions about Julian's arms, his hands.

> So you say he held down your wrists; which hand was on
>   which wrist?

I am reliving the trapped feeling, the fear of dying, not breathing
properly. I can't escape. I try to answer the questions.

> I don't know which. He had one hand over my mouth, I
>   could barely breathe.

He looks at me like I am not speaking the same language as he is.
Speaks loudly.

> Well, that's just not right, Ms. Ensler, because he was
>   holding your wrists, you said? So I'm afraid you are
>   mistaken, aren't you?
> No. No, his hand was over my mouth.

He is repeating back to me some of the answers I gave Richard in
the examination in chief. I am tangled up. Trying, but not catching
up. Where is this leading? Then I realize: Julian's KC is trying to say
that if Julian had one hand on each of my wrists, then he had no
extra hand to cover my mouth. That I was mistaken, I wasn't actually
pinned down, and of course I could breathe. In fact, the hand on
my mouth clearly must have been mine. I was just self-conscious
about my bad vomit breath, wasn't I? The KC is saying that if it was
my hand on my own mouth, as he 'suggests,' then I could have just
taken it away, and pushed Julian away. Or, I could have removed my
own hand from my *own* mouth and just screamed.

He is looking at me quizzically. Time seems to stop. The jury relax
a little, this seems to make sense to them. My mind is messy. I can't
catch up.

> No. No. I tried to get away.

I look over at the jury pleadingly.

> I told him. I said 'no.' I said 'stop.' I struggled. It was his
>   hand on my mouth.

I want to explain, but I'm stuck. The KC continues.

> How did you struggle?
> Yes, as best I could.
> How?

I take a moment. This is important to get right.

> I pushed him as best I could, I tried to kick—

I relive it. I feel the terror.

I tried to kick, and I tried to squirm.
I know it sounds bad. I have to say more.

He was squashing me. He was on top of me, bearing his
weight down on me.

I add:

I thought I was going to suffocate.

My mind is scrambled, I can feel a terrible wrong being done to me right now. This line of questioning is making me look confused, because I am, I am. I'm really confused.

Julian told his lawyer, or did his KC think it was a better story . . . that I had put my own hand over my own mouth, and therefore I was the only one stopping myself from screaming or speaking, and that I could have taken it away at any stage to speak up, or to push him away, or . . .

The KC is still speaking, he has me pinned like a butterfly, and he suggests, calmly, with nonchalance, that it was my hand over my own mouth, as if it were a game. Like the game of having sex in chambers. I'm shocked. That's what Julian's instructions are? A game! I look about me briefly. Thinking. Thinking. I see Adam's face in the gallery, I can see he is willing me to remember. He knows I am stuck. And then. Right there in court, I remember. I speak with complete clarity.

Julian had both of my wrists in one of his hands, pulled
high above my head.

I push my hands high above my head, merge my wrists together. I am illustrating what happened to me. There's a pause. I am here in court showing what he did. I continue. I don't move.

And his other hand over my mouth and nose at the same
time. Pushing down hard, with his hand, with his body,
trapping me. His hand hurting my face, I could barely
breathe.

I'm shaking. My eyes on Julian now. Fury rising as I remember it all, how I was trapped like an animal. How I tried to fight, then froze. The pain, the fear. 'How dare you, how dare you?' I think as I stare at him. 'Why am I the one up here being made to look like a liar?' Julian doesn't meet my eye; he is looking straight over at his family. I follow his gaze, see his dad give him a confident nod back. I sit. I take my arms down, I hold my elbows. I feel spent, worn, empty.

The KC's voice again.

He is apologizing to me for possibly making me feel uncomfortable.

I am just trying to get to the truth.

His voice is gentle, he is being nice to me now. And like every victim I have cross-examined before, I fall for it. I ache for niceness. He is gently completing the events of the night, very gently. I feel so broken I just want to go with him, just to get it over with, I want to be reeled in. The questions start again, he is not harsh. His voice has a beautiful, compassionate melody to it.

I understand that it was a terribly difficult and confusing night for you. You were ill.

I sway a bit. I feel sorry for the woman I was on that night. I feel tears well up but push them right down. He must have sensed it, or seen it even; he steers away, this time his voice is flattering. The KC suggests to me that I am a top barrister, a woman other barristers speak about in such high terms. In spite of myself I lean into this. I like that he knows this. He goes on.

A barrister who was seen to be easily the smartest in her bar call, perhaps of her generation.

I am suddenly alert. 'Hang on, this is going somewhere awful.' I can feel it. All my senses kick into action. The KC brings up my new chambers, calls it a larger and more prestigious chambers.

He waits for me to agree.

Yes.

He then says:

You were in competition to receive such a prestigious tenancy, weren't you?

I'm computing this, it's all new information, I don't know what he means. I don't answer.

He continues:

Indeed, the two contenders for the tenancy for your large new room were yourself and Mr. Brookes.

My mind is spinning. Without looking he picks up a sheet of paper he has strategically placed next to his file. He holds it up.

In fact, I have the short list in my hands right now. It only
    has two names on it.

He reads them out before tendering the document into evidence. He
reads out my full name and Julian's full name. I panic, look around;
Richard is on alert, looks grim. I have never seen this list; I never
knew about it. I realize I wasn't yet asked a question, but I speak
anyway.

My name might be on that list, but I, I . . . I never applied
    for a room in those chambers.

The KC is intimating, telling me he doesn't need me to speak, but I
ignore him, speak on.

I never applied for that position. I never saw any reason to
    have such a large chambers room when my old one had
    more space than I have ever had to myself in my entire
    life.

I see that Johnny's and Mum's faces are agreeing with me. I had a
corner of Johnny's room, with a fold-up screen between us for most
of my growing up. Barely room for my single bed, Mum had to buy
a secondhand Ikea short bed, and my feet as I grew hung off the
end. I am staring down the KC. I note the tiniest moment when the
KC does a mental shift. He assumed that I, as a successful barrister,
wanted the big room, the prestigious chambers at any cost. I hear the
jury members shift in their seats. They understand. I think back to
law school induction, how all the boys in that room looked like the
KC standing right here before me: white, privileged, so sure of themselves, so convinced that they were winners. I feel my skill set rise,
mentally nod at the dean for her words all those years ago, grateful to
the scared girl I was for the notes she took and remembered. 'Don't
ever trust your own instincts, sir,' I want to say. 'Day-one law school.
Only trust your LEGAL instincts.'

He computes, then his voice almost a snarl.

Well, I see you are enjoying that room now, aren't you, Ms.
    Ensler?

There is no time to answer, the next question comes fast to cover up
for what he didn't see coming. He fires right at me.

I can understand making up a story, or embellishing a
    story, to punish Mr. Brookes. After all, he told his

friends and even some of your colleagues about having
sex with you on his sofa in his room that night. It
embarrassed you, didn't it?

Slap.

This is what Julian was telling people while I was talking to Mia and
Cheryl about a potential relationship. That we fucked in his chambers.

I fade just a little, catch my breath, then find my way. My body has
been turned inside out with the evidence I have had to give; this final
humiliation is just a small cut.

> I can honestly tell you, sir, that I had no idea Julian had
> spoken to anyone about me like that.

He does an about-turn. Did I admit that moving to my new chambers was a strategic move for me to increase my income?

I snap back:

> I was offered the new chambers by a KC I admire. And I—

But he cuts me off. Annoyance, perhaps even tones of anger back in
his voice. He implies I made up a rape story to discredit Julian and
be the one offered the new tenancy. I can't help myself.

I interrupt:

> I moved chambers to get away from Julian, to be able to
> work without fear. Do not forget, sir, that I made my
> statement to the police on the very morning of the rape.
> No delay. Only hours after it occurred . . .

He interrupts me:

> This is not relevant to my question, Ms. Ensler, please
> refrain from elaboration.

But Richard rises. He's on his feet.

> Let her finish.

The judge lets me.

> I don't know any woman who would happily drink with
> a man, eat a meal, with all witnesses saying how much
> we laughed and got along, talked easily together, and
> then . . .

But Julian's KC interrupts me. He is on his feet addressing the judge.

> My Lord, I submit that this be struck from the record.

The judge responds.

Application granted.
The KC goes further.

Would My Lord please remind the witness to answer the
question and not make speeches.

I speak anyway.

And if you are implying that I planned the entire night so
that I could stage something like this, then I have no
words.

The KC is making further submissions, trying to drown me out.

My Lord . . .

But I continue.

The last seven hundred and eighty-two days have been
something I would never wish on any human being . . .

I can still hear him: 'My Lord . . .' and faintly somewhere I hear the
judge.

Ms. Ensler . . .

But I speak on, addressing the KC.

For you to stand there and suggest to me that I am in some
way holding a vendetta against Mr. Brookes is to suggest
to me . . .

KC again.

My Lord, the witness is not responding to any question.

I keep talking. This time I look at the jury.

Mr. Julian Brookes's KC here will at some stage tell you the
jury about what Mr. Brookes might have lost. But I will
tell you what I have lost; I have lost my dignity and my
sense of self. I have lost my career path, friends, peace
of mind, my safety. I have lost the sense of joy in my
sexuality.

I don't stop to take a breath. I can hear Julian's KC calling out now.
I speak on.

But most of all, I have lost my faith in this: the law.

I hear my voice shudder, the losses are hard, but this one I have only
just realized. I continue.

The system I believed would protect me. The system I have
dedicated my life to . . .

The KC is calling for an intervention. But after 782 days, after doing everything right, after being the best witness there could be, after telling the truth, I can feel something. I can feel all ten tracks in my brain lighting up. I have found my voice. It's a different voice, but it's mine. I keep speaking. Repeatedly I hear the KC's outrage.

My Lord. My Lord.

He is trying to drown out my voice, but I do not waver. I talk about how the law was the one thing I had believed in, that I had worked so hard, had fought hard for clients, believing that the system had its own checks and balances. How it gave me so much yet . . . now. . . . The judge addresses me directly, as a witness, not as a barrister.

Ms. Ensler, I must ask you not to speak unless you are answering a question. Those are the rules in court.

I look at the judge respectfully.

My Lord, there are some things I am going to say.

Julian's KC is on his feet, there are arguments to be made; he does not want the jury in the room, he calls for a voir dire. It's where the jury are sent out so they don't hear something that might be prejudicial. The judge nods. Strangely, the phrase's original meaning is 'to speak the truth.' I smile wryly as I recall this. Sit there quietly, watching as the jury begin to file out. They are confused, not sure exactly, in spite of the judge explaining it to them, why they must leave.

I notice that there are extra journalists taking up the media seats. In a boring day of court trials, it must have gotten out that someone was speaking out of turn, that there was drama in court one. I watch as the court artist looks at me and sketches again. No eye contact, nothing personal. I wonder what their images will look like. I feel a buzz. I wait. There are other onlookers moving into the public gallery, a group of female students, possibly law students, taking whatever spare seats are still available. I wait.

CHAPTER 44

NOW

The last juror looks back at me as he exits. The media are poised. The judge is alert.

You have limited scope here, Ms. Ensler, please be concise.

I breathe slowly. In, out. I find the face of Constable Kate Palmer. The young policewoman. She has her hand on my mum's shoulder. I let my eyes graze over all the people in the gallery, in my mind I see all the women who came before me, all the ones who will come after. Suddenly I see the image of Jenna. The woman I cross-examined as Phoebe watched on. I hear her voice before she collapsed. 'I'm not getting anything out of this. I'm just doing this to protect other women.'

I look up directly at Julian's 'boys' in the gallery. I look to the judge. I have nothing prepared, but somehow, I know exactly what to say.

My Lord, I am here in a unique position. Usually I stand at the bar table, sit with counsel, but now I am in this courtroom as a witness, a complainant, as a victim.

I say the last word with emotion. Then move on.

As a barrister I have questioned women in sexual assault cases on the assumption that the evidence can be delivered in a clean, logical package. But now I have seen, through my own attempts here today, that it *can't* be.

I pause. Continue.

I do not mean to implicate either the barristers or yourself, of course, My Lord, I am considering the system as a whole. And all my professional life I have participated in this system, and I have done this to women.

I take a big breath. The air is charged.

Now I know, this is not right. This is not 'reasonable.'

Because now I know, from my own life, as both a woman
AND a lawyer, that the lived experience of sexual assault
is not remembered in a neat, consistent, scientific parcel.
Yet the law insists that it must be. And without such
evidence the law too often finds testimony 'unbelievable.'

I look about me, I'm surprised that there is such stillness. I see something so clearly right now; I implore the others to see it too.

But this is not a car accident, a home invasion. This is rape.

A crime against the *person.*

Then with emphasis:

And now I know that when a woman says 'no,' when her
actions say 'no,' it is not some subtle, unreadable thing at
all. Yet, before this, I too would have stood in court and
suggested that 'she was mistaken.'

I look up, filled with something I haven't felt before. A need, a need
to be heard.

But when a woman has been violated, it is a corrosive
wound, one that begins with terror and pain deep within
the body, then it overtakes the mind . . . the soul.

I rest my eyes on Richard, who is watching me with interest.

Yet before, I would suggest that 'she was confused.'

I feel an ache in my heart, a physical ache.

The message is that if we do not deliver our evidence neatly,
in a clear linear story, with consistency in recall, then we
are lying.

I think back to my own practice in sexual assault cross-examination.
Everything I did was by the book, everything I did was with respect,
and yet, and yet . . . there was something amiss.

Before this, I too would point out inconsistencies as proof
of doubt in sexual assault trials; would tell the jury they
couldn't possibly be 'sure.'

I see Johnny, seated in the gallery. He has no idea what I am saying
but he is leaning forward, wanting me to feel that he is with me.

I gaze at all the lawyers seated before me, talk to them as well.

As a lawyer I know the law can't jettison consistency

entirely, but in sexual assault trials can we keep using it as the litmus test of credibility? Because, as a victim, let me tell you that the rape and the perpetrator are vividly recalled, the peripheral details not so clearly. If a woman is rattled by reliving the nightmare in court, if a woman's experience of rape is not *the way the court likes it to be*, then . . .

My voice catches slightly.

We conclude that she is lying, that she must be disbelieved. How can the victim ever win? Why do we believe consent exists until it is taken away to begin with? Are women such commodities? And then, when the woman does not consent, we are somehow not believing her? Despite everything she does and says? Could we not start with asking of the accused, 'What did he do to determine consent existed in the first place?' Could we not ask him to speak to it? To let the jury see what they might disbelieve in his story?

I look about me questioningly. The media are scribbling, Julian's KC is talking to his instructing solicitor, making out it is nothing to him, that if the jury aren't there, this doesn't add to anything. He's right. I know I don't have much time before he is on his feet again.

So I speak up, loudly.

So here in court, I want to call it out.

There's a flurry about the gallery as the onlookers recognize the drama.

The law of sexual assault spins on the wrong axis. A woman's experience of sexual assault does not fit the male-defined system of truth, so it cannot be truth, and therefore there cannot be justice.

My voice sounds confident now. It buoys me.

The law has been shaped by generations and generations of white, heterosexual men.

There he is, the KC is up on his feet. He is speaking but I can't even hear him anymore.

I continue.

There was a time, not so long ago, when courts like this

did not see nonconsensual sex in marriage as rape, did
not see that battered women fight back in a manner
distinct from the way men fight. Did not see the unfair
questions asked of rape victims around the color of
their underwear; the assumptions based upon types of
underwear offering some indication of consent. Yet.
Once we *see*, we cannot *unsee*.
I look about the court, settle on the media.
Can we?
Julian's KC won't sit down, he is standing. I ignore him and whatever
it is he is saying to the judge. I feel myself fly; I am speaking with
passion.
Now I see through my own experience, that we have it
all wrong when it comes to sexual assault. We do not
interrogate the law's own assumptions, instead we persist
in interrogating the victim.
I let that sit in the air, then:
The law is an organic thing, defined by us, constructed by
us, in light of all of our experiences. All of ours. And so,
there are no excuses anymore, it must change. We must
do better. Because the truth is that one in three women
are sexually assaulted, we need to know they have a
chance of being believed so that we know justice can be
done.
Julian's KC is talking to the judge, his face is red. The judge addresses
me. I can hear him again. I know I have gone beyond what I am
allowed to say, well beyond. But one last thing as I look up at the
court gallery. I remember Richard telling me all the figures around
sexual assault. The number of women who have been raped, like
me. Who have been sexually assaulted, harassed. My voice is a loud
whisper, one with great feeling.
One in three women.
I feel my eyes prick with tears, and hear myself say:
Look to your left, look to your right, one of us . . .
I'm looking at the women in the gallery. I feel my cheeks hot hot hot.
I am done, so done. I look over at my mum. Then down to the KC
and Richard. I feel a wave of sadness. Not despair, just pure sadness.

I know I haven't won my case. But a weight has been lifted. Media are still madly writing. I realize I have completely forgotten that Julian was in court through the entire thing. The judge speaks to me, tells me sternly not to speak again until I am asked a question. Declares that he is bringing the jury back in. Voir dire over.

I hold my head up. I see Adam standing at the back of the court-room. He nods at me. I see the open face of the young police officer. This young woman in a uniform usually worn by men. She locks eyes with me, and in this brightly lit, suffocating courtroom, standing in front of everyone, while my mum clutches her straw beach bag, right here, right now, meeting the eyes of that one young woman makes me feel . . . something good.

CHAPTER 45

LATER

I have been a criminal barrister for long enough. I know when the jury come back fast that someone is 'Not Guilty.' Still, when we are called in, I carry hope. The judge asks the jury whether they have reached a verdict in the matter, the foreman hands up the verdict before reading it out. Julian's KC and Julian are both standing; I'm seated, very still.

When the verdict is read out, the defense team are thrilled. There is a roar from his boys in the gallery, even clapping, which the judge admonishes quickly. Julian comes out from the dock and hugs the KC. Richard is telling me something, but I don't compute. Kate Palmer materializes beside me, puts her hand on my shoulder. I know I must stand but I can't, don't. I won't look at Julian. The jury files out, I look up as they do, not one of them can meet my eye. Something feels stuck in my throat. All of this and, and . . . they didn't believe me. The legal system made me look like a liar. Julian will never have to admit what he did, will never have to . . . I hear Richard.

I'm so sorry, Tessa.
The system feels faulty, not fit for purpose.
The legal system feels broken.
I feel the words as they flash across my thoughts. '*Look to your left, look to your right. I am broken too, but I am still here, and I will not be silenced.*' Richard is beckoning to my mum, who is now standing on the sidelines. She gathers her straw bag, stands, and comes over to me. I can't help but smile.
She speaks gently.
Come on, love.
I don't know how to stand up, how to leave the courtroom. I don't

know how to leave the building. I stay sitting, eyes on my mum as she waits. Richard standing by everyone, waiting for me. I look at Richard.

All this and they didn't believe me.

Richard responds:

You gave it an almighty go.

I'm still unable to stand when Johnny appears with Junie. I hear my niece's joy at seeing me ring through this ancient room. I suddenly stand up automatically, she runs to my arms as soon as Johnny places her on the ground. A clatter of shoes. As I hold Junie, I feel that I have somehow let her down. I know I will keep trying to work toward change, I have to believe I can make a difference. I have to believe that when she is older, juries will be able to believe the stories of women. I have to know the law will reflect women's experiences one day. But I feel so alone, so exhausted. There is no one fighting for me anymore. The case is done.

I imagine that Richard and Mum are relieved when I finally walk out of the courtroom; I know by now that Julian and his people are well gone. Celebrating somewhere. Mia promised me that after the case, whatever the outcome she would be cabbing it straight to mine, drinks, food, and a listening ear. I am keen to hear her thoughts on what she saw. I know she will make me smile when she imitates all the voices in court. She's a perfect mimic. We will continue to plan a trip when the weather is warmer. Part of what- ever new 'Operation Tessa' she has planned. I hug Richard farewell, thanking him profusely. He did a good job, a great job. When we are at the foyer, Cheryl is there with a huge hug, telling me, 'What an asshole that defense barrister was.' I laugh, there's no point in telling her he was just doing his job, that the wrong is something much deeper in the system and within the society the jurors come from. Besides, right now it feels good to hear that the man I have been battling for so many hours is 'an asshole,' he drove me hard. I wonder about the jury, each going home to his or her separate home tonight. I think about the judge and wonder if he believed me or not. But mostly I just want to get home. Johnny asks me if I am coming home with everyone right now. Mum waits anxiously for my answer. I tell them, 'No.' I think to myself, 'My home is in London now.' Mum side-eyes Cheryl, who jumps in.

> We all think you should come back with us. Just for
> tonight.

Junie is jumping about, excited at the prospect. I speak loudly.

> Well, I can't, can I? Because 'someone' turns two on
> Saturday and there's a party to celebrate. I need to stay in
> the city to buy her something special!

Junie beams.

> Me, me.

Mum holds on to my arm. I kiss her and whisper in her ear.

> Thank you.

Mum tries to speak. She manages a sentence.

> I'm so proud.

It makes me want to cry; I pull away.

> See you all on Saturday.

Cheryl hugs me again.

> Fucking champion, you are.

I hug her back. So grateful for them all. Johnny is looking up train times as I leave the court building. I walk out into a cold but blue-skied London afternoon. The crisp air on my face feels good.

CHAPTER 46

AFTER

As I walk outside, I turn and look back at the Old Bailey. Eyes up to the statue of justice, Lady Justice, standing up there, eyes blindfolded. She has stood there for over a hundred years. She proudly holds the scales in one hand and in the other a sword, a symbol for the power of justice. I wonder who decided justice was a woman. I remember learning it was something to do with clear-sightedness, and I laugh grimly after all that has happened today. The awful irony.

I decide to walk some way, then jump in an Uber. I feel my phone vibrate with a text, Adam. 'I'm so sorry. You were ducking great though. Let's meet for lunch next week? I'm so proud to be your friend. Adam x.' I smile at the autocorrect. Send him a thumbs-up emoji. Then I giggle and send him a duck emoji too.

I hear a voice calling my name. My full name.

Tessa Ensler. Ms. Ensler.

I see a woman running toward me, I recognize her and brace myself. She stands in front of me. The journalist from the *Times*, Rachel Myers. Strong, professional woman, intelligent glasses, dark hair tied back off her face.

I'm sorry, I'm not making any media statements right now.

I think I said all I have to say in court.

She wears trousers and a blazer, dark hair on her face when the breeze catches it.

I know. I wrote it all down.

She waves her notebook.

I'm writing something for the *Times* this weekend. About the trial.

I'm so tired, I nod at her. I'm just looking forward to seeing Mia at home. To sleeping. To walking away. Rachel stands still.

> I don't want a statement. I just wanted to tell you
>> something.

I don't know Rachel. I know who she is, but I don't know her. I'm also wary of the fact she is writing a story. She meets my eye.

> I wanted to say thank you.

I'm surprised. She continues calmly, with intent.

> I'm also one in three.

It takes me a moment to hear what she just said to me. I realize she is telling me she has also been raped. My eyes soften. I see her. Really see her. And nod. She just holds my gaze.

> You started something in there. Shown us that it doesn't
>> work; and then passed the baton to me and others to
>> show more people. I am writing down every word you
>> said in that voir dire.

I'm all out of words today. I stand there before her. Rachel continues.

> And it doesn't stop till everyone sees. Until they can't not see.

Rachel then turns, and walks away.

I watch her go, feel myself smile. This is not something I am doing alone. I feel the fight, the passion in my gut rise. I know something has to change. Not just with the law, but in society.

One in three is a lot of women who have something to say.

Too many to ignore.

ACKNOWLEDGMENTS

Prima Facie—*A (Latin) legal term meaning: On the face of it.*

The writing of this novel has been a true pleasure of creative exploration—a very different form of writing to the ones I have been accustomed to in theatre and screen. There was, for me, a true sense of being permitted to stretch my wings, dig in deep, and the feeling of coming home as a writer. There are so many people who made this possible, people who quietly behind the scenes read every word I wrote and offered their responses with such personal investment and enthusiasm, those who delivered endless of cups of tea, friends who walked and talked ideas with me, and the brilliant publishers of Henry Holt at Macmillan in New York who made this book possible.

I want to acknowledge especially the following people: Serena Jones and Lori Kusatzky from Henry Holt, who have been thorough and supportive and have offered their smart advice and great humor at every turn. Together with their team from Henry Holt at Macmillan they have made this process exciting, fun, and a great New York experience. I specifically mention: Hannah Campbell, Gregg Kulick, Meryl Sussman Levavi, Clarissa Long, Emily Mahar, Jason Reigal, and Alyssa Weinberg.

I further thank Jane Novak, my Australian and US literary agent, who has always had such strong faith in my prose and has been a friend throughout this publishing process, and Jane Finigan, my UK literary agent at Lutyens & Rubinstein in London, a wonderful comrade throughout; it was a joy working with a literary agency who runs the incredible bookstore in Notting Hill, a place I often visited before I was represented by them. I want to acknowledge the team of publishers from both Australia and the UK who have collaborated with Serena and Lori and brought the first edition to the fore: Cate Blake, Danielle Walker, and Tracey Cheetham and their team from Picador at Pan Macmillan Australia; and Venetia Butterfield, Helen Conford, and the team from Cornerstone at Penguin Random House.

I am grateful to my theatre and film agents: Zilla Turner (HLA Australia) and Julia Kreitman and Tanya Tillett (The Agency, London), who have shepherded me through the process that was *Prima Facie* the play, in all its productions around the English- and non-English-speaking world, but especially in Australia, London's West End, and on Broadway in New York.

The story of this book began as a long writing experience that was transformed into a play and a screenplay before it came full circle and is now this novel. In its other iterations, there are many people to thank, including Lee Lewis (director), Sheridan Harbridge (actor), Justin Martin (director), Jodie Comer (actor), Caleb Lewis (dramaturg), Griffin Theatre Company and its chairperson, Bruce Meagher, in Australia, James Bierman (producer), Empire Street Productions, and all of the designers, stage managers, and teams that surrounded those formative productions. The conversations with all these people have informed this story in ways they probably cannot fathom, as have the conversations with Susanna White (director of the upcoming film), Greer Simpkin, David Jowsey (producers, Bunya Productions Australia), Jenny Cooney (producer), and Elizabeth Haggard and Robert Kessel (producers, Participant USA). I am grateful for them all.

In my previous profession as a human rights and children's criminal lawyer there have been so many people who supported me, and they remain some of my closest and dearest friends and supporters. They are too numerous to name. However, there are also lawyers (judges, barristers, solicitors, academics, and ex-lawyers) who specifically supported the writing of this story and who work or have worked in, and continue to advocate around, human rights law.

I acknowledge the too-many-to-list artist friends I have made while working in the theatre—one of the joys in a theatre life is collaborating with like-minded people, and all over the world there is a sense of family in that community. There have been countless other people, those who have emailed, messaged, and written letters to me:

each of you have shared something of yourself and I thank you for it.

I am grateful to all those who offered their homes around the world—this book has been written in those homes and under your nurturing: Lizzie Schultz Willoughby, Trish Wadley, Julia Heath in London, Poppy Adams in Oxford, Jenny Cooney in Los Angeles, and Valerie Artz in New York. I am further grateful to the following libraries who have unwittingly housed me in my writing process: the New York Public Library and Marrickville Library in Inner West Sydney. Public libraries are a resource to be protected. I acknowledge Soho House in Notting Hill, London, as another of my nomadic workplaces.

A few people must be singled out for their early readership or inspiration around the pages of this novel: V (formerly Eve Ensler), Hilary Bonney, Karen O'Connell, Caleb Lewis, Jodie Comer, Sheridan Harbridge, Lee Lewis, Justin Martin, Nicole Abadee, Danielle Manson, Anna Funder, Rochelle Zurnamer, Vanessa Bates, Sally Murray, and Bain Stewart.

I also remember my mother, Elaine Miller, the original inspiration of a woman who comes from a background where education and prospects were never available to her, who fought and worked until she had a voice and was seen. Her sister, June Cooney Ferguson, is my precious aunty and godmother, and she, together with Joan Beech-Jones, Trish Bowditch, and Lois Simpson, has tried to fill the gulf left after the death of my mother. I love and appreciate them all so very much.

I have been blessed with the most incredible friends, who are generous, kind and loyal—every day I am grateful for them and marvel at their big hearts, humanity, and sheer brilliance; they have stuck by me through all of life's ups and downs. Some of them have traveled across oceans to support me and celebrate my work.

Most important, I thank my family. They have patiently bought me cups of tea, cooked my meals, and kept me constantly in touch with the world. I am beyond grateful for the fun, vulnerable, sensitive, sometimes wild, sometimes messy, and always loving home they offer me. My children, Gabriel and Sasha Beech-Jones, are my constant inspiration; they are sensitive, thoughtful, and loving people who I am more in awe of than they could ever know.

Lastly, my husband, Robert Beech-Jones, has been more than my rock, he is my great love, my "home-coming arms," and a man who is more authentically himself than any other man I have met on this earth. Robert's whip-smart, extraordinary intelligence is only matched by his humble nature, loyalty, and gentle ways.

ABOUT THE AUTHOR

Suzie Miller is a contemporary international playwright, screenwriter, and novelist. Based in both London and Sydney, Australia, Miller has had her work produced around the world, winning multiple prestigious awards. Her smash hit one-woman play *Prima Facie* ran critically successful seasons in London, selling out in the West End and winning the 2023 Laurence Olivier Awards for Best New Play and Best Actress, and on Broadway, where it received four Tony Award nominations and a win for Best Actress in 2023. Miller is educated in science and law, with a doctorate in drama and mathematics. She practiced human rights law before turning to writing full-time and is currently developing major theater, film, and television projects across the UK, US, and Australia, including feature-film adaptations of her plays. *Prima Facie* is her first novel.